ONE LAST CHANCE

D0615754

Other books in the Chance series:

ONE LAST CHANCE

Trapped by a Blowdown *by Ron Gamer*

DISCARDED

Adventure Publications, Inc.
CAMBRIDGE, MINNESOTA

dedication

For wonderful daughters, Kristine and Darlene, who continue to make their parents proud.

One Last Chance is set in the Boundary Waters Canoe Area Wilderness of northern Minnesota. Although the plot is purely fictional and set in the present, the story is based on the devastating winds that swept over the region in 1999. Now referred to as the "Blowdown," the storm flattened hundreds of square miles of forest. For clarity in crafting the story, the exact storm path and a few geographical features have been altered.

This is a work of fiction. Although inspired by an actual event, the names of all persons, characters and public or private institutions are inventions of the author's imagination. Any resemblance to people living or deceased is purely coincidental.

Cover and book design by Jonathan Norberg

All rights reserved. With the exception of short excerpts for review purposes, no reprint of this work may be done without notification and permission of the author.

10 9 8 7 6 5 4 3 2 1

Copyright 2007 by Ron Gamer
Published by Adventure Publications, Inc.
820 Cleveland Street South
Cambridge, MN 55008
1-800-678-7006
www.adventurepublications.net
Printed in the U.S.A.
ISBN-13: 978-1-59193-211-6
ISBN-10: 1-59193-211-4

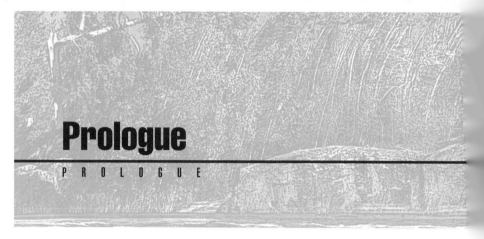

Prologue

P R O L O G U E

Never had Travis felt so frightened. The inside of the tiny tent was darker than an ink spot. So black, it was like being in a closed coffin. But the teen didn't dwell on the image. He was already terrified. He didn't need his imagination adding to the fear.

The boy burrowed into the sleeping bag as far as his long legs would allow. A wind snapped and licked at the thin fabric, blocking other sounds. Earlier in the evening, animals had been fighting near the tent, bumping it, scaring him half to death.

From the sound of their yips and growls, Travis thought they must be timber wolves. The large, meat-eating predators roamed freely in this part of northern Minnesota. With a breeze billowing the tent fly, it would be hard to hear if they returned.

But Travis could picture them sitting outside, waiting patiently for him to come join them in play. Winners take all.

Eventually his breathing eased and his heart stopped pounding. At least slow enough that he could consider dozing off. Yet he knew falling back to sleep wasn't likely—not at least until first light—many long dark hours distant.

The teen worked at tucking his terror into the corner of his mind. He tried desperately to think about other things, good things—safe things.

He thought about school and his friends, about food and his family, about cars and girls—anything to keep his brain busy. Yet, no matter how hard he tried, his mind kept wandering back to his situation—a terrifying state of affairs he couldn't have imagined a week or two earlier.

Had he really been the one to suggest a canoe trip this late in the season?

He hadn't meant one so long, one so far from home. That had been Seth's idea and Travis had been too timid to disagree. He went along as he always did when his buddy offered up a new adventure.

And look where it got them. They were in trouble—terrible trouble. They were in such serious danger that they might wind up as headlines in the local paper.

The young man rolled over, trying to find a position his aching shoulder would accept. He listened attentively, his ears straining to hear if the unwanted visitors returned.

Hearing only the wind buffeting the fabric, Travis flashed back to the day Seth and he embarked on this portage canoe trip. Was it only a week ago?

Somehow, it seemed longer than that—so much longer.

Chapter One

C H A P T E R   O N E

The old yellow bus squeaked to a stop, hesitating for a moment, as if unsure which way to turn. Then after coughing out a puff of smoky exhaust, the vehicle lumbered onto the blacktop. Moments later, the weary transport labored as it climbed the long grade west of Grand Marais. Through the rear window, the postcard view of Lake Superior quickly became a memory.

With a jerky lurch and a mashing of metal, the driver shifted gears. She tightened her grip on the wide wheel, directing the bus along the tree-lined Gunflint Trail. Behind her a dozen students chatted noisily. They were being returned to remote homes located on the edge of Minnesota's Boundary Waters Canoe Area Wilderness. Most were overjoyed. They were looking forward to a four-day break from school.

Travis Larsen and Seth Springwood, best pals since kindergarten, were sprawled across the broad backseat. Busy planning a canoe trip, their eyes were trained on a map. The fifteen-year-olds lived near one another on the shores of Poplar Lake, some twenty miles farther up the "Trail." Each had taken paddle trips before, but this outing would be different. This would be their first portage travel without someone looking over their shoulders.

Although the calendar read October, the weather made it feel more like July. Leaving the cool air of the inland sea behind, the bus plunged into the muggy warmth of the upland forest. The abrupt temperature change made the windows fog over like pitchers of ice water on a hot summer day.

"Can you believe this heat?" said Travis. "The guy on the radio said it's broken about every record for a hundred years."

"You know," Seth said, "this warm weather is supposed to stick around for the next week. Instead of just a short overnight, why don't we go south right from your dock? We could head down to Brule Lake. That should make for a pretty easy three- or four-day paddle."

"Really? Can we go that far in three days?" Travis asked.

"Yeah, shouldn't be hard at all. If we want, we can call it quits at Brule. We could phone home from the landing at the end of the Caribou Trail. One of our folks could drive down the main highway and then back up Caribou to get us. But, if we feel like staying out until Sunday afternoon, we'll tell them we're going to continue through the Swan Lake Chain. They could meet us at Trail 152."

Travis used a finger to trace a series of blue blobs dotting the map. "I see what you mean. I like the looks of this Brule Lake route," he muttered.

He took a deep breath and added, "But aren't there some long portages if we circle back through Swan? Your old canoe's pretty heavy. It won't be the easiest thing to carry. Besides, that's getting pretty far from home. What if we had an accident or something?"

Seth scrunched his brow and shook his raven-haired head. "Don't be a wuss, Trav. Lighten up, we'll be okay. And with the two of us sharing the load, my canoe won't be a problem."

He paused, thinking of what to add. He needed to convince his pal everything would be fine. "Hey, what with this terrific weather, how much gear do we need? We'll probably be paddling in cutoffs. And we won't have to bring much in the way of food. We can use freeze-dried meals. Rollie the outfitter told me he had a couple of boxes he'd just as soon use up."

Travis retraced the proposed route with his finger, then said, "Well . . . I guess it'd be okay. If you're sure that all we need is freeze-dried."

He sat up and looked at his friend straight on. "You should know, Seth. You're the one who went on all those group trips last summer. I just hope we catch some fish. Just thinking about all that paddling makes me hungry. Still, I hope everything goes all right."

"Hey, we'll just do it. I can make a copy of the route to leave with my mom. We're supposed to have a permit to enter the BWCA. But hey, we're starting right from our own docks. How illegal can that be? Besides, if we applied for a permit the rangers probably wouldn't approve. They'd say we're too young. So who has to know? It's nobody's business where we go and where we camp. We don't need big brother telling us what to do."

"Yeah, you're probably right. Of course, there are always our sisters' big mouths. You know how they can be. We'll have to think of some way to bribe 'em. No way do their friends need to know what we're up to."

The boys each had a sister seated closer to the driver. Sarah was Seth's twin. She was a slender redhead who shared neither Seth's wide frame nor dark features. Travis's little sister Beth was a gangly ten-year-old he affectionately called "Little Booger."

Travis had no sooner expressed his doubts when one of the girls turned around. "Hey, Boy Scouts! Sarah says you guys are taking off this weekend. What's the matter? Afraid a few young women around the resort might contaminate you?"

"So much for keeping it to ourselves," Travis moaned.

Pretending to be more upset than he really was, Seth stood up. "Oh, it's not that we're not mature, Andrea, it's just we're both allergic to seeing so much ugliness at one time."

"Uh-huh! You're gonna be sorry you said that," the pretty blonde fired back. "Girls don't get mad . . . we get even."

Seth's sister, Sarah, couldn't resist joining the friendly teasing. Turning in her seat, she yelled, "You Danny Boone wannabes better behave in the big wild woods. Word is, the wolves and bears are fattening up for winter. I hear they just love to snack on chickens. I'm sure they'd enjoy a pair of fourteen-year-old roosters sleeping in little tents."

With a shrug of his broad shoulders, Seth grinned at his friend. "Trav, this trip is the best idea since sliced pizza. Even if we only get to the other side of the lake, we'll be away from Sarah's mob of motor-mouths."

Brakes began to squeal. The bus ground to a stop alongside a white post topped with a mailbox with "Larsen" stenciled on the side. Stuffing the map into his school pack, Travis unfolded his long limbs, stood tall and brushed back his sandy brown hair.

He beamed at Seth. "See ya at first light. I still have a few things to get ready. Dad's still over on Isle Royale finishing up this summer's research stats. I'll need to double-check the packing list with Mom."

* * *

Linda Larsen reviewed the camping list while supper dishes dried on the counter. She seemed satisfied her son had packed everything needed for the weekend. Walking over to the entry closet, she plucked a small package from the top shelf.

Travis paid no attention. He was intent on attaching his packsacks to the aluminum pack-frame. With the box behind her back, his mother sidled over to her son, smiled and said, "Surprise! Your dad and I had planned on giving this to you for Christmas. But I thought you might make good use of it now." After setting the box on the table, she removed a wallet-sized leather case.

"What is it?" Travis asked, looking up.

"Why don't you open it up and find out? I think you'll like it."

Unsnapping the flap, Travis pulled out a thick, stainless steel device that resembled a pair of pliers on steroids. "Jeez, Mom, I'd been planning to save for one of these. How'd you know I wanted a survival tool?" He marveled, turning it over in his hand.

"Wow! This is the best one they make—two knife blades, pliers, screwdriver heads and a can opener. It has everything. Thanks!"

"There's something else. This is a compass with special flint under the back cover. It even has a cord you can attach to your belt or wear around your neck."

Travis only gave the compass a fleeting glance. His attention was on the shiny multi-tool. "Oh, we shouldn't even have to use a compass. Seth's borrowing one of the GPS units the guides take along on the summer trips. Our route's already programmed. All we have to do is stay on track."

"Well, make sure you bring an extra set of batteries. Electronic gizmos don't always work. Relying on them could get you lost."

"I hardly think we'll get lost. We have the topo map, a couple of compasses, and the GPS. We have everything but a cell phone, and you know they don't work around here. Even E.T. couldn't phone home."

"All I know, Travis, is that I won't get much sleep until

you two get back. Remember what I told you earlier. Trouble, just like bananas, sometimes comes in bunches."

* * *

It had been over a year since family friends, Kate and Rollie Kane, had coaxed Sarah and Seth's mother, Lynn, into selling her Poplar Lake cottage. The older couple insisted the Springwoods move in at the Kanes' lakeside resort. That had been several months after the twins' father had been killed in an auto accident.

Sarah's slumber party had forced Seth to seek refuge in one of the resort's vacant cabins. He now found himself alone in the dark, staring up at the pine-paneled ceiling, unable to doze off. His lack of sleep had nothing to do with the upcoming adventure. His thoughts were focused on his mother's recent behavior.

Following the death of their father, the twins' grief was eased by the return to school and activities with friends. It was their mother who was having the hardest time coping. Lynn Springwood could hardly get through a day without crying or being reminded in some sad way of the family's loss. After moving to the resort, her mood swings gradually waned. It was like a new start for her, and that's what she called it, her "new beginning."

Much of her sorrow seemed to evaporate as she became more and more involved with handling resort business. She worked hard during the day, and as far as Seth could tell, slept well at night. She seemed rested and happy in the mornings.

But lately things had changed. For the past few months, his mom would go out on Friday or Saturday night. She never said where she was going or whether or not she had company. And she returned late, really late, usually too late for Seth or Sarah to stay awake. In the morning she'd be there, humming in the kitchen, making break-fast. She'd pump the twins with questions, but remained elusive about her own mysterious evening outings.

Seth tossed and turned, wondering if the gossip he had heard at school was true. One of the older students had taunted him several weeks earlier. "Yo, Sethpool! Saw your ol' lady leaving the Blue Ox the other night. You got a pretty hot momma!"

Seth tried to ignore the remark. The slur of his name didn't bother him. He realized older guys took pleasure teasing freshmen. But the part about his mother cut him to the core. He'd wanted to leap off the locker room bench, slam the senior jock against the wall and make him eat his words.

Yet, he knew that wasn't the answer. Fighting would only make matters worse. Instead, with ears burning, he stuffed his gear into his locker, slammed the door and rushed off to the next class.

Now, alone in the darkest part of the night, Seth lay awake, thinking about what the jock had said. Was their mother going out bar-hopping on weekends? Was she hoping to find someone to take their father's place by acting like some college co-ed looking for a date?

She has no right, Seth concluded, no right at all. Their father hadn't been gone long enough for her to think about another man. If what the jerk had said was true, their mother had been avoiding telling the truth. That hurt more than physical pain.

Seth brushed his hand across his face and realized he was wiping at his eyes.

* * *

Travis eased through the side door of the Larsens' lakeside home. The pale blush on the eastern horizon gave promise of another pleasant day.

He stood on the deck munching a caramel roll, amazed at how warm it was for six a.m. This time of year it wouldn't have been uncommon for the ground to be covered with frost. Instead, it felt more like summer than

14

fall. Pushing the last of the pastry into his mouth, he stood quietly, listening as woods and water awakened.

Tree frogs chirped in the brush beyond the yard. On the lake, a loon's long, mournful cry echoed across the water.

Travis couldn't help thinking how strange this was. These sounds should have ended weeks ago. Loons still this far north in October? Tree frogs thinking it was still summer?

Maybe there was something to the global warming they'd talked about in science class—although he knew he'd have a hard time believing that in January. Travis picked up the frame that held his two packsacks, tent, rod and sleeping bag. Then he followed his feet down the steps to a long, L-shaped dock.

The plan had been for Seth to load the food and cooking tools the night before the teens set off on their trip. With first light, he was to paddle his newly repaired canoe along the shoreline to the Larsens' dock. From there the adventure would officially begin.

Setting down his gear, Travis peered along the shore. A small, forested finger of land stuck out like a dark wall. Seth would have to paddle around the point before Travis would see him.

Anxious, Travis was about to head up the steps when he caught a glimpse of a dim shape. In the foggy vapor the shadow appeared ghostly, as if floating above the placid surface.

Travis retraced his steps, and then knelt by his equipment. Soon the shape transformed from a mirage to reality. In the predawn light he could just make out a long, skinny boat sliding through glassy water.

Travis imagined that Seth's Native American ancestors had played out the same scene several centuries earlier. Except his relatives would have been paddling in a birch-bark canoe—the type they used to fish and hunt these very waters. Travis waited quietly as Seth approached. Only small gulps of the paddle disturbed the peace.

"Thought you were gonna sleep all day," Travis teased as the canoe eased alongside the pier.

"Didn't sleep much at all, how 'bout you?" Seth replied. "I shoulda stayed here last night. The girls made such a racket I moved to an empty cabin. By then it was early morning and I just couldn't fall asleep."

"Right . . . couldn't be you're tired because you were hoping to get a chance to be alone with Maria?" Travis taunted.

"As a matter of fact, wise guy, she wasn't at the party. What d'ya say you quit yakking and get your stuff and skinny butt in the canoe?"

"I don't know. Should I wear waders to keep my feet dry? You did the repair work, right? I don't want to get wet before the sun comes up."

"It's watertight. But if you don't get yourself in gear you'll never find out," Seth snapped back. "Hand me your pack. I'll stow it in the middle."

"Listen, why don't you load the canoe. I'm gonna run up and say goodbye to Mom. I haven't told her about our change of plans."

Travis dashed from the dock and up the steps. After slipping through one of the two large glass doors fronting the deck, he padded to his parents' room.

"Mom?" He whispered. "You awake?"

Hearing no reply, he turned on the hall light and pushed the door open. With light spilling from the hall he could see that the bed was empty.

"Say what?" he muttered. "Did I miss something?"

Traipsing back to the kitchen, he switched on the ceiling light. Spotting a note nestled on the floor, he reached down and picked it up. It was a message from his mother.

The note said that she had received a call from the sheriff's office requesting all medical staff to report to the hospital. There had been a multi-car accident and she was needed in the emergency room. Mrs. Larsen had written that Travis should go ahead with the trip, but to make sure they watched the weather. They were to head for home at the first hint of a change.

"Great," Travis mumbled. He was planning to tell his mom about their new plans right before they left. He figured that way she wouldn't have much of a chance to change her mind.

"Oh well, Seth's mom knows where we'll be. And what's the difference?" he rationalized. "Once past Poplar Lake it's all wild country, anyway." Shuffling to the kitchen counter, he pulled a pencil from the holder to write a reply.

Laying the pencil on the paper so the note wouldn't blow off again, he retraced his steps to the lake.

"Thought maybe you went back to bed," Seth said impatiently.

"No chance," Travis replied, easing into the front of the canoe. "Let's get this tub to the other side before the wind picks up."

"We're doing it, pal." Seth declared. "Three days of sun and fun. No books, bothers or brats."

"You got it! It'll be just you, me and the last of the loons. But by all rights they should have headed south by now. I guess this warm weather has their flight plans all screwed up."

The words had barely left his mouth when a loon's laughing call shattered the early morning quiet.

"Sounds like they want to talk to you," Seth laughed. "You do speak loon, don't you?"

"Only when I'm around 'loon-na-tics' like you," Travis shot back.

"Good comeback, slacker. Now start pulling on that paddle or we'll be on the water after sunset."

As if having been coached, a second loon called somewhere in the distance. Its primitive voice sounded much like an eerie echo of the first.

Soon the sun peeked above the horizon, officially opening the day—a fiery red sphere lifting above the speckled forest on the far shore. The canoe sliced water, leaving only a ripple to mark its passing.

Both boys pulled hard, eager to put miles between themselves and their backyards.

Chapter Two

C H A P T E R   T W O

By the time the young adventurers reached the opposite shore, the sun had climbed into a clear, blue sky. A smart wind had awakened with the morning light, slowing the pair's progress to the first of the many portages ahead of them.

Released from the birches and aspens bordering the beach, yellow and gold leaves danced in the breeze. Most fluttered to the water where they became toy boats, chasing one another atop white-tipped waves.

After beaching the canoe, the crew of two swapped sweatshirts and jeans for cut-offs and T-shirts. The front of Seth's light-blue shirt showed an outline of an antlered deer, encircled by the message, "Take a kid hunting." Underneath in smaller print it read, "and you won't be hunting for your kid." Travis's faded gray tee pictured a giant mosquito underscored by the words "Minnesota State Bird."

"Man, it must have warmed up twenty degrees since we left the dock. Hard to believe it's almost the middle of October," Travis panted, tugging the bow on shore.

"One good thing, those hard frosts we had a couple of weeks back killed off most of the bugs," Seth responded, adding, "Let's have a snack before we load up for the hike to Meeds Lake."

"Sounds good. Nothing loony about that idea."

"This is the longest portage of the trip. If we finish by noon, we should be in great shape to make Henson Lake before dark. Maybe in time to do some fishing."

Seth reached into a pack to retrieve a couple of energy bars. Handing one to Travis, he flashed a smile and said, "Who's gonna haul the canoe on the uphill part of the portage?"

"It's your boat, dude. I'd never deny you the pleasure of making the first carry. Of course, if it's too heavy for you we can always go back and get a few of the girls at your sister's party to give you a hand."

"Yeah, right. Let's just get to it," Seth mumbled, chewing the last of the bar. "Grab the packs and I'll get the canoe. It's time to get moving."

Straining under the weight of their loads, the boys began trudging up the slope. Each had portaged before but there had always been older and stronger adults to help with the task. It wasn't long before they realized what a big job they had taken on.

"Need a break," Seth wheezed. "This thing is heavier than I thought."

"Deal. These packs are all I can carry. I don't remember this much work portaging with my dad."

"That's 'cause he probably did most of the heavy lifting," Seth moaned, setting one end of the canoe on the ground. "We're at least thirty minutes into this portage and I doubt if we've gone halfway. Check the chart; see how much farther 'til we hit water."

"According to the map, the portage is about three quarters of a mile long. We can do it. We'll just have to stop more often than we thought. I'll take a turn with the canoe, I just wish it was one of those new aluminum lightweights you have at the resort," Travis groaned, lifting one end. With Seth's help, he balanced the skinny boat on his narrow shoulders. Looking much like a tall turtle, with only long legs visible under the green shell, Travis shuffled forward.

Seconds later, Seth exploded with a blistering string of four-letter words.

"What's the problem?" Travis's voice boomed from under his load.

"You won't believe it! A huge blowdown is blocking the trail. It's so big it must have tipped over from old age. Lose the canoe and help me figure out how we're gonna get around the mother of all pines."

Travis couldn't believe his eyes when he rounded the bend. In front of him was a wall of green. It had to be an old growth tree more than a hundred years in the making. And it couldn't have fallen in a worse place. The path at this point passed between a rock-faced cliff and a steep hill filled with the skeletal remains of other fallen trees. The enormous evergreen blocked the only level ground.

"We have two choices," Seth grumbled. "We can go back the way we came or we can chop a tunnel through the branches. I vote for chopping."

"Me, too, I guess. We should only have to hack half a dozen branches to slide the canoe through. I'll get the hatchet. Why don't you bring the canoe up here while I get started?"

Travis unbuckled the back of his top pack and pulled out a small hand ax in a leather sheath. Trotting up the path, he stopped in front of the green wall of needles and tried to figure out where to start. When he decided which branches would be the easiest to cut, he began chopping. Several minutes later he had managed to cut the limb and throw it to the side.

"One down!"

In an hour of taking turns they managed to cut a channel under the fallen giant. Chips littered the ground as if a family beavers had been busy. The boys slumped to the ground to discuss their next move.

"Let's put the gear in the canoe, then one of us can crawl ahead with the rope and pull while the other pushes from behind," Seth suggested.

"Good idea. It should work."

With Seth pushing and Travis pulling, the canoe slid through the narrow opening like a long, green toboggan. When the boat cleared the pine, Seth yelled into the forest. "You have to do better than that to stop us. We have places to go and things to do!"

"I wouldn't push it," Travis advised. "It's not nice to fool with Mother Nature. After a few moments of reflection, he added, "We must have lost over an hour to that tree. We better get our butts in gear or we'll fall so far behind schedule we'll be paddling in the dark."

"I hear you. Grab the packs and help me with the canoe. We can't be far from the next lake."

The last of the hike was mostly downhill. Twenty minutes later, Travis spotted the glitter of sun-sparkled water filtering through the underbrush. Soon, both teens were standing at the water's edge, sweat soaking through their shirts.

"I can't believe the temperature!" Seth exclaimed, bending down to splash water on his face. "It must be in the high seventies, another record-setting day."

"No doubt. Now let's try setting a record getting to the next portage," said Travis. "We still have a long way to go before dark—and it comes pretty early this time of year."

"I'm ready," Seth answered, pushing the canoe into the water. Then, holding the bow so Travis could climb in and work his way to the back, he added, "Your turn to drive."

After a few minutes of silent paddling, Travis spoke. "What time is it getting to be?"

Seth laid the paddle across the gunnels and unfastened the small nylon pouch attached to his belt. Pulling out a black leather case, he turned toward Travis and flashed a toothy grin. "Not only can I tell you the time and our exact location, I can tell you to the minute the sun will set. This GPS Rollie let me borrow is amazing."

Opening the case, Seth removed what looked like a cell phone. The top half held a tiny video screen. "I didn't turn it on this morning. No sense draining the batteries until we need to use it."

Seth pressed the startup button. Then, holding the device high in the air, he waited for the unit to lock onto satellites orbiting far above them.

"It's one thirty-four," Seth said in his best announcer's voice. "Sunset is at six-fifteen, central daylight time. Anything else you need to know?"

"Yeah, since that thing's so good with numbers, what'd I get on my math test? And how does that little box know so much, anyway?"

"It's all in the operator," Seth fired back. "Guess I better handle it."

Soon they reached the next portage. Just before the bow struck the rocky shoreline, the boys paddled backward to slow the canoe.

"Well done, if I say so myself," Seth said, scrambling from the bow to a large, flat boulder. "Nary a bruise on this magnificent craft of mine.

"Sit tight," he instructed. "I'll pull the bow up on that sand between the rocks."

"How long a carry we got this time?" Travis asked.

"This is a short one, only about a quarter mile or so. Let's hope it doesn't involve any chopping. I still can't believe the size of that tree back there. It must have been a hundred years old."

"That's what I'm going to feel like tonight after all this work."

"What are you talking about?"

"My body's gonna feel a hundred years old from carrying this pack of yours," Travis replied. "What did you put in it, bricks?"

Rolling the canoe upside down, Seth lifted the bow over his head. He walked his hands down the gunnels until he came to the middle. Quickly pushing the canoe upward, he used the palms of his hands to catch the inside bottom. With a second thrust, he spun in the opposite direction and again caught the bottom with his palms. Lowering the padded crosspiece to his shoulders, he balanced the canoe.

"Quit whining. You want me to tell everyone at school what a rookie I took along? I loaded the *Titanic* by myself.'

"That was quite a trick," Travis admitted. "Where did you learn it?"

"Most of the college guys Rollie uses as guides do it that way. Big difference, though, those canoes are a lot lighter. Why didn't you talk me out of using this tub? It weighs as much as a pregnant moose. So stop complaining about a couple of extra pounds in my pack."

This time the trail was clear of fallen timber. The trip to the next lake went well. In no time at all they had the canoe packed and were crossing the slim body of water. After a ten-minute paddle, they pulled the canoe onto the next portage landing.

"There's good news and bad news, Trav. The good news is that this is the last long carry of the day. Then it's mostly water to tonight's campsite."

"So what's the bad news?"

"The bad news is, it's your turn to carry the canoe. And guess what? I'm not helping you load it on those skinny things you call shoulders. You're on your own."

Seth picked up his pack-frame and slipped his arms into the carry straps. Squatting, he grabbed Travis's pack and in one smooth motion, lifted it high in the air. He balanced the second load on his head using his arms as support braces. "I'm outta here. See ya."

"Hey, man! Help me with the canoe. I've never loaded one by myself."

"There's always a first time," Seth's voice bellowed as the packs vanished into the forest.

"Gimme a break!" Travis yelled up the trail. "You've been doing this all summer. I admit it; compared to you I'm a rookie. Get your butt back here and give me a hand."

Seth reappeared at the trailhead. "Gee, Trav, I've got my hands full right now. But when you get to the other end of the portage, I'll be happy to give you a hand. Maybe even a standing ovation."

Then like a deer at the edge of a meadow, he disappeared.

Travis muttered under his breath, "Seth the comic. But if he can do it, so can I."

He clutched the side of the canoe and rolled it over. Then picturing what Seth had done, he grabbed the bow and lifted. He began to inch his hands along the gunnels. When he reached the brace he gave a hard, upward thrust. Catching the bottom with his palms, he bent his elbows and gave another push skyward.

The teen started to turn so he would be facing the front. Unfortunately the tip of a shovel-shaped rock caught his toe. Travis lost his balance. He tried to catch himself, but with his hands over his head, he tipped sideways. Falling to one knee, he managed to keep from landing face first on hard ground.

The canoe continued to drop, hitting his hand and shoulder. Travis grimaced as the canoe rolled off and with a jolting thud, crunched on the rocky ground. Dazed, the youth lay flat for several long moments.

After a time Travis slowly pushed to one elbow and then to his knees. His palm pulsed in agony, as did his shoulder. Holding out his arm, he opened and closed his fist. All his fingers seem to work. He flexed his shoulder. Jolts of sharp, searing pain shot through his upper body.

"Perfect. Just what I need, a broken arm."

Rising like an arthritic old man, Travis got to his feet. He flexed his shoulder a second time, only more slowly than the first attempt. The ache was definitely there, though not quite as sharp. Stepping back to the now upright canoe, he ran his eyes along the bottom. Despite the cracking sound it'd made, nothing seemed damaged.

"No way am I going to load this thing by myself. It was Seth's joke and now he's laughing it up while he's lugging his own boat." Travis unstrapped a paddle from the seat supports and squeezed it with his sore hand. Satisfied that he could get a grip on the shaft, he used it as a walking stick as he shuffled down the trail.

* * *

Seth lowered the pack he'd balanced onto his head and let it plop on the beach. Squatting, he leaned back until his pack-frame was touching ground. Then he freed himself of the straps.

"Whew!" he exhaled loudly. "Seth, you deserve a break today. Sit down and cool off. Wait for the rookie to bring the canoe."

The sweaty teen loosened a side pocket on one of the packsacks. He reached in and pulled out a plastic container. "Yep, you deserve a reward," he announced to no one but himself. He popped the lid and poured a handful of mixed nuts and dried fruit onto an open palm.

Licking the last bit of trail mix off of his fingers, he decided to go back and help with the canoe. Maybe the rookie couldn't carry it this far.

Munching the last kernel of mix, he turned and began retracing his steps.

Chapter Three

C H A P T E R   T H R E E

Seth hadn't gone far before he spotted Travis hobbling down the trail. He wasn't all that shocked to see him empty handed. "Say buddy, didn't you forget to something—like, a big, green canoe?"

Drawing closer, Seth noticed the grimace distorting Travis's face. "Where's our ride? And why are you limping?"

"The canoe is right where you left it. And I'm walking this way 'cause my shoulder feels like I was mauled by a moose."

Seth pulled up short. "What happened?"

"I tried loading the canoe like you showed me. But it didn't work out. I tripped and it crunched my shoulder."

Seth turned serious. "Are you okay? Anything broken?"

"I think I'm all right. I don't know about the canoe. It fell pretty hard but I didn't see any cracks."

Seth scuffed the earth with the toe of his tennis shoe. He looked up and asked, "What do you want to do, camp here and head home in the morning?"

"I think we can keep going. That is if you don't mind lugging the boat. I think by the time you lug it over here, my shoulder and hand should feel better."

"Your hand? What happened to your hand?"

"Same trick. The canoe bounced off my hand before it hit my shoulder. It hurts, but I think it's just bruised."

"Well, if you're sure you're all right, I'll get the canoe. We should still make tonight's campsite with enough daylight to fix supper. We probably won't get any fishing in, but we can fish tomorrow or Saturday. Why don't you soak your hand in the lake while I'm gone? Maybe it'll feel better."

Travis trudged to where a flat section of volcanic bedrock angled into the water. Then he gingerly lowered himself down on his side and dangled his throbbing hand in the water.

As he lounged in the sunshine, movement across the narrow bay caught his eye. It was big and black, almost the size of a Volkswagen and Travis knew instantly he was looking at a huge black bear.

Travis had seen dozens of bears. They were common in the region. But even at several hundred yards he could tell this was no ordinary animal. This was a giant of a bruin.

"Ho-ly cow!" Travis exclaimed. "Talk about your king of beasts. That big boy gets the right of way anytime he wants."

"Who you talking to? Did the canoe hit your head, too?" Seth's voice boomed, startling Travis. He had been so intent on watching the bear, he'd failed to hear his friend's footsteps.

"Across the bay, over by that broken birch," Travis said, gesturing with his good hand.

"What am I looking for?" Seth asked, dumping the canoe with a groan.

Travis returned his gaze to where he'd last sighted the animal. "It's gone," he sighed.

"What are you talking about? First you mumble to yourself and now you're seeing things. You sure the canoe didn't crack your melon?"

"There was a monster black bear over there a minute ago. It was the size of a Chevette."

"Oh, really? Don't flake on me, man."

"I'm serious, Seth. There's a bear on the other side of this bay as big as a dumpster. I didn't think they got that big. I'm not so sure we want to go over to that side of the lake."

"Trav, unless you want to head back the way we came in, we don't have a choice. Besides, when was the last time you heard about a camper being attacked by a bear? They like to raid the food supply, not eat people. We'll be fine. We'll just make enough noise to scare it away. The bear will be long gone before we get there."

Travis turned to study Seth. "You're serious, aren't you? But I suppose you're right. Let me take care of my stomach before we move on. How about you show me where the snacks are hidden? But wait a minute; I thought you said this was the last carry for the day. Now you're saying we have to paddle and portage some more?"

"So I lied. The trip over to Henson Lake is only a couple hundred yards. We really can't count it as a portage. Finish up. We need to get our rears in gear."

Travis stared across the water. "What about the bear?"

"What about him? He won't bother us, especially if we make a lot of noise. By the time we paddle over, he'll be long gone."

"Uh-huh, sure," Travis mumbled. "He's probably already headed for our campsite."

They slid the canoe into the water, climbed aboard and set off. For Travis, each stroke was painful. If he paddled on the left side, his shoulder ached. If he paddled on the right, his hand hurt.

"Sorry to say it, but you're going to have to carry most of the load today. I'm a hurting machine."

"So what's new?" Seth grinned. "Haven't I been doing the heavy lifting anyway?"

"Whatever. At least I can help scare that bear away."

Travis turned, cupped a hand to his mouth and bellowed. "Eaaah! Eaaah!

"Impressive. I think they heard you in Grand Marais. Has that bear rattled your nerves?"

"If you saw how big it was, they'd hear you in town, too. I swear it could just about look a moose in the eye. And that's just standing on all fours."

Seth couldn't help but laugh. "Might you be stretching it a bit?"

"Well, maybe a little. But I'm telling you, that bear's a monster."

It only took a few minutes to cross the skinny arm of water. A short carry through the forest would lead to Henson, another long slim lake.

In no time at all they were back on the water. As they were approaching a small rocky point, movement caught Seth's attention. Letting his paddle drag, he studied the dark shape moving along the edge of the forest. It had to be the bear Travis had seen.

"Whoa, Trav! Look over by the point. There's your buddy. You're right. He's a beast. I've never seen one that big. What do you think he goes? Five hundred pounds?"

"At least that much, maybe more," Travis answered. "And did you notice?"

"Notice what?"

"He's going the same way we are!"

Seth considered the remark. "I'm not going to worry about it. We don't have any tasty-smelling food with us like bacon or steaks. And if we build a big enough fire, there's not much chance of *any* bear bothering us."

"Ahhh, Seth, not to change the subject, but have you been dripping water in the canoe?"

"No, why?"

"There's a puddle under the packs. I was hoping you'd splashed water in when I wasn't looking. 'Cause if you didn't put it there, I'd say our ship is leaking."

Seth glanced down. Sure enough, water lapped at the bottoms of the aluminum pack frames.

Seth's teasing smile was suddenly replaced by a scowl. "How hard did you drop my canoe?"

"Not that hard. How well did you fix the crack that made Rollie give it to ya in the first place?"

"It was done right," Seth growled. "I filed the crack, set in a fiberglass patch and put on a coat of resin. If you hadn't dropped it, there wouldn't be a problem."

Seth studied the puddle, and then added, "At least it doesn't look like the leak's too bad. We'll be at the campsite before there's enough water to get our feet wet. Right now, our problem is finding the campsite."

"Did you forget the GPS?"

"You're right, I did."

Seth laid his paddle across the gunnels and unclipped the GPS from his belt. Then he studied the screen for a few seconds. Looking up, he said, "According to this, our first campsite should be along shore about half a mile up."

Travis nodded, relief written all over his face. "By the time we set up camp it'll be too late to go fishing. What's the backup plan for dinner tonight?"

"We have plenty of freeze-dried meals. They're pretty slick. All we do is add water, heat and stir. Instant supper. You ever try 'em camping with your dad?"

"Nah, we always used a cooler to carry fresh food. Dad likes his steaks with the bone still attached. Sometimes Mom sends a pot of stew we can use for several meals. When you're hungry nothing tastes better. Speaking of hungry, I wonder where our big, black friend is. He probably wants to join us for supper."

"Jeez, Trav. Would you forget about the bear? We'll be fine. Freeze-dried ain't on his menu." Seth grinned.

"Now, if we had some of those steaks you and your dad pack along, that'd be another story. We'd have to eat them tonight or he'd be all over us. If the wind is in the right direction, a bear can smell cooking meat for miles."

"Thanks for sharing. It makes me feel so much better knowing that critter can smell us a mile or more away. I'm gonna sleep like a baby tonight."

Travis took a couple of pathetic pulls on the paddle, then blurted, "Over there, in that cove. Is that the campsite?"

Seth paused his paddle long enough to look. He beamed. "What'd I tell ya, rookie? We made it here with daylight to spare. And we didn't even sink in the process. There's hardly any water in the bottom. You sure you didn't put it there when you were worrying about that bear? It does seem to have a yellow cast to it."

Despite his pain, Travis laughed. "Nice try, bud. But if anyone wets his pants, it'll be you when old Blackie tries to share your sleeping bag tonight. But hey, take it easy. You better slow down before we hit shore."

Seth backstroked, bringing the narrow craft to a stand-still just as it was about to touch land. After thrusting his paddle to the bottom to help steady the canoe, he said, "Okay pal, end of the line for day one. How's that old saying go? All's well that ends well."

"That's the saying, Seth. But the trip is a long way from being over. Let's get out, set the tents up and get a fire going. I'm starving. I can hardly wait to sample your camp cooking."

Chapter Four

C H A P T E R   F O U R

"Sarah, did the girls enjoy the slumber party?" Lynn Springwood queried. Mother and daughter were busy in the kitchen. Through the wide window over the sink, a panoramic view of Poplar Lake was on display.

"Yeah, it was fun. But none of us really got any sleep," Sarah yawned.

Day was fading to twilight as the two finished the last of the dishes. Earlier, Lynn had driven Sarah's friends home. Now she was hoping to have a serious chat with the female half of her twin offspring.

Lynn stared at the lake through the window glass. Poplar had calmed to a satin finish. The first stars of night were beginning to twinkle, casting reflections on the shiny water. Only a single loon broke the glassy surface, trailing a thin line of wake as it glided past the pier.

"I wonder how your brother's day went. The boys sure had a sunny start to their adventure. I don't ever remember weather this warm in October." Lynn stalled, hoping to find a natural opening to switch topics.

She set a plate on the counter, stared out the window, and then started over. "If Seth hadn't helped on so many canoe trips, I don't think I would have let him go so far. At least Seth and Travis have each other to look out for them. I think that's important, don't you?"

Sarah spun around to face her mother. "Are you asking for my opinion? It's a little late for that, isn't it?"

"Well, yes. Your opinion is important to me. Why would you think otherwise?"

"Really, Mom? How could I think it's important to you when you go off 'who knows where' on the weekends? You don't say where you're going or where you've been. I gotta' tell ya, Seth and I have been pretty bummed out about it."

"That's what I need to talk to you about. I think it'll be easier for me to tell you first. Then maybe you can help me find a way to tell Seth."

"Tell Seth what? What are you talking about?"

"Sarah, can you understand how much I miss your father? How lonely I get for someone to share my feelings . . . someone to talk to when I have a problem?"

"What are you saying, Mom, that you can't talk to Seth or me? How's that supposed to make us feel?"

"Oh no, Sarah! You and Seth are the most important part of my life. It's just that I miss having a partner my own age. You know . . . someone to share life's ups and downs."

Sarah took a step back and stared her mother. "So what do you do, Mom, go man-shopping on weekends?"

It was Mrs. Springwood's turn to react. Her chin dropped with a gasp. "No Sarah, it's not like that at all. Do you remember in early summer when you stayed over at a friend's cabin, the same weekend Seth helped guide a canoe group?"

Sarah nodded but kept her lips locked.

"Do you recall I was teasing you before you left? I said

my babies had grown so old that they were leaving poor Mom home alone?"

Again, Sarah only nodded.

"Well, something happened that weekend that's changed my life. Changed it for the better, and I hope you and Seth think so, too."

"What is it? Did you win the lottery?" Sarah mumbled sarcastically, no longer able to look her mother in the eye.

"Gosh no, nothing like that. That Saturday afternoon, I drove into town to pick up supplies. While I was in the grocery store, pushing my cart around one of the aisles, I bumped into another cart. The carts really clattered. I was shocked when I saw the face of the other shopper. It was a boyfriend from my high school days. Doug Davis. He was just as surprised to see me. We stood there looking at each other with silly grins on our faces. After a few minutes of chitchat, we agreed to catch up over coffee."

"Mom," Sarah blurted. "Are you telling me you go down to the cafe every Saturday night and play catch-up with this guy?"

"No, it's more involved than that. We're both single parents. He lost his wife a year ago to cancer. He's raising his seven-year-old by himself. Doug's a journalist. He writes short stories and feature articles for several magazines. He wanted to live where he knew his daughter, Cindy, would be safe while he was on assignment. His brother's family lives near Grand Marais. Cindy always has a safe place to stay when Doug's out of town."

"Get to the point, Mom. Where are you going with this?"

"We agreed to meet for dinner the next weekend. A week later I drove to his place for dinner and to meet his little girl."

"Are you saying that every Saturday you go down to this Doug guy's place and let him cook for you? There's more to the story, isn't there?" Sarah asked, eyes blazing. "There has to be more or you wouldn't have kept it so secret!"

"I'm getting to it, honey. Please hear me out. Yes, for the first couple of weeks that's exactly what I did. We'd have dinner and then watch a video or play Chinese checkers with Cindy. Several times we went out to eat. But after running into some of the kids from your school, I didn't think that was such a great idea. The last few weeks we've driven to Duluth to catch a concert and a play. That's why I got dressed up before leaving and returned so late."

Sarah turned to face her mom. With hands on hips she snapped, "Is it serious? Are you and this man with two first names an item?"

"The truth . . . yes. I care for him very much."

"How could you? Dad's only been gone a little while!"

"It's been almost two years, Sarah. Don't you think it's time I get on with my life?"

"What about Seth and me? How's this going to change our lives? Jeez, Mom, I'm confused. It seems like we were just getting to be a family again, and now you're throwing us a stinkball—because this really smells!"

"Honey! How can you say that? You haven't even met Doug. I know he can't take Dad's place and he knows that, too. He's dying to meet the two of you. I haven't let him because I was afraid of the way you kids might react. You seem to be proving me correct. Please, give it a chance. I know you'll like him, and Cindy's the sweetest little girl."

"What, has he asked you to marry him or something? Is that where this little mother-daughter chat is going? Don't tell me that. I don't want to hear it!"

"Yes and no. Yes, he's asked me, and no, I said not until you kids were okay with it."

"Even if I was okay with it, Seth won't be. He worshipped

Dad. He won't let anyone take his place!"

"Sarah, don't you think you're being a little selfish. Doesn't what your mother wants or feels count for anything? Let's leave it there for the night. Sleep on it. Maybe you can see things a little more my way in the morning."

"I doubt it. But you're right. I think I've heard enough about this this guy for one night. I'm going to bed."

* * *

As the sun set over the far shore with a finale of flaming oranges and reds, the campers hurried to finish their supper chores. Seth was kneeling on the lava flow that sloped to the lake. He was rinsing the pots used to heat their meal. Travis was busy reorganizing his packsack.

Finished scrubbing, Seth looked up and asked, "How's your hand?"

"Sore, but I think it'll be better by morning. What, you worried you'll have to do all the paddling? My shoulder still hurts, though. Any chance you brought aspirin along?"

"Check the first aid kit. It's in the side pocket of my bottom pack."

Travis shuffled to Seth's pack. He dug around for a moment before removing a white container. He smiled as he pulled out a small bottle of pills. "Ahhh, good news. These should help."

"You're welcome," Seth said. "Not to change the subject, but can you believe the sun already went down?"

Seth was right. The sun had dipped below the horizon, leaving behind smears of blood red sky. As if jealous, the placid lake mirrored the colorful sunset. But the day's warmth was escaping like heat from an open oven. As soon as the sun sunk out of sight, the air took on a sharp chill.

The boys had pulled on jeans and sweatshirts before starting the fire. Now they returned to their packs seeking a second layer of clothing. Seth donned a blaze-orange jacket. Travis slipped into a green waterproof windbreaker.

"Wow, Seth. If we get lost you'll sure be easy to spot. That jacket is bright enough to direct traffic. When did you get that?"

"I got it for my birthday last summer. Mom said if Rollie would take me, I could try deer hunting next month. You need blaze-orange to be legal."

Travis nodded. "Cool. My dad isn't into hunting. He doesn't see anything wrong with it. But with all his outdoor research, it's not something he's interested in. I guess I can see his point. He captures a lot of wildlife with his camera, though."

"Not much protein in a photo. Hard to digest, too," Seth laughed. "I'm gonna get some more wood. Why don't you round up some pine needles to stuff under our tents? But we better get a move on it. Until the moon comes up, it'll be blacker than the inside of that bear's belly."

"Don't remind me. Speaking of bears, shouldn't we hang the packs from a tree limb?"

Seth gave it a quick thought before shaking his head. "Nah. We don't have any real food with us. The food packets are sealed and don't have any odor. That old bear's probably more afraid of you than you are of it. We never had any trouble all summer. Let's just keep the fire burning for awhile. That'll keep the critters away."

The words had barely escaped the boy's lips when a wolf's howl rose in the distance. Starting with a low moan, the call rose in pitch, and then slid down the musical scale before fading away.

"Welcome to the Boundary Waters," Travis exclaimed. "Sounds like my dad should be doing his wolf research out here. If he hadn't taught me that wolves don't attack people, I'd say we sleep in the canoe tonight."

"Not to burst your bubble, but they do—attack, that is," Seth corrected him. "It's really rare, but it happens. A lone wolf attacked some kids on a beach in Ontario last summer. And a pack tore into some guys and their hunting dogs in Idaho. I read about it in *Outdoor Life*."

Travis didn't argue with his friend. He was more concerned about the bear they'd seen than any long odds of a rogue wolf making trouble.

Hearing no answering reply to the solo call, the boys went about their chores. Seth ranged in search of firewood. Travis gathered large handfuls of needles from under a nearby pine. When he was satisfied he had enough, he lifted one side of his small tent and spread them generously on the ground. He was finishing the job when Seth returned with an armload of wood.

"I'm going to hoist my pack into a tree," Travis said as Seth dropped the fuel near the fire. "Want me to pull yours up, too?"

"Nothing's going to bother it. You're just wasting time and energy. Here's what you can do. Put the cooking pots on top the packs. If a critter gets to close, the pots will hit the ground. The noise will either scare it off or wake us up. We yell and whatever's out there turns tail."

Travis's forehead wrinkled. "Have you ever tried that trick before?"

"No, but it should work. And while you're at it, put some rocks next to your sleeping bag. You can always thump Big Blackie on the rump. That'll get his attention."

"Oh, yeah! Probably a lot more notice than we want!"

For the next hour the twosome sat near the fire swapping school stories. Seth finally chose to risk sharing his mother's behavior. When finished explaining how different she seemed, Travis remained silent.

After a long pause, he said, "Aren't you being a little hard on her? She is an adult. And as long as she takes care of you and Sarah, she deserves some private time, too."

Seth stared straight ahead, as if reading a distant road sign. "How do you figure going out at night, doing who knows what, is private time?"

"You don't know what she's been doing, Seth. I understand your concern but don't jump to conclusions. Jumping without knowing where you're gonna land is a good way to get hurt."

"Yeah. Easy for you to say. You have both your parents. Without Dad around, Mom is my responsibility."

Travis slowly shook his head. "Is that right? When did she appoint you her caretaker? I think you need to trust her on this one. She hasn't let you and Sarah down yet, has she?

A waning half moon had climbed high enough to begin filtering light through branches. The floor of the campsite was a mix of ink-stained shadows. Without looking at Travis, Seth grabbed a stick and stirred the fire. He broke several branches into small pieces and then tossed them on the hot coals. Offering only a half-hearted "good night," he crawled into his tent and zipped the door shut behind him.

Travis remained seated, staring vacantly at the glowing embers. He was pondering his remark about Seth's mom. It was obviously not the one Seth had wanted to hear. But thinking it over, he still felt it was the right response.

Anything else wouldn't have been truthful. Only after standing and stretching did Travis react to Seth's final words. "Yeah, sleep tight, buddy. And don't let the timber wolves bite."

"Funny. Don't call me when old Blackie crawls in your tent."

Chapter Five

C H A P T E R   F I V E

The teenagers lay awake, mulling over the day's events. Travis was troubled about his sore hand and shoulder. Seth's brain bounced around his buddy's remarks about his mother. But despite their ponderings, it wasn't long before the effects of the exercise and fresh air caught up. Within minutes of each other, both teens nodded off. Outside, the moon continued its western journey, a giant nightlight repeated on the lake below.

Occasionally a swirl would ripple the glassy water as fish rose to snatch an errant insect. But except for the far-off hooting of an owl, the campsite was as quiet as a back road cemetery.

The boys quickly settled into deep slumber.

As the campers slept, the sharp snap of a breaking branch broke the silence.

Then all was quiet.

There was a second cracking sound, this time muffled and closer to camp—followed heavy breathing. Close, closer, *crash*! The pots and pans on the pack tumbled to the rocky ground with a clatter. Startled, the boys were instantly awake.

Seth was the first to react. "Hey! Get out of here! Get!"

Both teens fumbled frantically for their flashlights. Though alarmed, they unzipped their tent doors and aimed the beams of light toward the gear. It was exactly what Travis had feared, the monstrous black bear. The huge animal was clutching the food pack in its claws and trying to tear it apart with its sharp teeth.

"Hey!" Seth screeched, throwing a rock in the bear's direction. The stone bounced off the bear's rump with no effect. The hulking omnivore continued ripping at the bag. Seth took aim and hurled a second stone. The rock struck the bruin square in the face. Dropping the pack, the bear let out an enormous bellow, its large canine teeth catching the moonlight.

The bear rose on its hind legs, the coal-black hair on its broad back bristling with rage. Raising its massive head, it growled a warning.

"Get out of here!" Seth bellowed. "Come on, Trav, make some noise."

As if awakened from a bad dream, Travis finally realized he had to help. He started yelling at the top of his lungs.

The bear suddenly became aware he had more than one human to deal with. Dropping to all fours, it snatched the pack in its massive mouth and without looking back, lumbered into the darkness.

"Is he gone?" Travis whispered.

"Yeah, and so is our food," Seth growled. "We're off to a flying start. I hope you're half the fisherman you say you are. Otherwise we're going be two hungry campers."

"You think he'll come back?" Travis croaked, visibly shaken by the encounter. "Maybe we better get the fire going again."

"I doubt it. But yeah, a fire wouldn't hurt."

With the bear gone, the forest behind camp remained

dark and mysterious. Travis stirred the coals hoping to rekindle a few flames. Seth danced his flashlight beam along shore until he spotted a piece of driftwood. Talking loudly to himself, the teen nervously shuffled toward the prize. Reaching the goal, he quickly snatched one end of the weathered log. Then with firewood in one hand, flashlight in the other, Seth backed his way toward the tents, eyes busy scanning for danger.

By tossing sticks on top of the hot embers, Travis had managed to bring the fire back to life. "Here, "Seth said. "This driftwood should burn for a couple of hours."

Placing one end on a rock, Seth stomped the log into two pieces. He laid both halves across the coals, picked up a branch and stirred the ashes. After a long moment the edge of the log flickered orange and yellow. Seconds later, much like a gas fireplace, it burst into flames.

"It's going to be a long night," Seth observed. "Why don't you crawl back into your bag? I'll keep first watch. There's no sense both of us losing sleep."

"I can't sleep now. Why don't we both stay by the fire? Maybe later, when my heart stops hammering, I'll be able to get some rest."

"Suit yourself. But I don't think we have anything to worry about. That damn bear isn't gonna come back as long as the fire's burning. Let's see if we can scrounge up some more wood. One log isn't going to make it to morning."

Switching on the flashlight, Seth headed for the forest's edge. He had just disappeared into the shadows of thick evergreens when he gave out a loud whoop.

"All right! Blackie didn't get everything. Trav, bring your flashlight. Some of the food bags must have fallen out of the pack. Help me find them."

"You sure it's safe to be in the woods right now?" Travis replied weakly.

"As long as we keep making noise, we'll be fine."

Travis aimed his slice of light toward the wood-line. The beam wobbled in his shaky hand. "Keep talking, I don't want to be bear bait."

"Look," Seth directed, shining his light on the ground. "There's scuff marks where the pack was dragged through the pine needles. Hey, there's another packet."

Seth followed his flashlight beam and retrieved the plastic pouch.

"I wonder how many more fell out before he stopped to finish ripping the pack apart." Travis asked in a voice still nervous with fright. "Maybe we should just get more firewood and look for our stuff in the morning."

"Yeah, good idea. No sense pushing our luck. We can pick up the trail at daybreak. At least we have a few meals to go with the fish you're gonna catch. Who knows, maybe we'll get lucky and find a few more once the sun's up."

* * *

The night lingered like a bad movie, the scene with the bear replaying in the boys' minds. Travis finally tried to sleep. He had just dozed off when it became his turn to keep watch. Now wide awake, he sat by the fire, constantly adding wood to keep the flames dancing.

Above camp the sky was a black bowl. Clouds had moved overhead, and except for faint fire flickers, the campsite was enveloped in darkness.

Travis began to wonder if this camping trip had been such a great idea. He was so weary. His shoulder and hand throbbed. Then there was the leak in the canoe to think about. How bad was it? And the bear—was he still hanging around camp? Food, what were they going to eat?

These questions and more were on his mind as the first hints of morning began lifting night's dark veil. Travis knew that true sunrise was at least an hour away. But its promise let him breathe a little easier.

"Soon," he whispered. "Soon it'll be light enough to see if that brute is still hanging around."

"What are you mumbling about?" Seth asked from inside his sleeping bag.

"Oh, you're awake." Travis said, embarrassed about muttering out loud.

"I wasn't until some fool started jabbering. Why don't you crawl back into your bag, try to get a little rest?"

"Think it's safe?"

"Yep, I do. Full light's on our doorstep. Nothing should bother us now. Go ahead and get some sleep. I'll keep an ear open for unwanted visitors."

Travis didn't need prodding. He went into his small shelter and soon nodded off. Later, when he awoke, the tent was filled with light. He lay still, listening. Nothing. All was quiet.

"Seth, you awake?"

No reply.

Travis called again, louder. Same result.

The youth's pulse began to race. Travis ripped open the zippered door to scramble outside.

This time he bellowed. "Seth! Seth! Where are you?"

"Yo, sleeping beauty, keep your cool. I'll be with you in a minute."

Relief flooded over Travis. He stumbled to a stump and plopped down, waiting for his heartbeat to slow. For a panicked moment he'd felt what it would be like to be alone so far from home. Seth's yell startled Travis before he had time to dwell on that image.

"We're in luck!" Seth hollered. "I found the pack. My things are pretty much all here. But I only found two pouches of freeze-dried, and they both have tooth marks in them."

Approaching one another, Seth held up the pack for Travis to inspect.

"Where was it?" Travis asked.

"Not far from where we found the other stuff. It wasn't hard to find. I just followed a trail of socks and underwear, and there it was, lying in the leaves. I can't say it's as good as new. Well, it is, if you don't count the ripped flap and the bite marks."

"What's missing?"

"Ahh, well," Seth stumbled. "A couple things. Like the GPS I stuck in the pack. And the extra energy bars I forgot were in there. I guess they probably were what the bear smelled in the first place. And a couple of Snickers I was saving for the last day."

"What?" Travis exploded. "You had candy bars in the pack and you wouldn't let me hang it from a limb? What were you thinking? You know bears love chocolate. It's one of the first things my dad taught me when I started camping. Never keep candy bars around unless you want a bear hug in the middle of the night."

"Chill, man. I packed 'em this summer, all the time. No problem," Seth growled in return.

"Yeah, but you camped with big groups. Even Blackie wouldn't try a night raid with a bunch of people around. Jeez, Seth. I can't believe you of all people did something so stupid!"

"Hang on! Who you callin' stupid? Okay, so I made a mistake. Big deal. Like you're Mr. Perfect. What about dropping the canoe? You hurt yourself and cracked the bottom of my boat."

Travis spun away, his mouth set in a tight-lipped grimace. After taking a deep breath he turned to face Seth and said, "Hold on a minute. You left me to carry the canoe by myself. Maybe if you'd fixed it right in the first place, it wouldn't have cracked. Don't blame me for your mistakes."

This time it was Seth's turn to suck air. After a long pause he made one final remark. "My mistakes, huh? How do figure they're my mistakes? Sometimes stuff just happens, Trav. It's part of life."

Chapter Six

C H A P T E R   S I X

Tempers cooled and the teens went about starting the day. Seth searched the woods and underbrush hoping to locate the GPS. Travis busied himself at the fire, preparing one of the remaining freeze-dried packets.

Wearing a long face, Seth trudged back into camp with empty hands.

Travis stopped stirring to look up. "No luck finding the GPS, huh?"

"Nope. It must have flipped out of the pack when the bear was running away. Rollie isn't going to be too happy. Those things are pricey. But there's not much we can do about it."

Changing the subject, he asked, "So, what's cooking?"

"Turkey and potatoes."

"About ready to eat?"

"Almost. Just have to let it cool," Travis answered, giving each pot a stir with a stick. "Soon as we eat, we better think about moving on. I thought I'd get my fishing rod ready and drag a lure behind the boat. Maybe we'll get lucky and catch lunch."

"Better hope so. We're going need more than a couple of freeze-dried meals to fill our tanks."

Travis sensed the heated words they had earlier were bothering Seth. "Look," Travis said, turning to face his friend. "Sorry about what I said before. To be honest, I'm a little scared."

"Really? Why? We'll be okay. Except for the food packets and the GPS, we have the same gear as when we started. Well, that and the fact you hurt yourself. I won't even mention dropping the canoe on your head. Are you able to paddle today?"

"Not sure. My shoulder still hurts but my hand feels better. I think I can give you a hand. But I'm going to be so busy pulling in fish, I won't have much time to paddle."

"Yeah, right. Let's finish eating and get going."

Soon after wolfing down the meal they went about stowing their gear. Finished packing, Travis extended the telescoping rod borrowed from his father.

"I'm ready to cruise. I just need to find the map," Seth said, digging through a pack.

"You won't find it in there. I tucked it away before we landed." Travis said, reaching into his bag. "Good thing Blackie didn't get to this last night. We'd definitely have an 'unbearable' problem."

"Unbearable . . . funny. Okay, that's it; I'm ready to go. Let's make a wake."

The boys eased the canoe into the water. Seth took up his position in the rear. He reached under the seat, pulled up a strap from a life preserver and snapped it to a belt loop.

"What, you plan on tipping us over? You didn't hook up yesterday," Travis said, preparing to shove off.

"Just in case you hook on to Jaws and it attacks the canoe. Seriously, I thought I'd play it safe. It might be a good idea if you do the same. We always wear them on the summer trips. Water's a lot warmer then, too."

"You're probably right," Travis agreed, getting in.

"So long, sucker! Hope you get a gut ache from stealing our food!" Seth yelled at the forest.

"And don't come around again or we'll kick some bear butt!" Travis added. Then, turning serious, he said, "Funny, isn't it?"

"Funny how?" Seth asked.

"How brave we are during the day. And how quickly things change without sunlight. Speaking of sunshine, what's gonna happen to ours?" Travis asked, gazing up as he let out his fishing line.

During the time it had taken them to get on the water, dark clouds had lined up the horizon.

"It looks like we won't be stripping down to shorts today. This time of year it's hard to get the temperature to rise without sunshine," Seth said, studying the graying sky over his shoulder.

"Bring the canoe closer to shore," Travis requested. "There's probably a big bass waiting for breakfast right next to that drowned tree."

Seth did as requested. Travis made an ideal cast. The lure landed alongside the skeletal remains of a pine that had tipped into the water.

As if a small stick of dynamite exploded, spray erupted behind the lure. Travis was startled by the sudden action. The rod was almost yanked from his grasp. Recovering, he jerked back on the rod back to set the hooks.

"All right! All right! You're mine!"

"Give it line, don't lose it!" Seth instructed excitedly. "That's our next meal!"

The young angler played the fish like a pro. While Seth kept the canoe in position, Travis slowly worked his catch toward the boat. When he thought the fish was played out, he brought it alongside the canoe. Then he reached down to lift it from the water.

"What is it?" Seth asked.

"Smallmouth," Travis replied, grinning ear to ear. "Biggest one I ever caught."

Travis jammed his thumb into the fish's mouth, pinned its jaw against his forefinger and hefted it out of the water. But as he was laying the fish on the floor, the bass made one last attempt at freedom.

"Ouch!" Travis yelped.

When the fish flopped, it had slipped from Travis's grip. One of the treble hooks sunk its needle-like point deep into the boy's thumb. Reaching down and grabbing the back of the fish with his free hand, Travis held on with all his strength.

"Seth, get us to shore, fast!"

Seth pointed the canoe toward the bank. With swift strong strokes, he quickly closed the distance, guiding the craft alongside the downed tree.

"How bad is it?" he asked.

"Don't know. I won't know until we get the hooks out of its mouth."

Seth kicked off his sneakers and jumped into the knee-deep water along shore. Splashing to the bow, he tugged the canoe tight to shore. Then he sloshed alongside Travis to check out this latest emergency.

Travis held the fish up for Seth to inspect. A quick glance showed that two of the three hooks were firmly embedded in the fish's lip. The third hook was buried to the bend in Travis's thumb.

"Seth, grab my survival tool. It's in the case on my belt. It has a wire-cutting pliers."

After making certain Travis had a solid grip on the fish, Seth removed the survival tool. Without wasting a second, he used the needle-nosed pliers to remove the hooks from the fish's lip. Then, after tossing the bass far up on shore, he snipped the line from the lure.

Travis held up his hand, the bright bait dangling down like an early season Christmas ornament.

"What now? Can you pull the hook out of my hand?"

"I think I better get the treble apart first. Then we can see about pulling it out."

Seth snipped the offending tine where it joined the other two hooks that formed the treble. He tossed the bait to the middle of the canoe, then examined Travis's predicament.

The hook was buried deep in the meaty part of the thumb. To yank it straight out would be painful and bloody. The barb would not want to vacate its new home without ripping flesh.

Seth explained what he planned to do. "I think the best solution is to use the pliers to twist the hook around so the point comes back out."

"That sounds nasty. Painful, too."

"Well, unless you want to keep it for a souvenir, I don't see any other way."

Gritting his teeth, Travis nodded. "Yeah, okay. Do it."

Travis climbed from the canoe and straddled the tree trunk. Seth kneeled alongside. Placing the hooked hand firmly on one knee, Seth gripped the exposed shank tightly with the pliers. Then he twisted until the tip poked up and out through taut skin.

"Man, that hurts!" Travis winced, flinching.

"Yeah, well, there it is," Seth said, giving the hook another twist. "Almost done."

Enough of the barbed point stuck out for Seth to squeeze it with the pliers. "Hold tight," he instructed, giving an upward thrust. "Gotcha!"

Better let that bleed a bit, Trav. Fish have nasty germs. It's probably best to let a little blood run to wash 'em away."

Travis let his arm dangle and shook his hand as if trying to get rid of something yucky. "Thanks for the opinion, Dr. Springwood."

"Don't be a wise guy. I'm not the wuss with all the little owies."

Seth stood and added, "Isn't that the same hand you hurt yesterday?"

"Yes it is, doctor. How much blood should I let drip before wrapping up my thumb?"

Seth put on a smug smile. "Squeeze out three or four gallons, then rinse it in the lake."

Travis recalled nicked fingers from removing hooks from northern pike. What seemed like a nothing scratch often took days to heal. He let the wound bleed few more seconds. "Three or four gallons, huh? How 'bout I wash it off before I bleed to death?"

"Whatever. It's your thumb," Seth said, striding up the bank to recover the bass. "This is quite a catch. What d'ya think, four pounds?"

"All of that, enough so we won't starve. Why don't you throw it in the canoe? There's enough water in the bottom to keep it fresh for shore lunch. Soon as I put on a band-aid, we can get moving."

"You gonna start with that leak business again?"

"Nope. Just stating a fact. It's not seeping in fast enough to sink us, though. Not yet, anyway."

Travis paused, eyeing his friend. "You look goofy with that orange vest dangling from your belt. Afraid you're going to fall in the lake?"

"Nah, it's just that my partner needs to be rescued every few hours. If you're done whining, let's get going. It looks like we're gonna be in clouds for the rest of the day. We'll need to make the best use of our daylight."

Wrapping his hand in a handkerchief, Travis carefully grabbed the paddle. And although his shoulder ached, he didn't complain. He had caused enough delay as it was.

Travis let his eyes wander. Like sheep in a distant meadow, woolly clouds were roaming, blocking out the sunlight. The morning air remained cool. Sweat shirts and jeans would remain the uniform of the day.

With Seth providing the bulk of the power, the canoe continued tracing the forested shoreline. After lull in the conversation, he said, "We should make the next portage in a little while. Do you want to do the fish before or after the carry?"

"How long ya figure to do the portage?"

"Depends on how much help you're gonna be. If I have to do all the carrying, it'll probably take an hour. If you can manage the packs, we'll be to the next lake in half that."

"How's this for a plan. We both make the trip, you with the canoe and I'll carry part of a pack. While I get a fire going, you can return for the rest of the gear. That way we shouldn't lose any time."

"Then that's what we'll do," Seth grunted, gazing across the lake. "Hey, look! There's a huge moose over there feeding in the shallows. Look at the size of that rack!"

"Man, sure glad he's on that side of the lake. One swat from his antlers and we'd be bottom-side up!" Travis exclaimed. "A Big Mac doesn't have anything on that guy. We're 100 miles from McDonald's, and all the critters come super-sized."

"Seems that way. Maybe the lack of hunting pressure

this far from the roads lets them live to a ripe old age. Rollie has a set of moose antlers tacked on the boathouse at the resort. I thought they were huge. But that guy's hat rack makes Rollie's horns look sick."

"My dad says there are some real monsters over on Isle Royale. If they get big enough to fight off a wolf pack, they're pretty much kings of the island until old age or disease take them down. Speaking of Dad, I wonder if he's through working the island for the season. I kinda miss him when he's gone."

The words had hardly left his mouth when Travis realized his blunder. Who was he to complain about a working father when Seth didn't have one at all?

"Sorry . . . I wasn't thinking."

"Forget it. Don't ya remember? You dropped the canoe on your head yesterday. So today, you get a pass."

They paddled on without further comment. Overhead, clouds continued closing ranks—heavy clouds, thick vapors dressed in fat, dark bottoms and tall, white hats. Every now and again a finger of cool air blew over the lake, raising goose bumps on the paddlers' necks. On the lake's face, nervous white-tipped wavelets danced along the surface.

Mother Nature was planning a surprise party. But she hadn't informed the two young adventurers. The boys paddled on, sensing something was changing, something was different; neither of them was certain enough what it was to want to talk about it.

That would come later—after the fact.

* * *

It was just after one o'clock Friday afternoon when Roger Larsen drove his blue Suburban into the double garage. Gathering his briefcase and a bulging overnight bag, he trudged to the side entrance of his lakeside dwelling.

Finding the door unlocked, the man entered without knocking. "Hello, anyone here?" he called out.

"Dad, you're home!" Beth yelled.

The gawky ten-year-old raced from her bedroom reading perch. "You're back early. We didn't think you'd be home today."

"You're right. I was planning to come home tomorrow but I changed my plans."

"How come?"

"Couldn't wait to see my two beautiful women," he smiled, picking Beth up like a doll and then twirling her around.

Setting Beth down, he asked, "I take it your mother's still at work?"

"She should be home any minute. She's only supposed to work 'til noon."

"Terrific, then we can all have lunch together. What d'ya say we make some sandwiches and heat up some soup? Have it ready when she gets here."

Mr. Larsen put his things in the closet, washed his hands at the kitchen sink, and then poked his head in the refrigerator. "I see some tomatoes, bacon and lettuce. How 'bout BLTs? Does that sound good to you?"

"Sure, Dad. I'll heat up a frying pan. You slice the tomatoes—they squish when I do it."

By the time Linda Larsen's car pulled into the driveway, the house was filled with the scent of fried bacon.

"Your timing was perfect, Dad. You knew she was coming home, didn't you?"

"Yep, I did. I called her at the clinic as soon as I got into town. Your mother and I are worried about the latest weather report. Seems our warm sunshine is about to end. Forecasters released a completely new outlook for the weekend. A big change is on the way."

"A change? What kind of change?"

"The report was confusing. It seems a Canadian cold front is pushing a low pressure system much farther south than earlier predicted."

"Say it in English, Dad. What's a low-pressure system? And why are you worried?"

"Okay. First we could get some really heavy thunderstorms. Much colder temperatures could follow them. It'll make for some nasty weather for camping. I'm worried about the boys being so far from home without a way for us to reach them. If there had been a hint of this change earlier in the week, we'd never have let your brother take off. It's not like in the middle of the summer. This time of year, the temperature can drop like a rock. I sure hope they brought their warm clothes."

Talking stopped when the door opened. Linda Larsen stepped into the kitchen. She closed the door and then turned, smiling. Sniffing the air, she said, "Mmm. Smells like lunch is in progress. Let me guess, BLTs, right?"

"Right, Mom. They're almost ready."

Sidling over to her husband, Linda gave him a quick peck on the cheek and said, "It's good to have you home."

Then she turned serious. "But Roger, I just heard the latest forecast. They're saying before the weekend is over we could see snow on the ground. Can you believe it? It's over seventy out right now. How could we get such a drastic change in such a short time? I'm concerned. Travis's note said they're going farther than they first told us. What can we do to make sure they'll be okay?"

Roger placed his hands on his wife's shoulders and gave them a gentle squeeze. "For the time being, there's not much we can do. They're experienced enough to keep an eye on the sky. I'm sure they'll cut the trip short and paddle for all they're worth when they see the weather changing."

He released his grip and flashed his bride a reassuring grin. "How often do forecasters get it right, anyway? The kids might be home in their own beds before there's anything to worry about."

Even as he spoke, the words seemed to have a hollow ring. Roger wasn't all that certain. It was the middle of October in the North Country.

This time of year any kind of weather was possible, even snow and ice.

Chapter Seven

C H A P T E R   S E V E N

This was one of those times the weather people had it right. As the late-season campers were busy portaging to the next lake, Mother Nature was brewing a bomb-shell. But without a radio, the boys hadn't a clue what was in store for them. They had just finished loading the canoe and were about to head out on the water.

The portage had taken longer than it should. When Travis tried hauling his share, the injured shoulder screamed in agony. Jolts of pain surged down the side of his body. He ground to a stop, slipped off the pack, and then stood flexing his upper arm, considering his choices.

He wrapped his good arm around the pack frame and hugged it to his chest. Then he began waddling forward like a wounded duck. But the load was heavy and the arm soon grew weary. A timeout was in order.

Despite carrying the canoe, Seth was soon out of sight. Travis had only traveled a few yards when he was surprised by Seth's quick return.

"You've already carried the canoe to the next lake?" Travis gasped.

Seth stopped alongside Travis and frowned. "Nah, there's a broken birch up ahead that made an easy spot to lean the bow. I thought I'd check on you and then go back and get my gear. By the way you're struggling, I'll be making a couple of trips."

"Sorry 'bout that. My shoulder really hurts when I try to carry this on my back. I'd hoped it'd be better today. It wasn't so bad when I was paddling, but it really hurts when the strap cuts across it."

Seth scowled. "Slacker. You'll use any excuse to get out of work."

As Travis opened his mouth to protest, Seth grinned. "Just playin' ya. No sweat, buddy. I can hack it."

Travis studied the ground. He was feeling guilty enough about his inability to help. After a moment he looked up. "Maybe I'll return the favor someday. Things usually even out in the long run."

"Whatever you say. You keep going while I make a dash for my pack. Be back in a flash to check on you. Don't get lost," Seth barked, trotting past Travis and on down the trail.

Nearing the end of the portage, Travis caught glimmers of water ahead. Just then, Seth caught up. He gave out a grunt of warning and then passed Travis as if his pal were standing still.

As soon as he reached the lake's edge, Seth slipped out of the pack-frame harness. Turning, he muttered to the wind. "There's no rest for the weary. I better run back and get our ride."

Travis continued struggling with his gear. When he reached the beach he dropped his load along with an inflated sigh. Plodding a few yards along the shore, he plopped down on a small plot of grass and weeds.

Lying flat on his back, he squeezed his eyes shut while sucking in deep breaths of pine-scented air. After a time Travis raised his head to look around. The lake offered a wide view.

As his gaze swung to the north, he suddenly felt as if fish were flipping about in his belly. He was witness to a drastic change in the sky's wardrobe. Instead of wearing a pretty blue party gown trimmed with splashes of white as it had at sunrise, the distant horizon was dressed in dark funeral colors.

A chill swept through his body that had nothing to do with the temperature. Travis had experienced enough Boundary Waters thunderstorms to recognize an extreme weather shift was about to take place.

"Jeez, so much for the stable weather forecast. Who can you trust?"

Having promised to make a fire, Travis wearily pushed himself upright. Then he ambled along the lake. He began picking up rocks to form a fire ring. That completed, he gathered armfuls of twigs and dead limbs. Next he walked over to a recent birch blowdown and began pulling off thin strips of its paper-like bark.

After placing the shreds in the center of the rocks, he surrounded them with a tiny tepee of twigs. He pulled a lighter from his pocket, bent down and held the flame to the nest. The thin strips began to blaze, passing the flame to the larger pieces of fuel.

When Seth trudged into camp, he was greeted by a cheerful blaze spiraling up a plume of friendly gray smoke. Travis's bass was dangling from a stringer tied to the rear of the canoe.

"Yoo-hoo, gimpy. You want me to clean the fish, too?"

Travis stopped breaking branches long enough to reply. "I can do it. But you'd probably do a better job, what with the hook in my hand and all. I'll fry the fillets, though."

Once he set the canoe down, Seth untied the fish and placed it on the flat portion of one of the paddles. "Don't know how good a job I can do. My knife isn't long enough to reach across a fish this fat. You did good catching one so big."

Seth stuck his hand into a pocket and pulled out a folding knife. Opening the blade, he made a cut in the fish's belly, and then turning the fish in the opposite direction, started slicing along the backbone. A few more deft strokes freed two slabs of tawny-tinted meat.

"Without any batter to coat these, it might be better to cook them with the skin on. What do you think?"

"If you didn't pack any batter or cooking oil, I think you're right. Once they're fried, the skin should pull right off."

By keeping the pan closer to the rocks than the fire, Travis made sure the fillets didn't char. When he was certain they were cooked, he declared, "Soup's on!"

The boys sat side by side at the water's edge. The pan rested between them.

"Not bad for a rookie. Glad you could do something to contribute," Seth grinned around a mouthful of bass. "It won't win any blue ribbons for presentation, but it sure hits the spot."

"Thanks," Travis replied. Seth's kind words helped ease his guilt at not pulling his weight. "You check out the weather lately?"

"What do you mean?" Seth asked, stuffing another forkful of fish into his face.

"That way," Travis nodded toward the foul-weather front looming behind Seth. "Looks like it could get ugly."

Looking over his shoulder, Seth gulped. The distant sky was a deep, dark, blackish blue—nearly the color of night. "Ho-ly cow!" he blurted, spraying bits of fish into the air. "When did that sneak up on us?"

"It's still quite a ways off. But it looks like we'll get wet before the day's over. The question is . . . what's the quickest route out of here?"

Seth chewed, swallowed and then paused, thinking. "Well . . . time-wise we're more than halfway to the pickup point on Brule. If we head back the way we came, there's all that portaging. Going on to Brule Lake is almost all paddling. We have to get through the Cone Lake Chain, then cross the big lake. Wouldn't want to be out there, though, if a storm hits. Big water means big waves."

"Yeah, but if I remember right, Brule has quite a few islands. We could always take cover and let the storm pass."

"Hmm . . . maybe. Maybe not. Let's finish eating and get back on the water."

Soon they were paddling the narrow bay leading to the main body of water. This was another long, confined lake. Its thickly timbered hillsides sloped sharply to shore, giving it a stadium effect.

Without sunshine, the wavelets didn't seem nearly as welcoming as earlier. Sticking to business, the duo cut straight across the lake. They would follow the opposite shoreline for the next mile or two. From there they would take a shortcut to reach the first of the Cone lakes. According to the map, that chain would take them into Brule Lake, one of the larger bodies of water in the region.

Paddling nonstop for a half hour brought them close to the next portage. The burning sensation in Travis's shoulder grew more intense with each stroke. The thumb and palm of his right hand also hurt—almost as if they were being pinched with a pair of pliers. The young man wasn't having a good time. But, determined to pull his own weight, he didn't whine.

Seth broke their rhythm. "Let's get closer to shore so we don't miss the landing."

"There," Travis pointed with his paddle. "I think it's up ahead a couple hundred yards. It looks like there's a path heading into the woods on the other side of that boulder."

Seth stopped stroking long enough to stare, and then nodded. "Great, just a short carry and we shouldn't have any more portages. We should be able to use the canoe the rest of the way."

Travis let his paddle drag while he asked, "How many hours of canoeing do we have left?"

"Lots. It took us the better part of two days just to get this far. Once we get in the Cone Lake Chain, we have some creek paddling to do. You never know how that's gonna go. If the water's high and there aren't too many blowdowns blocking the way, we could make it by mid-day tomorrow. But, if the current's not running or if there're lots of trees tipped into channel, it could be slow going. Especially since I gotta do all the carrying."

Seth was correct about the length of the next portage. The good news was it was only a short hike to the next bay. The bad news was that it was mostly uphill, and then down a very steep slope to the water. Seth had all he could handle.

"Jeez, this may be a short haul, but it's one of the toughest so far," Travis griped as he labored uphill.

"Quit whining," Seth wheezed. "I'm doing most of the work. Let's just hope it's the last." Then he disappeared over the crest of the hill to retrieve a second load.

Despite the difficult carry, the canoe was soon floating. The boys stood near the bow, peering at the map.

"Here," Seth pointed. "These little lakes are connected to each other, then to Brule. Since it's already mid-afternoon, we'll never make it that far today—even if the creeks are clear of windfalls. But I think we should at least try to make it to the second lake. Hopefully we can get the tents up before we're caught in a monsoon."

A moment later, staring at the darkening sky, he added,

"Because it sure looks like it's going to pour before the day is done."

The narrow waterway they were about to paddle was really an extension of Winchell Lake. Their next target was at the far end of the bay. Winchell's excess water supposedly spilled into an outlet stream that flowed into the Cone Lake Chain.

Fifteen minutes of persistent paddling brought the pair to the end of the bay.

"I don't understand. The map shows the creek dead ahead. I don't see it," Travis wondered aloud.

"It's gotta be there. I think we need to pull up on shore and scope it out on foot," Seth suggested.

Selecting a place to beach the boat, the boys churned to shore and scrambled out. Seth stepped to the right. Travis went left.

Seth had traveled only a few yards when he let out a bellow. "Damn! This can't be!"

"What? What is it?" Travis yelled.

"We've got a problem. Come here."

Travis jogged along shore to where Seth stood shaking his head.

"No wonder we couldn't see it. Look. That's supposed to be our path," Seth said, pointing at the meager trickle of water meandering around boulders and rocks.

Apparently the extended warm weather had lowered the lake level. What should have been a fresh flow was now an almost arid bed of gravel. The only exceptions were a few pools fed by the puny ooze seeping into the channel.

Frustrated by the sight, Travis kicked at a loose stone, skittering it into the lake. "Cripes! What now? It's like we're trapped."

Seth swiped a hand across his brow and frowned. "We're

not trapped, but we sure have our work cut out for us."

Travis took several steps past his buddy. Then as if he could will the water to rise, he stopped and stared down the dry creek bed. After a moment he said, "What do you mean?"

"I mean, instead of paddling, we'll have to carry the gear to the next lake. And with all those rocks and boulders, it's not going to be easy."

Travis turned to study his partner. "You mean use the creek as a portage trail?"

"Exactly. Unless you have a better idea."

"No, but that's really going to eat up the day."

"Speaking of eating, let's see if we can get to the next lake in time to catch a fish or two. I'm about running on empty again. I'll start with the canoe. You try carrying our packs. No way I can get both the canoe and the gear over these rocks without burning most of our daylight. Let's see how it goes."

It didn't go well. Unlike many of the portage trails that had been cleared of toe-trippers, the stream bed was a hiker's nightmare. Struggling with the heavy canoe on his shoulders, Seth began picking his way over and around rocks, jagged stones and waterlogged tree parts.

Travis didn't fare much better. His plan was to carry one pack until his good arm played out. Then he'd set it down. Hopefully, the arm would recoup while he trudged back for the other pack.

The scheme worked for a couple of carries. But soon his shoulder and arm ached. He needed a timeout. While resting, he pulled out the map. It was a short half mile to where the creek drained into the first lake.

Tucking the map away, he flexed his arm and rotated his shoulder. Then he made a vow. "I can make it that far. I gotta. I don't have a choice."

Seth refused to rest. He remained hard at work, tiptoeing around puddles and rocks. It wasn't long before he was far ahead of his friend. Several hundred yards downstream, the channel made a sharp turn. While Travis was taking a breather, Seth disappeared around the bend.

As long he was already in world of hurt, Travis decided to try carrying both packs at the same time. Squatting, he slipped on Seth's rig. Straining to stand, he shrugged his load so the strap pulled on the good shoulder. Once satisfied that the pack was secure, he grabbed his pack and held it tight to his chest.

Hugging the load as if it were an overgrown baby, he began shuffling between rocks and puddles. First his left foot got wet, then his right. "Oh, well, I'm probably gonna get soaked before the day's over anyway," he muttered, and like a blind mule, stumbled forward.

He hadn't gone far before he realized the folly of the effort. In a matter of minutes all energy was spent. Another timeout was needed. But then ahead, through overhanging branches, Travis caught the glimmer coming off bigger water. The sight gave him hope, renewing his will to go on.

He took several stumbling forward steps and then stopped, a lump rising in his throat. Because he suddenly realized that although he could see the next lake, he couldn't see Seth.

Scanning ahead, his focus came to rest on something long and green. The canoe—its bow was pointing up like a tilted skyscraper.

Travis breathed a little easier. Seth must have set it there. His buddy must be taking a break. Or maybe he was just scouting ahead.

Relieved, Travis called another timeout. Plodding to the bank, he stripped off the packs and plunked butt-first on a flat boulder.

As the teen rested, sucking wind, the silence was shattered by a human howl.

"Trav! Trav! Help!"

Leaping to his feet, Travis yelled, "What's the matter?"

"Just get over here!"

Travis left the packs where they lay. Ignoring the puddles and meager flow, he started trotting down the channel. Closing in on the canoe, he noticed that something looked out of whack. The boat was wedged between a pair of big boulders, tipped at a bizarre angle.

Pulling up short, Travis swallowed a breath and bellowed, "I'm at the canoe, Seth. Where are you?"

"Right here!"

Travis looked all around. No sight of his pal. "Where is right here?"

Seth's deep voice boomed out with a hollow echo. "I'm right here, under the canoe!"

"What are you doing under there?"

Travis hurried to the front. He gasped when he saw his friend lying face down with one leg slanted west, the other pointed north.

"I hope you're just resting, waiting for me to lift that green monster off your sorry butt," Travis croaked.

"That would be the place to start," Seth moaned. "And then you can look at my leg."

"If I wanted to look at legs I'd watch the cheerleaders." But even as he joked, Travis knew this was bad. From the way Seth's ankle was twisted, it was obvious they had new troubles—big time.

Ignoring his own aches, Travis grabbed the bow and then hefted it up and out of the way. "What's the problem?" he asked, biding time to push down panic.

"Pretty obvious, isn't it?" Seth groaned. "My ankle's pointing the wrong direction."

Travis forced himself to look. "Think it's broken?"

"Don't know. But it must be. Help me turn over and we'll find out."

Travis dropped to his knees, and then using both hands, freed the foot from where it was wedged between two rocks. "Can you roll over?"

"Oh man, does that hurt! Help me!" Seth pleaded.

In the ten years they'd been best friends, Travis had never heard Seth complain about pain. Seth was one of those rare kids who refused to cry, regardless of how far he'd fallen or how hard he'd been bumped. So Travis knew that if his pal was whining—he was in a world of hurt—a really big world of hurt.

Travis grimaced, as if by doing so he could share some of Seth's agony. "How d'ya want my help? What can I do?"

"Hold my legs together while I roll over. I can't lie here all day."

Travis did as asked. Slowly, and in obvious anguish, Seth managed to roll over.

"Help me sit up. Let's have a look at my ankle." Seth muttered between clenched teeth.

Like a cupboard door with a loose hinge, Seth's foot drooped out at an odd slant. His ankle was either broken or badly sprained. Whichever, Seth wouldn't be walking anywhere in the near future.

Travis fought to quell the second wave of dread. Frightening images flashed. They had a real predicament. If this had happened during the regular canoe season, it wouldn't be much of a worry. They could set up camp and be fairly sure another group would be passing by in a matter of days.

Not now. They were the only campers for miles, probably the last to travel through the area until next season.

What about food? What were they going to eat? An image of two starving teens flickered in his mind.

"What do you think?" Seth moaned.

As if to erase the mental images, Travis shook his head, returning to reality.

"What?" He muttered.

"How bad is it? Broken?"

"Don't know, can't tell. I'm not a doctor. But it doesn't look good. Don't think you'll be dancing anytime soon."

Despite his discomfort, Seth lips formed a feeble smile. "That's okay, I hate dancing. But do you think I can walk on it?"

Travis shook his head. "I don't think that's such a good idea. But I know you can't stay here."

Understanding that he was the one who had to take charge, Travis fell silent, pondering his next move.

After a pause, he said, "First thing we have to do is get you to a better spot. Let me check out the area ahead. Maybe there's a good place to set our tents for the night. Hang on while I unhitch the life preservers. You can use them for pillows while I'm looking."

Ignoring his own troubles, Travis snatched the canoe with both hands, and then flipped it over. He unsnapped the life jackets strapped to the seats. Gently lifting Seth's injured leg, he placed a life jacket under the ankle. Then after handing the second one to his friend to use as a pillow, he said, "Back in a minute. I'm gonna go look for a campsite."

Without a load on his back it took little time for Travis to dash to the lake. One side of the stream was unsuitable. The bank was a tangle of brambles and brush. But on the west side he stumbled upon an existing campsite. From the look of it, the place had been used many times before.

The spot was a natural. About thirty yards from the stream lay a grassy clearing. Guarding the far edge of the opening—rising some fifteen or twenty feet straight up—was a steep cliff. The rock wall would give perfect protection from any northerly winds.

"Terrific!" Travis mumbled. "It's about the first good news of the day."

Standing open-mouthed, gawking like a kid on his first trip to a carnival, Travis conjured up a plan. He'd carry Seth to the campsite. Then he'd return upstream to retrieve their gear. Their belongings were hanging on the pack frames. They'd need the all the equipment to set up camp.

Satisfied with what to do next, Travis trotted back to his friend. "Seth, you ready to rock? If you can stand, you can ride on my back."

Seth peered up, shaking his head in disapproval. "That ain't gonna work. My hip got wrenched when I went down. It'd hurt too much to wrap my legs tight enough to stay on, much less lock my ankles. Better you move me with a fireman's carry."

"Huh? How d'ya do that?"

"Simple. If you can get me standing, I'll flop over your good shoulder. You know, like a rolled up rug."

"Yeah. You're right. It does sounds like the best way."

Glancing upstream, Travis realized that they had to get moving. The threatening clouds were almost overhead. But now—instead of a blue-black cast—they had taken on a ghoulish green hue. Travis was no weather expert, but he knew that clouds that eerie color couldn't be a good thing.

Getting Seth to an upright position wasn't easy. Every

little movement caused pain. Hard as he tried to avoid it, Seth couldn't keep himself from groaning.

With Seth up on one leg, Travis bent and offered his good shoulder. Seth's weight was all he could support. Travis struggled to stay upright.

Taking careful, tiny steps, the overloaded teen battled his way down the channel. When they arrived at the campsite, he wheezed, "What now? No way I can climb the bank with you on my shoulder."

"Find a soft spot to dump me. While you go for the gear, I'll use my good leg to push my way to the top."

Travis shuffled to a rock-free opening on the slope. Bending until he thought he was going to topple over, he let Seth drop on his rear.

"What do you think? The packs or canoe first?"

"If you can handle the canoe, get it. It's close. And if bad comes to worse, we can always crawl under and use it as a roof to keep the rain off."

Travis agreed. Careful to avoid tripping, he trotted back to the canoe. By ignoring the discomfort, he was able to load it by first setting the bow on the bank. Then he crawled underneath and stood tall—aches and all—with the canoe resting on his shoulders. By treading softly the entire way, he made the return trip nonstop.

Meanwhile, Seth managed to scoot himself up the slope. Once on level ground he moved along like an inchworm. Sitting tall, he pushed off with his good leg, letting the injured limb drag behind like a lifeless branch.

Peering out from under his load, Travis was surprised how far Seth had crept. "See you made some progress. Where do you think we should put the canoe?"

Seth swiveled his head, looking the area over for the first time. "There," he said, nodding toward the rock-face. "If you can do it, I think you should turn it upside down along the bottom of the bluff. The cliff should protect it in case we get strong winds."

Travis used the creek bank to hold the bow, then knelt and crawled out. Rolling the canoe right side up, he lifted the stern, and with a hard thrust, propelled the canoe onto high ground. He scurried up the bank, grabbed the bow and dragged the canoe like a big sled.

He tugged the canoe parallel to wall and turned it over. After taking a quick glance at the sky, he walked the end of bow rope to a small spruce, wrapped it around the base and tied a simple knot.

Then he hurried back to Seth. "You gonna be okay while I go after the packs?"

"Have to be, go ahead . . . go get 'em."

Travis took another look at the sky. "Man! It looks like it could pour any minute! Hold the fort buddy. I'll be back as fast as I can."

With one last fleeting glance over his shoulder, the teen headed upstream. He was just about to pick up the packs when Mother Nature's October shocker multiplied the boys' troubles.

Chapter Eight

C H A P T E R E I G H T

"I know. I know. They should have applied for a permit. That's exactly why I'm talking to you now," Roger Larsen barked into the phone.

"They didn't, and it's as much my fault as theirs. With the weather being so mild I gave my permission for the trip. The forecasters hadn't given us a hint that things would be any different this weekend."

Roger paused as he listened to the voice on the other end. "Okay then, we'll check back later. Thanks anyway."

He set the phone on its cradle before turning to face his wife. "They don't have any aircraft available. And if they did, they wouldn't send one up until this weather system passes over. Besides, they won't do anything until we know for sure the kids are in trouble."

Earlier, the Larsens had received a call from Lynn Springwood. She had also heard the forecast. Did Roger know if there was any way to check on the campers?

That's when Roger decided to phone the permit office. The ranger was not at all happy to learn about the boys' outing. He'd informed Mr. Larsen that the single-engine airplane used for Forest Service operations was in Duluth for repairs. All other aircraft were based at the Ely airport, many miles away on the far side of the BWCA.

Regardless, if an air search was needed, it would have to wait until the low pressure system moved out of the area. At this time there wasn't any emergency, even with the possibility of bad weather. Until it became a fact the boys were in danger, there was nothing to be done but wait.

"But Roger, it's supposed to freeze by morning. The boys didn't take enough clothing to stay warm with the temperature that low. Couldn't they be met from the other direction? They must have traveled more than halfway by now. We have to do something."

"About the only things we can hope for is that they'll find a safe campsite and keep warm and dry."

Without warning, the inside of house was lit by a brilliant flash of light. A booming crack of thunder quickly followed. The light over the stove flickered, and then went dark. Roger picked up the receiver. "So much for the phone . . . no dial tone."

The words had barely passed his lips when a violent gust of wind shook the house, rattling the windows and doors.

"We better get to the basement!" Roger directed, yelling to be heard over the sound of debris being dashed against the dwelling. Herding Beth and Linda down the darkened stairs, he glanced out the cellar window. Just then the top portion of a large birch broke in the wind. It crashed onto the driveway, its golden crown blocking Roger's view.

Linda let out a scream and clutched hard at her husband's arm. Beth hugged in tight against both. They stood huddled together, hearing the wind come in waves, battering everything in its path. The sturdy log home shuddered and shook as if a freight train rumbled overhead.

The sound of breaking glass and furniture being moved came from the open stairway. Linda circled her arms around her daughter. Roger threw his arms around both.

"My God!" He uttered. "What's happening up there?"

They stood holding onto each other for several long, terrifying minutes. As the wind began to let up, a new noise took its place. The sound of pops, crackles and bangs came from the deck end of the dwelling.

"Dad, Dad, what is it? What's that weird sound?"

"Hail, large hail. Usually that means the worst of the wind has passed. You two stay put. I'm going up to see what's happening outside."

Entering the living area, it was hard for Mr. Larsen to take in the damage. For several seconds, he stood in a trance. One of the sliding glass doors was shattered. Cushions, several overturned dining room chairs, along with bits of glass, shreds of leaves and other odds and ends littered the rug.

Hailstones the size of golf balls were pounding the deck. A few bounced through the opening in the broken door, joining the layer of debris already deposited on the living room carpet.

He crossed the room to the second set of doors. Wet leaves and twigs were plastered to the glass. He peered out and what he could see was not pleasant. In the yard, bent and broken trees leaned against each other for support. Several lay on the ground, dirt-covered roots jerked from the earth, exposed to the heavy rain.

Through the debris and downpour, Mr. Larsen could barely see the water's edge. He could just make out the overturned dock, its support legs poking out of the water like frozen road-kill.

"Oh man, what a mess, what a mess!" he muttered. "The boys are in trouble if they get caught in this storm. Big trouble."

Chapter Nine

C H A P T E R   N I N E

Determined to recover the gear, Travis chugged up the streambed like a locomotive. He zigzagged with head down, breathing hard, completely focused on each step. The last thing they needed was for him to stumble and duplicate Seth's trick. By the time he reached the equipment, his lungs had joined the list of complaints. He stood with feet spread, bowed at the waist, hands on knees, gulping air.

The tired teenager was oblivious to what was about to happen. As he recovered, bent and panting like a pup, the first gust of wind raced down the channel.

The sudden blast hit Travis like a sledgehammer, nearly knocking him off his feet. To keep from falling, he lunged forward and then collapsed on the packs. More gusts followed, faster, stronger. Instantly alarmed, Travis squirmed between the pack frames, an arm around each, pulling both snug to his chest.

Like a jet engine on takeoff, the wind howled even louder. Then a new noise added to the din. Travis didn't recognize the sound—didn't know what was happening. Close by, an aspen snapped with an ear-splitting crack. The tree crashed into the channel opening, filling the space with limbs and leaves.

Through his fear Travis recognized this was no ordinary rain squall. This was a violent storm, a dangerous storm. A storm with a devastating wind, the kind you read about in the paper or see on the news. This was a tempest you wouldn't want to be out in, alone, far from help.

Although his circuits were overloaded, Travis knew he had to move. Throwing an arm around each pack-frame, he struggled to the edge of the creek. What he needed was a safe place—somewhere to hide—something to hunker behind.

A few yards further upstream a pair of boulders nestled together like twins, their backsides tucked into the bank. Somehow Travis managed to stay upright long enough to fling his body between the giant stones.

Overhead, the wind kept wailing, acting more like a hurricane than a North Country thunderstorm. Around the terrified teen, the air filled with a blizzard of orange and gold as the colorful leaves were ripped from the trees and forced into early retirement.

The gunshots of tree trunks popping added to the clamor. Shaking, Travis cowered between the boulders, uncertain what to do.

An old aspen gave up the struggle, snapping with a cannon-like boom. The now nearly leafless crown crashed down, its upper limbs striking mere feet from where he huddled in horror. Never—never in his fourteen years had he been so scared.

Travis clutched the packs, closed his eyes and wished with all his heart that he were home, in his room—safe and secure—all in one piece.

When the wind began to ease, a new noise filled its space. It was a strange sound, like that of unskilled drummers striking sticks together—none able to keep a rhythm. A huge hailstone hit Travis on the back of the head, causing instant piercing pain. The young man now knew what was producing such a strange beat. What he needed right now was a helmet.

Too terrified to move, Travis pulled in his legs and curled in a ball. Then he tipped the tops of the packs until they touched, forming a roof, protecting his head and shoulders.

The minutes passed like centuries. Pebble-sized ice balls continued pelting down, soon carpeting the ground with a thick layer of cold, white stones.

At last the hail finished its horrific act. Unfortunately, it was time for rain to take the stage. Large drops—huge drops—drops the size of fat nickels and dimes. A waterfall of wind-driven rain drenched Travis. In no time, the teenager was as soaked as if he had jumped off a dock or fallen out of a boat.

Cold, wet and scared stiff, Travis stayed tucked between the boulders. He had no idea of what he should do or where he should go. Eventually the raindrops became smaller. But what they lacked in size, they made up for in numbers.

And as time dragged on, Travis became aware that his feet weren't just wet. They were actually resting in water! Whether he wanted to or not, he had to leave this safe haven. The downpour was beginning to fill the creek bed.

Unable to absorb such a huge volume of water, the surrounding high ground shed the excess like a raincoat. Hundreds of miniature streams raced toward the channel. Reaching their goal, they joined forces, spreading a dirty blanket that quickly covered the rocks and shallows.

Poking his head above the boulders, Travis acknowledged his latest quandary. He grabbed his pack and with a huge effort, threw it up on the bank. He did the same with Seth's. Clutching a branch from the blowdown, he pulled his chilled and soaked body after them.

Then he lay with his face burrowed against wet earth. He didn't know if he should cry tears or cry for help. Somehow he retained enough sense to know neither would be of any use. Because he was out here alone.

No, that wasn't true.

They were alone. Seth was nearby—only a few hundred yards distant. His pal would know what to do. No matter the situation—big or small—Seth always seemed to come up with a solution.

But wait! That wouldn't work. Not now! This time Seth was part of the problem. This was a predicament Travis would have to solve on his own.

Exhaling an audible sigh, Travis raised his head and opened his eyes. The rain had slackened. He saw countless broken or uprooted trees in every direction. It was as if the storm had trapped him in a forest prison.

Turning toward the creek provided another amazing sight. What had been a dry channel was now a raging river. Soiled water surged past, boiling and churning, carrying limbs and branches along as if they were nothing more than carelessly discarded bottles and cans.

New alarm welled up. Travis wanted to close his eyes, make the scene go away. He did close his eyes, and then to keep from being sick, took long deep breaths.

Think, think . . . you have to do something . . . you can't stay here!

He stood that way for a time like a stone statue, afraid to reopen his eyes. But when he finally did, he saw that the light was leaking out of the day.

Earlier, the afternoon had been dimmed by woolly clouds, and then later, the storm itself. But now the darkness of real night was seeping into all the corners.

"C'mon, move!" he told himself. "You gotta get going!"

The mixture of the cool temperature and the wet clothing had started a shiver attack. Becoming aware he was shaking like a leaf, Travis flipped open a pack flap. He reached in and pulled out a sweatshirt, along with his waterproof windbreaker. Ripping off his soaked Tee, he stuffed himself into dry clothing.

But pulling on the sweat shirt recapped other problems. For when he lifted up his left arm to slip into the sleeve, pain slashed down his side, making him cry out.

The fact that it did so made him grunt in disgust. He was tougher than that. He had to be. This wasn't the time or place to act like a sissy.

He spoke his thoughts aloud. "Quit whining, you big baby! There's not a damn thing wrong with your legs. Pick up a pack and go!"

The temperature had fallen so drastically that when he spoke, his words came out as little white clouds.

Daylight was fading fast—really fast. Travis accepted that he wouldn't be able to lug both packs over, under and around the jumble of tangled tree trunks.

"Okay. Now think! Think about tonight. We have to get through tonight."

Studying the pack frames, he pondered what things he might manage to carry. What items were most important to survive a cold, wet night?

After giving it a moment of careful consideration, Travis decided on the sleeping bags and a warm shirt or two for Seth. Spreading his waterproof windbreaker to shield off the drizzle, Travis knelt over the pack-frames. As quickly as he could manage, he unhitched the packsack. Then he stuffed the sleeping bags, Seth's orange rain shell and an extra sweatshirt into its wide, mouth-like opening.

Next, he undid a side pocket to reclaim his flashlight. After making certain all the flaps were secured, he

83

dragged both frames well away from the stream. Satisfied they wouldn't be washed away, he leaned the packs against one of the few surviving trees. Standing, he slipped an arm through one of the slings on the packsack.

Finally, a bit of relief—the pack acted much like a large purse. The lightened load could be carried on his good shoulder.

He hadn't taken more than a few steps before bumping into a tangled barrier. Twisted branches clung together like the limbs of a giant pretzel, forming an impassable barricade.

"Go slow, you can do this. Keep calm, keep cool."

Travis reasoned that if he stayed near the creek, he wouldn't get lost. So the mission was really rather simple; he would travel a few hundred yards downstream and arrive back at the campsite.

"Not far, two football fields," he mumbled, trying to talk panic out of taking charge. "How hard can that be?"

But as it turned out, the trek was more than hard—nearly impossible—more difficult than one could have imagined. So many broken or uprooted trees littered the way, his forward progress slowed to a crawl.

The last remnant of daylight dwindled as Travis struggled through the twisted and tangled mess. Darkness continued poring into every corner, increasing his urgency to rejoin Seth.

Full night enveloped Travis as he slithered snakelike under a fallen pine—its fat branches holding its massive trunk clear of the earth. He paused then, resting. An hour or two earlier the trek would have been an easy hike. But not now. Covering the short distance had taken nearly an hour of intense toil.

A bit of benefit came from the hard work—the exercise had warmed him—put the brakes on the shaking. And

Travis knew that was a good thing.

But when he figured camp was close, a terrible thought filled his brain, causing a different type of shudder.

What was he going to find? Was his pal dead or alive? Did Seth escape the fury unharmed? Or did a tree crash down and break more bones—or worse?

Summoning his last reserve of courage, Travis sucked in a breath and bellowed. "Yo! Seth! You okay, man?""

The reply was sudden and closer than Travis expected.

"Hey buddy! 'Bout time you got back. I'm kinda lonely here all by myself."

Travis's heart skipped as relief covered him like a warm blanket. His legs suddenly went rubbery. He had to drop to one knee or chance toppling over.

"Thank God!" he muttered, turning his gaze toward the darkened sky.

"Thank God!"

Travis traversed the final few yards by climbing through the tops of several small, uprooted aspens. Although the forest was black as a Halloween cat, being near the lake, the campsite opening clung to a smidgen of light.

Enough so, that Travis could see the cliff had been a good guardian. The opening had been shielded from the worst of the wind. The canoe hadn't moved much, if at all. It was resting alongside the rock wall, right where he had put it.

"Seth? Seth? Where are you?"

"Right here. Where else would I be?"

Travis flashed his light in a circle.

"Are we gonna play this game again? Where is here?"

"Look under the canoe. You think I don't know enough to get out of the rain?"

Travis stabbed the beam below the overturned boat. Sure enough, his pal was there, lying on his side, wide eyes shining in the shaft of light.

"Hey! Turn that thing off. You're blinding me."

Travis switched off the flashlight and hobbled to the canoe. "Man, am I glad to see you!"

"That goes double for me! When I heard the wind come roaring over the trees, I managed to roll under the canoe. But hey, I had the boat and this cliff to protect me. I was really worried about you. How'd ya manage to stay in one piece? I thought for sure you'd be trapped under a tree or blown into the lake."

For the umpteenth time since they'd left home, Travis let out a weary sigh. "Later. I'll tell you about it later. But here, in the pack, I brought you some dry clothes."

"Thanks, but I'm really not wet. The canoe makes a great roof. Bet you got a bath, huh?"

Although Seth couldn't see him in the dark, Travis nodded. "You got that right. Let's just say I'm lucky to be alive. I've never been so scared in my life. Not even when we were little and I saw your face for the first time."

Travis paused, pondering. "Seriously, if you can get along without me, I'm going to try starting a fire."

The teenager was slowed by both darkness and the foul weather. It took nearly an hour before he had enough dead sticks and limbs to get a fire blazing. Shuffling about in a wind-driven drizzle, Travis widened the search for suitable fire material.

It didn't matter that the forest was a gold mine of broken timber. Earlier in the day the tangled mass of tree parts had been alive and growing. That meant the wood was wet, green and unsuitable for a campfire.

Satisfied there was enough fuel to keep the fire going

for a few hours, Travis returned to Seth. He was curious about the injured ankle.

"Awful! It's either broken or badly torn," Seth answered to the inquiry. "There's no way I can walk. It's already puffed up double the size of my other ankle. We've got trouble, buddy. And I don't know what we're going to do about it."

Dredging up grit he never knew he possessed, Travis snapped back a reply. "Hey partner. We'll take it one night at a time. We'll deal with tomorrow when it gets here. Now then, there better be room for two under that green roof. 'Cause I have a surprise. I brought our sleeping bags."

Once cocooned under the close cover of the canoe, two nervous teens talked over their plight. Several times Travis slipped out of his bag to tend the fire. It'd been built too far from the canoe to give them any warmth. But the meager light seemed to be the only bright spot of the day. He did not want it to go out.

As they talked, the day's hectic workload tracked Travis down. The weary teen was unable to keep his eyes open. In the middle of a sentence, he nodded off. Within minutes he was in a deep sleep.

Sometime later he experienced a weird dream, one that seemed real. He dreamt he was home, lying near the fireplace—reading. The book was an outdoor adventure. The saga revolved around a couple young fellows out on a wilderness trip. Like all good yarns, Travis couldn't wait to get to the end, see how the tale turned out. He was almost through, but when he turned to the last chapter, the pages were blank.

That's when he awoke, startled and confused. Sitting up, he banged his head on the bottom of the boat. He cursed softly.

"What? What's the matter?" a voice asked from the dark.

Shaking away the cobwebs, Travis remembered where

he was—under a canoe—far from home—much like the story in his dream. And that's when he recognized the reason for the blank pages. The final chapter had yet to be written.

It was up to him to author a happy ending.

Could he do it?

"Nothing Seth, just talking in my sleep. Get some rest. We'll deal with our troubles in the morning."

Travis wanted to fall back to sleep. But he couldn't. His brain was a beehive of worry, buzzing from one scary thought to another. Finally, just before first light, he drifted off again. Only this time he fell into a deep, dreamless slumber.

He awoke to dazzling light. He peered from under the canoe and received a shock. The disheveled forest had been covered with an ivory bedspread. While he and Seth slept, the drizzle had turned to snow—heavy, wet snow. The kind of snow that sticks like glue to anything it touches.

The tattered landscape was frosted in wedding cake white. Trees that hadn't been tipped or torn had branches bowed in prayer. From under the canoe Travis's sightline was toward the lake. Although he was warm in the sleeping bag, a shiver tingled down his spine. Even the water seemed to have changed overnight. It had lost its friendly blue sheen, and now cast a cold, steely gray.

Travis tucked his head into the sleeping bag. This was worse than the bad dream; it was the ultimate nightmare. This was the real thing, a vision that didn't end when he opened his eyes.

The youth burrowed deep into his bag, and then cradled his face in his arms. He squeezed lids tight to avoid spilling tears. He felt like a little boy—like the time he was six and got separated from his mom at the big mall in Minneapolis.

He wanted to cry then, too, but was afraid everyone would think he was a baby. He felt like that now, lost and helpless. But he wasn't a baby and crying wouldn't help. They had to get up and get on with things.

"Seth, you awake?"

From deep inside Seth's bag came a guttural grunt. "Yeah. I've been awake for a while. Just waiting for you to tell me it's time to stick my head out. Is it morning yet?"

"Yep, and guess what—Mother Nature is at it again."

"What now?" Seth asked, looking like a tortoise in a shell because only tousled dark hair poked from the end of his mummy bag. Sticking his head out, he turned away from the cliff. "Oh great, just what we need. I guess now we can use the canoe as a bobsled instead of a boat."

"Yeah, right. Like I could pull you through that tangled mess out there. Maybe I should just stay in bed a little longer, practice my prayers. Anyway, how's your ankle?"

"You don't wanna know. It hurts like crazy. I can hardly roll over. My stomach feels pretty hollow, too. Think you're up to catching some fish?"

"And how am I supposed to do that when my rod and reel are still back with our other stuff?"

"I forgot. Well, you better get the packs 'cause I'm sure not going anywhere."

Travis wiggled forward to pull himself free. The arrangement of the cliff and the canoe had managed to keep the ground dry where they slept. Pulling on wet shoes, he shivered at the thought of crawling over and around snow-covered tree parts.

"Seth, I don't have a choice. I'm going after the stuff. Here, I'll pull my bag on top of yours. You might as well be toasty while I'm gone."

"Thanks. Good luck and be careful. It looks wicked out there."

Travis pulled his bag over his buddy. Then he slithered through the narrow opening between the gunnel and the ground, getting a face full of snow as a reward.

Pushing up with his arms caused a grimace. Now he had cold hands to go along with an aching shoulder. He was already wet and chilly, and hadn't even left camp.

Trudging to the stream, Travis saw that during the night the water had receded. He stood, staring, trying to determine the easiest route. He chose to follow the creek bank. A foray into the forest would be foolhardy. It would be too easy to get turned around, too easy to get lost.

He hadn't gone far before his jeans were thoroughly soaked. But there was no way to prevent that from happening. He had to keep going.

Travel was faster in the light of day. After twenty minutes of tedious work, he thought he was getting close. But with every tree and bush wearing a white coat, nothing looked familiar.

If he hadn't been so miserable, Travis might have appreciated the landscape. It was a photographer's delight. Thick vanilla icing covered everything in view. But the youth failed to see the beauty. To Travis, it looked more like a scene from a horror movie.

He stopped and tried to picture where he had been blasted by the first gust of wind. He recalled the boulders that protected him from the falling aspen. But coated with snow, everything looked very much the same. He saw lots of big snow covered rocks, many look-a-like twisted trees—each dressed in a lacy, white dinner jacket.

"Okay, think!" he whispered. "Think about where you were when the wind blew. Think about where you were when the hail hit. And imagine where you crawled up on the bank."

Pulling himself over a pair of downed poplars, he spied two out of place lumps. "Gotcha! Thought you could hide from me, did you?"

After brushing off the snow, he faced a new dilemma. How could he possibly lug both packs in a single trip?

"Okay, slow down. Make a plan," he encouraged himself. "Take one thing at a time. Think!"

Having removed one of the packsacks the night before, his own pack felt light enough to carry on his back—as designed. Grabbing the top bar of Seth's heavier pack frame, Travis began dragging the rig like a sled. By lifting, tugging and sliding it over and around the abundant blowdowns, Travis retraced his steps toward camp.

The sky above remained a gray wool overcoat. A marriage of drizzle and wet snow, propelled by a brisk wind, slapped at Travis's cheeks. But he trudged on, ignoring the throbbing shoulder and cold, achy hands. He finally reached the last obstacle, and like so many times already on this adventure, he was exhausted.

Travis towed Seth's pack frame alongside the canoe. He slipped off his own pack and called out, "Hey, sleeping beauty . . . I thought you'd have breakfast ready."

"Huh?" A muffled response escaped the green roof. "You back already? You just left."

"What are ya talking about? I've been gone for more than an hour. While you were dreaming, I was playing pack-mule to our gear."

"You mean you were able to get everything in one trip? That's great!"

"I don't feel so great. I'm wet, tired and starving."

"Check my lower bag. I had some leftover trail mix that didn't fit in the container. It's in a baggie stuffed in one of the small side pockets."

Travis knelt in the slush and started examining the

openings. In the second pocket his fingers grasped plastic. Never had a mixture of fruit, nuts, and chocolate bits looked so inviting. He untwisted the tie and shook out a handful. They were delicious, better than anything he could imagine.

Seth watched as Travis savored the treats. "Hey man! Leave some for me. I'm hungry, too."

Travis poured out another fistful. Then he bent and passed the sack under the canoe.

"Okay. It's time to get to it. First thing is to get the fire going. Once that's done, I'll set up the fishing rod . . . see about hooking some protein. Need anything first?"

"Pain-killer. Get some aspirin from the first aid kit. And water, I'd like a drink."

For the next half hour Travis labored on camp chores. By stirring a few active embers, he was able to ignite a tepee of small sticks. Once the fire was burning, he stood as close as he dared, letting the heat touch his jeans. The blaze had flared and soon the Levis began to steam. But they felt so wonderfully warm, Travis was reluctant to leave.

The snow had begun to melt. Although it was cloudy, the temperature remained above freezing. Because of warm ground, the sugar coating quickly changed to liquid. Plips and plops sounded as broken birches and aspens shed the premature winter wrap.

Travis reclaimed the rod from his pack-frame. He extended it to its working length. Next he attached a hook and bobber. But he had a problem. What would he use for bait?

He was traipsing to the fire for a second warming when the idea hit. Grub worms. Grubs burrow into rotten wood. Locate a rotting log and he should have his bait.

With renewed oomph, he stalked the cliff face until he spotted the remnants of an old pine. The once-mammoth conifer was encased in soft-looking moss and lichen.

Travis struck the deadfall with the hatchet blade. A hunk of the soggy wood flew off, exposing only soft, yellow innards. He whacked the log a second time. Pay dirt! Curled up for a long winter nap was a large, white worm.

Travis held the prize in his palm as he carried it to the canoe. He informed Seth of his plan. He'd use the worm to catch a sunfish or perch. The small fish often lived close to shore in hungry numbers. Then by using guts from the first fish, he should be able to catch more.

"Rookie, I'm proud of you," Seth admitted. "It should work. And the wind is in your favor. The bobber should float out from shore. You won't have to keep casting. Go on; catch us some big ones for breakfast."

Travis jostled more wood on the fire, and then stood stone-like, warming his jeans. When they began steaming, he trekked to the lake. He threaded the grub onto the hook and adjusted the bobber. Satisfied it was secure, he cast the rig out.

Shivering, the rod clutched in his fist, he let his eyes roam the surroundings. Except for the campsite area, protected by the cliff, the shoreline looked like it had been used for bombing practice.

The lake wasn't large. Travis could see most of the shoreline. The storm had surged in from the northwest. Trees were bent or slanted toward the southeast—as if a giant's hairbrush had been dragged over the top. The squall hadn't played favorites; trees were broken or tipped all the way around.

That Seth and he hadn't been blown away or crushed was a miracle. Tree parts were bobbing up and down in the center of the lake. Then his eyes focused on something else—orange—bright orange. It occurred to him that he hadn't picked up the life preservers. Apparently they'd washed out of the channel and floated out into open water.

He was thinking it was better that the preservers were in the lake than the boys using them. Suddenly he became aware of a slight pulling on the pole. Snapping to attention, Travis let out line, waited a heartbeat, and pulled back with a quick but gentle tug. He felt a fish struggling at the other end.

"Bingo!" He yelled. "We will eat today!"

Travis slipped the survival tool from its holster, opened it up and slit the perch's stomach. He cut the tiny intestines into small, gooey bits. He had bait. After a half hour of angling, a dozen tiny fish lay in the wet grass. When he had enough for a meal, he reeled in and carried the pole to the canoe.

"Hey Sleeping Beauty, you awake under there?"

"Yup. How ya doin'? Catch anything?"

Spirits lifted by his angling triumph, Travis attempted to brighten the mood. "Ya, sure, you betcha," he answered in his best imitation of what many think is typical Minnesota speech.

"Caught us a fine mess of dem fishes fer ar breck-fast. Just hafta clean dem now, ya know."

"Fishing must have been great if you feel good enough to kid around. What'd you get?"

"Perch . . . sunnies . . . even a few little smallies. We'll have them for breakfast. Then I'll see about catching enough to feed us for the rest of the day . . . maybe some for tomorrow, too."

"When you're finished with that, take a look at this ankle. I can't stay under the canoe all day. And we better make some plans."

"You want me to look at it now or do you want me to start fixing the fish?"

"My stomach comes first. Until the snow melts, I think I'll just stay right here and watch you work."

Travis went about cleaning the catch. When he finished there were enough tiny pieces to satisfy the bottom of two pans.

Red-hot coals had dried the wet wood. The fire snapped happily with heat. Small fingers of orange licked out along the rocks. They were perfect flames for cooking a warm meal.

Like a bear peeking from its burrow, Seth observed his pal. He wished there was something he could do to help. His stomach gurgled, pleading to be fed.

But the teen wasn't certain the growling was all about hunger. Fear might be adding notes to the song. During the night he'd had ample time to ponder their predicament. It was scary enough to be hurt and far from help. But the storm and the snarl of blowdowns had trapped the two of them. There was no way out.

Even if a rescue party knew where to look, how would they reach the campsite? The portages had to be trashed. It'd take days to cut the tangled mess. In the black ink of that long night, he'd experienced dreadful images—lingering, freezing and wasting away—skeletal remains not discovered until the next summer. But now in the light of day, observing Trav frying fish, he felt better about things.

Seth had mused over other mental images. He had thoughts about his mom and her situation. What'd he call it the other night? "The lie—the lousy lie." But maybe Travis was right. Maybe his mom had a good reason for her secrets.

Sometime during those deep, dark hours he'd made a vow. If they survived this disaster—and watching Travis, he was beginning to believe they would—he wouldn't bug his mom about Saturday night outings. She could come and go as she wished, no questions asked.

What Travis had told him was true. She had a right to her own life. She was the adult. All the wishing in the world wouldn't bring his dad back. He'd have to settle for fond memories.

That quandary and a dozen others buzzed had about in his brain like a swarm of angry hornets. Then Travis broke into Seth's private thoughts.

"Hey, bud! You ready to eat?"

"What? Oh, yeah, been ready since last night."

"Okay, then. Just remember, there's only two things on the menu—fish and more fish," Travis quipped, setting a pan in front of his pal. "Watch it. I'm gonna swing the canoe out of the way. You can sit up and have breakfast in bed."

The on-again, off-again drizzle had petered out. Except for a few sheltered areas, all snow had melted. The area the canoe had covered had remained dry.

"Can you sit up? Or do I have to feed you?"

"I can do a sit-up. It's my ankle that's got a problem, not my stomach muscles."

Travis snatched his sleeping bag off Seth's and quickly rolled it in a ball. Then he looked on as Seth struggled to rise.

"Hey, Einstein, wouldn't it be easier if you opened your bag first? Kinda tough to eat tucked in the way you are."

"Right. I was gettin' to it." Undoing the zipper to his waist, Seth placed the pan on his lap. "Thank you, sir. This smells terrific."

Travis sauntered to the fire to retrieve the second pan.

The twosome attacked the meal as if the fillets might swim away before they finished eating. When his pot was empty, Seth beamed. "Not bad, rookie. Regards to the chef."

"Thanks. It wasn't pretty but it sure helped fill the hole in my middle," Travis garbled between bites.

"How many packets of the freeze-dried are left? One or two?"

"Actually one whole packet and two or three others the bear bit into. But I think it's probably best we hold off using 'em until we have to," Travis mumbled, chomping down the last mouthful.

Setting down his pan, Travis turned serious. "Let's have a look at that leg. Maybe I can see if it's broken . . . or if you're just faking it."

"I'd like to be faking it. You're doing such a good job of waiting on me. Don't think so, though. I don't see how I can walk."

"Whatever. You're gonna have to crawl out of the bag. I can't check it out with you burrowed in like that."

As Travis tugged at the bottom, Seth squirmed out. Travis lifted the injured leg and then placed it on his balled-up sleeping bag. Next he removed Seth's sock, exposing the irritated ankle.

The joint was swollen twice its normal size. Ugly colors fanned toward the foot and calf. The region with the most swelling was a bruised purple. Shades of red and yellow circled the bulge like the rings around an ugly bulls-eye.

Seth waited patiently before asking, "Well? Is it broken?"

"What? You think I'm Superman? I don't have x-ray vision. It's your ankle. What do you think?"

"Not sure. I think I might have ripped those tendons you hear about when football players get hurt. Those stringy things we learned about in science, the things that hold bones together. It happened to one of the Vikings' running backs a couple years ago. Ended his career."

"It's a good thing you're not a Viking. You'd be riding the bench."

It was Seth's turn to be somber. "What do you think we

ought to do about it?"

"About the only thing you can do is to stay off it . . . see if the swelling goes down."

Travis paused. He let his gaze linger over the lake. Whitecaps were rolling in formation toward the opposite shore. He was glad the wind was blowing away from them, not the other way around. Looking at Seth again, he asked, "So . . . is that our new plan? Stay put 'til you can hobble; feast on fish a couple times a day? Wait for Search and Rescue?"

"You have a better idea? Look around. Where could we go even if I could walk? The trails have to be impossible to portage. If we tried to use the canoe, the creek out of here must be choked with blowdowns. Without a chainsaw, we'd never get through."

"Yeah . . . you're probably right. We'll have to wait until someone finds us. And if that's the case, I'll set up your tent. You can go back to bed if you want. No sense for you to get cold. That's my job."

Travis spent the rest of that gray, dismal day attending to camp chores. After dragging the canoe away from the cliff, he pitched their tents where the boat had kept the grass dry. Then he helped Seth wiggle into the tent before zipping him into the sleeping bag.

He spent much of the midday hours gathering fuel. Satisfied there was enough wood to keep a fire burning into the next day, he pondered other problems. Was there a way to keep the fish fresh until they became stomach stuffers?

Travis scrounged the shoreline. He was looking for a notch in the bank, a spot to build a rock corral. After some twenty steps he found the perfect place.

He began stacking rocks into a semi-circle. The teen labored nonstop until the stones were higher than the lake. Then he stood, hands on hips, applauding the effort. It would work. Fresh water could seep in—fish couldn't swim out.

A growling belly telegraphed a message: "Stop patting yourself on the back. Get busy stocking the corral." The fish-gut bait worked like magic. Nearly every cast brought back a colorful sunfish or wiggly green perch. When there were enough fish for a couple of meals, he decided to go after a real keeper.

Travis popped open the pocket tackle box. He selected the largest hook. Then he traded the small hook for the large one. Finally he trudged to the fish pen. A live perch would make an excellent lure. Though using live game fish for bait is illegal in Minnesota, he doubted anyone would fault him for trying to save their lives. And if a game warden did jump out of the bushes, the resulting fine would be worth getting rescued.

After pushing the hook's point under the perch's dorsal fin, Travis adjusted the bobber and with a flick of his wrist, flung the rig far from shore. Then he did something he'd regret. He propped the front end of the rod on a rock, so the reel hung below it on the ground.

He considered that unless he kept constant watch, a keeper could pull the whole affair into the lake. To make sure that didn't happen, he cut several finger-thick branches. He pushed both into the ground—each snugged up against the reel.

He gave the rod a tug. Satisfied a fish couldn't pull it loose, he decided it was time to take a break. His shoulder was throbbing. His hand hurt and his feet were a pair of cold sausages. Why not slip into his tent, crawl into the sack and snooze a few minutes? There was plenty of daylight left. He'd fix them some food after his nap.

Travis paused as he padded past Seth's shelter. The only sounds he heard were soft small snores, the kind caused by deep sleep. Feeling good about what he had accomplished, the tired camper looked forward to a short siesta.

He added wood to the fire, rotated drying sneakers and disappeared into his tent. Within minutes he was fast asleep.

Chapter Ten

C H A P T E R T E N

Lynn Springwood tried to call the Larsens. Holding the receiver to her ear confirmed that the phone lines were down—no dial tone—not even a hint of static.

Her next notion was to motor over in the pickup. A glance through a back window told her that wasn't an option. A snarl of downed trees littered the driveway.

After a moment of thought she told Sarah to hike to the lodge. The teen could tell by the look on her mother's face that it was best not to argue.

"Mom, do you think the storm was widespread? Don't thunderstorms just blow stuff down in a small area? The boys must be miles from here. They should be okay, right?"

"Sarah, I don't know. I just don't know. I pray that they're fine. Rollie has a generator for when the power's out. Maybe you can find out something from the TV in the lodge. I'm going to walk down to the Larsens' house. I know Roger has a cell phone. Maybe we'll get lucky and it'll work. I can't just stay here and do nothing."

"But Mom, what can you do? It's not like you can take the truck and pick the guys up. You don't even know where they are."

"I know. I know. I'm hoping Roger or Linda have an idea. I don't. Wear your jacket and watch for downed wires. Now go on. Get over to Rollie's."

Lynn had to thread through a clutter of limbs to reach the road. The highway was even a bigger mess. Bent and broken trees blanketed much of the blacktop. Many were tipped at crazy angles, their exposed roots holding tight to clumps of rocky soil.

She stopped, stunned by the damage. It looked like a bomb had gone off, a really big bomb. Remaining still as granite, she let her eyes roamed the ruins. Leaves, needles, the crowns of birches, aspens and evergreens layered the road. Nothing looked like it should. Only skinny saplings remained standing. But most of them stood naked and bowed, undressed by the wind.

Saddened by the sight, Lynn refocused on the blacktop. After wiping away a tear, she began picking her way through the debris. In the background, sounding like a swarm of monster mosquitoes, chainsaws whined relentlessly. Obviously, her neighbors were already at work.

She scarcely recognized the Larsen entrance. The only remnant of the mailbox was a stubby section of white post. Lynn shuddered. If this sturdy roadside marker could be sheared off, had a similar thing happened to Seth?

Roger was in the garage. Lynn trudged through the open double door. The man was at the workbench, sharpening the chain of a power saw.

"Lynn, I'm glad to see you endured the big blast. How'd you make out at the resort? Are all the buildings still standing?"

"Far as I could tell they are. But Roger, I'm worried about the boys. Have you heard how widespread the storm was? Is the damage just around Poplar or is it all over the region?"

"We don't know. I tried the cell phone, but as usual, it doesn't work this far from town. Let's use the car radio. Maybe there'll be a news update."

Roger slid into the Suburban and then lowered the windows. He turned on the radio and punched a button. Scratchy static rasped from the speakers.

"Well, I guess that tells us something. Either the tower is down or the power is off at the antenna. It's on top of the hill above town. If the power's off there, it looks like the damage is pretty spread out."

"Try the Thunder Bay station. Maybe they'll have some information," Lynn suggested.

"Good idea," Roger said, pushing the seek button. The speakers came to life.

"A ranger in Grand Marais reported widespread storm damage over the Boundary Waters Canoe Area Wilderness. Several outfitters contacted officials via short-wave radios. An outfitter based near Brule Lake had only one word for the destruction: 'devastating.' Others said that the wind had leveled entire sections of forest, bulldozing everything in the storm path. Another noted, and we quote, 'trees of all sizes are down . . . as if flattened by a gigantic roller.'"

"The sheriff's office reports it will be hours before sections of the Gunflint Trail can be cleared. Telephone and power lines are down, making communications with Trail residents impossible. The sheriff's spokesperson did say it was fortunate that this happened so late in the year. Canoe season is over. She indicated that if campers had been caught in such a fierce gale, their chances of serious injury, or worse, would have been great. An inquiry to the permit office in Grand Marais showed no active permits, certainly a lucky break for rescue personnel. Meanwhile, in other news . . . "

Roger switched off the radio. The account had sent

shivers down his spine. The man's natural boyish smile was gone, replaced by a clenched jaw. "I think we heard more than we wanted. Let's go in the house. We need to figure out a way to find the boys."

Lynn's face had gone pale. She was shaking like a leaf, not wanting to believe the broadcast. Yet she knew it was probably accurate.

"Roger, do you think . . ." she started, but couldn't find the words.

"Lynn, we have to be positive. The boys know what they're doing. They would have found shelter. I bet they're probably thinking of all the extra days they'll have to camp and fish while they're waiting for crews to clear the portages. For that matter, they're probably camped on Brule Lake right now and will paddle out tomorrow."

"You really think that's true?"

"Keep your fingers crossed," he replied. "I don't want to think otherwise."

Chapter Eleven

CHAPTER ELEVEN

The word was strategy. What they needed was a strategy. That had been one of Travis's thoughts that first evening huddled under the canoe. Both had been cold, wet, hungry and scared. But they had made it through the night, and now most of this new day.

Maybe that should be their strategy, he concluded—take one day at a time.

Other images swirled about so fast they made him dizzy. He thought he'd rather be just about anywhere else right now, even in history class. There it would be warm, and he could daydream, think about what he'd do after school. His stomach would be packed from lunch. He would tease the girls on the ride home, maybe flirt with Katie or joke with Seth in the back of the bus.

What he wouldn't do was suggest a canoe trip—a trip where things kept going wrong. An outing where they'd become stranded, hurt and helpless—unable to make their own escape.

Travis crawled from his tent. Although he was stiff and sore, the bag had been comforting. He stood, stretched tall and said, "Seth, you awake?"

"Yeah, but I'm starving. I think it's time to fry up some more fish."

Travis stared at the lake's gray surface before answering. "I suppose. But I'll need to clean some first. And before that, I'll need to tend the fire."

"Wish I could give you a hand. It's getting pretty boring just hiding out in my tent."

Travis took a couple steps and stopped to rub his stomach. Before moving on he said, "When we get home I'm gonna scratch fish off the menu. But you can serve me pizza, lots of pepperoni pizza."

The day remained dark and damp. The sky's pewter-colored belly continued to sag low and fat. Travis checked on his footwear. The fire had dried both the shoes and socks. They felt wonderful when he pulled them on and he relished their warmth. He stood quiet for a moment, savoring the heat from the hot coals. Then he went to work.

Once the fire was going, Travis trudged to the lake. The fishing pole had to be checked. He wasn't hopeful that the perch rig would attract a large fish in the middle of the day, though. Lunkers usually stayed deep until dusk. He found the rod as he'd left it. At first glance he didn't notice the miscue.

He scanned the choppy surface, trying spot the bobber. Unless the perch had dragged it toward shore, it should be floating in front of the rod. But as hard as he looked, he couldn't see it.

He decided to check it. Travis slid the reel away from the anchor sticks, but something didn't seem right. It took only a second for the problem to register. The reel was empty—not a hint of line remained.

"What the heck! What's going on?" he growled. Twisting off the reel's cover, he saw only a loop where the line had been attached.

"No way! It can't be! It's not possible!"

"Yo! What's all the yelling about?" Seth hollered. "What's the matter?"

"You don't want to know. You really don't want to know!"

Travis stood holding the now useless rod, trying to fathom what had happened. Like a TV warming up, the picture cleared. After he'd cast, he never turned the handle. The drag wasn't set; the line was free to keep uncoiling. A large fish must have snatched the perch and continued to swim away. The line ran out and snapped at the spool.

Damn! He'd made another rookie mistake. How could he be so stupid?

"Are you going to tell me or just keep me in the dark?" Seth yelled. "What's going on out there?"

Travis toted the rod to the tents. Slouched alongside Seth's shelter, he said, "I did a dumb thing. I made another stupid mistake."

Travis confessed to the blunder. Then he had a sudden thought. "Hey! You packed a rod. Didn't you?"

"Yeah, I did. I brought that stubby telescoping one I used on summer trips."

Travis's load seemed to lighten. "So where is it? I don't remember seeing it when I was digging around in your packs?"

"It should be tucked between the top and bottom bags."

Travis stuck his head in the tent and pulled out Seth's pack frame. He made a frantic search.

"Find it?" Seth asked impatiently.

Travis felt his load grow heavier again. "No. It's not here. Sure you brought it?"

"Absolutely. I used a checklist for everything. I'm positive I stuck it between the bags."

"I'm telling you, it's not here!" Travis snapped.

"You don't suppose it fell off when that bear stole my stuff? It never occurred to me to check. I assumed it was still there. Are you positive it's not between the packsacks?"

"More than positive. Oh, man! Now we have another hitch."

"Were you able to save a few fish from this morning?"

"Yeah, there's probably enough for a meal."

Travis let out a long, exasperated sigh and asked, "You want the fish or a freeze-dried packet?"

"Fish. We better use 'em before they go belly up. Or with our luck, some critter will sneak in overnight and enjoy a free, fish-to-go value pack."

Travis began preparing the one-course snack—his mood as foul as the weather. He'd hoped an airplane would be flying over, that they'd already be searching. But it wasn't to be.

The sky remained damp and dreary; gray clouds far too thick and low for little airplanes. No pilot would risk flying into the forested hills surrounding the chain of lakes. Seth and he had no choice but to spend another cold night in the bush.

When the fish were cooked, Travis carried the pan of fillets to Seth's tent. He bent, unzipped the fly and in a cheerless tone, said, "Soup's on."

Sensing his partner's murky mood, Seth sat up. He flashed his friend a fake grin and said, "You're getting' pretty good at this chef thing. Next year Rollie's gonna have to bring you on as a cook."

"Don't think so. I'm not having fun. This has turned into a disaster. Starting with the first portage, nothing's gone right. We should have turned back when we came to that stupid tree. Everything's gone wrong since then.

The bear, dropping the canoe, my hooked hand, low water in the creek, your ankle and worst of all, the storm. Now I lose the fishing line. Who knows? We might starve before anyone finds us."

"Stop it! Don't be thinking that way. This was supposed to be an adventure; we'll be laughing about it in a few weeks."

Travis stood and stared at the lake; its water was as dull as the sky above. After a moment he said, "Yeah, right. It's hysterical . . . a real barrel of laughs."

Under the thick clouds, darkness would come early. There would be no twilight. Travis made another excursion to gather wood. Returning to fire ring, he dumped the load and then stood motionless. He couldn't think of what else needed immediate attention. He decided to call it a day.

Before turning in, he asked Seth, "Need help with anything before I turn in?"

"Glad you asked. I gotta go to the bathroom really bad. It's one thing to pee outside the tent. But right now I gotta handle some serious business. I can't just walk over to the woods like you can."

Seth managed to inchworm out of his tent. Travis helped him balance on his good leg. Then Seth hopped along the cliff-face. Travis respected Seth's privacy. He left him propped against the outcropping.

To kill time, Travis ambled to the shore. He stared out at the dark surface and wondered what kind of fish had stolen their lifeline. For that was what it had been. It'd been a lifeline—a line to food, a line that could keep them nourished.

The quiet was shattered by a call for help.

"Trav, if you're not too busy, I could use a hand."

"Okay, be right there."

As he turned, his eye caught something breaking the surface. Whatever it was, it vanished just as fast. That was puzzling. "Maybe the fish came up to laugh at me," he thought. Perplexed, the youth trudged back to his pal. Then he got the only genuine laugh of the day.

Seth was propped forward on his good leg, leaning against the rock wall. His jeans and briefs were twisted around the good ankle. The swollen limb was painfully held off the ground. But what Travis saw most clearly in fading light was Seth's white, bare backside.

Laughing, he couldn't help razzing his buddy. "I take it you're all finished. But at least one good thing's happening tonight."

"Oh yeah, what's that?" Seth's baritone echoed off the cliff.

"The moon's out early and it's a full one at that."

After returning Seth to his bag, Travis banked the fire. As darkness tightened its grip, he threw in the towel and crawled inside his tent. He lay awake thinking about all that had gone wrong.

After a time he asked, "Seth, you awake?"

"Yup, I'm pretty much caught up on my sleep. What's on your mind? Still worried about losing your line?"

"Yeah, that . . . and a dozen other things. You think they're looking for us?"

"It's hard to say. It probably depends on how much got flattened. Thunderstorms don't usually damage a large area. But this didn't seem like an ordinary storm. I'd guess that when the weather clears, they'll fly over for an air search."

"Isn't it illegal to fly small planes over this part of the state? Some law about noise and disturbing the peace and quiet?"

"Right, but they can use them in an emergency. I guess it'll depend on some government yahoo giving the okay.

Maybe we aren't an emergency yet. No one really knows about our situation. We said we might not be back until tomorrow afternoon. Maybe they'll wait a while, see if we show up before they start looking."

Travis exhaled noisily. "That sorta makes sense. You told your mom what route we'd be taking, right?"

"Ah . . . not really. All I told her was we'd be heading for Brule Lake."

"Well, she should be able to figure out our route. It'd be easy to trace on a map."

Seth was quiet for a time. "Ahh . . . they might have a problem doin' that. We didn't use the regular route. Most people go through Horseshoe and Gaskin lakes."

"But wouldn't they come through this chain anyway?"

"Yep. I think they would. But the thing is . . . a search party would most likely check the other route first. That's miles from here, and if the portages are blocked, it could take days before they reach these small lakes."

"But they'd come through here eventually, right?"

"I think they would. You can verify it on the map in the morning."

For a time both went quiet. Travis broke the silence. "Seth, you notice that there aren't any animals around?"

"How could I tell? I've been in the tent all day."

"I haven't seen as much as a chipmunk. What happened to all the critters?

"No doubt some of the bigger ones got hurt or killed. Unless they live underground, I'm sure the small ones lost their nests. I haven't really thought about it."

Another quiet time followed before Travis quivered out another question. "Seth, are you scared?"

"Scared? Are you scared we won't get out of here?"

"Yeah. Aren't you worried that something else is going to happen? You know . . . like no one will find us in time?"

"In time for what? You got a date with Katie? Didn't you tell me to take one day at a time? What happened to that? The one thing we can't do is panic. Rollie tells the guides that they can never panic. Panic will doom you before anything else. We'll be all right. We just can't let our imaginations run wild."

"You learned a lot about the woods this summer, didn't you?"

"Yeah, Trav, I did. But we never had a storm like this. Think about it. Some of the trees blown over have to be a hundred or more years old. We lived through a once-in-a-lifetime event. It'll be something to tell our grandkids about."

"If we get rescued."

Travis went silent again, his brain an anthill of activity. Finally he said, "Seth, did you ever wonder why a tent shuts out wind and rain, but sounds come through louder than if you are standing outside?"

Seth coughed out a guffaw before asking, "Where'd that come from? Are you losin' it?"

"No, just changing the subject. The rescue thing worries me. 'Cause Seth, I'm scared. We've made too many mistakes. I'm afraid we might make some more."

"Stop tormenting yourself. Get some sleep. Things will look better in the morning."

"I'm trying, I'm trying."

"Good night. And Trav, don't let the bedbugs bite. I'm told they make you itch."

"Ha, ha . . . you're such a comedian you oughta be on stage. I just hope that nose horn of yours won't keep me awake all night. Sometimes you snore louder than a lovesick moose."

Chapter Twelve

C H A P T E R   T W E L V E

Travis awoke well aware his mattress was the hard earth beneath the fabric floor. Open eyes caught no evidence of a new day. The tiny shelter seemed as dark as a closed casket. Before nodding off he thought more about the strange thing that had surfaced on the lake.

Could it possibly have been his bobber? Would the fish that robbed the line still be attached? If so, could he use the canoe to locate and retrieve it? It was certainly worth a try.

He dozed off and on for the next hour. When at last a hint of light leaked into the tent, Travis slithered from his bag. Outside, the morning was a twin to the day before. Hefty dark clouds still hung low, canceling hopes for a colorful sunrise.

Travis rekindled the fire and checked on his pal. "Everything okay in there?"

"Still here. Not a hundred percent, though. What kind of day is it gonna be?"

"It looks about the same as yesterday. We must be getting some of Seattle's weather. Clouds followed by more clouds. Do you need me for anything right now?"

"Nope. Are you going somewhere?"

"Yup. I'm gonna take a cruise. Too bad you can't come along."

"Cruise? What are you babbling about?"

"I'm going to take the canoe and look for my bobber."

"When did you come up with that idea? You think there's a chance you'll find it?"

Travis told Seth about the splash he'd seen the night before. Seth agreed it was worth a try. "Just don't tip over. Paddle from the middle or put some weight in the front. It'll help keep the canoe from flipping."

"Thanks, but I already thought of that."

Travis slid the canoe to shore. Then he bit at his lip, pondering if this really was a good idea. The water was cool, too cool for safe swimming. He had been taught about hypothermia—how cold water can steal body heat in mere minutes. How it can bring certain death to the strongest of swimmers.

Yet he couldn't think of any other options. His blunder had caused the problem. Only he could fix it.

Once the canoe was in the water, Travis climbed in. Staying low, he used the paddle for balance.

He knelt in the center and stroked away from the beach, the ache in his shoulder reminding him to go easy. Without a load of passengers and gear, the canoe rode high. The youth quickly discovered that the slightest weight shift caused it to tip from side to side. Once away from the beach, he made several wide thrusts with the paddle, turning the craft parallel to the shoreline.

In order to keep the canoe on a straight course, he had to switch hands every few strokes. Lighter than usual, the craft skimmed the surface, leaving only a trace of wake. Between pulls, Travis scanned every direction, hoping to spot the float.

The teen was amazed by the destruction he witnessed. The majority of trees along shore were either broken off or tipped over. On the lake, bare branches broke the surface like weeds in a forgotten garden.

For a while, the search seemed fruitless. He had circled most of the lake when he made a sighting. He spotted an orange life jacket clinging to a partially submerged branch. With care and patience, he maneuvered the canoe alongside the half-sunken tree top.

Careful not to lean too far over, he untangled the strap and hauled the life preserver into the canoe. He felt a bit safer having the lifesaver on board. At least he wouldn't sink if the canoe flipped.

Travis had nearly circled the entire lake when he made his second find. Suddenly, there it was—the bobber— just ahead of the canoe, zipping across the water as if pushed by a propeller.

The red-topped nibble-teller was angling away from shore. Thrusting hard, Travis turned the canoe and paddled to cut in front of it with all the muscle he could muster.

The canoe shot forward as if it also had an engine of its own. A dozen pulls later, Travis was in position to make the grab. Just then the float bobbed by the boat. Travis leaned over to snatch it. He closed his fist on the plastic ball and gave a yank.

But the fish on the far end of the line had other ideas. Feeling the sudden jerk, the large pike made a powerful thrust with its tail. The sudden surge almost ripped the bobber from the teen's grip. And much more frightening, the canoe rocked over on its side, nearly capsizing.

Travis had known there was a fish on the line. He had prepared himself for a tug. But he hadn't prepared for the power of whatever was attached. If the canoe hadn't been so lightly loaded, the line would no doubt have snapped. And as it turned out, that would have been a good thing. But the line didn't break. Instead, the craft swung in the direction the fish was swimming. Travis clung to the bobber as if his life depended on it.

Even when the line began to crease his hand he held tight. Pumped by the possibility of actually landing the fish, he hollered out loud. "You're mine, fish! All mine! I'm gonna eat you for breakfast!"

Then the unexpected happened. Travis was concentrating so hard on the fight, he didn't notice the submerged tree trunk. Without warning the canoe smacked into the log. The tipsy craft stopped as if it had hit a wall.

Travis was thrown against the gunnels. The sudden shift in weight caused the canoe to roll, plunging its passenger face-first into the cold water. It all happened in the blink of an eye. For a few short moments, Travis had been king of the world, about to land a trophy. Then in a flash, he was fighting for his life under the overturned watercraft.

The plunge into frigid liquid sucked his breath away. It took several heartbeats to realize what had happened; he was trapped under the canoe. As panic rose, he began fighting for his life.

Grabbing a gunnel, he thrust skyward with all his strength. The canoe went up, but the effort pushed Travis deeper into the water. That's when he realized he could he could see light above. Kicking and pulling, he clawed toward the surface. Finally he broke free, gasping for air.

More panic. Where was shore?

Furiously treading water, he felt something bump his head. He spun around to push it away, but suddenly stopped. It was the life preserver, floating alongside, begging to be used. Travis reached out with his free hand and snuggled it to his body, unaware his other fist still clutched the float.

Shore, camp and the fire were at least a hundred yards distant. Instinct said to kick that direction with every once of energy his shivering body could generate. Because if he didn't reach land quickly, this would be the last swim he'd ever make.

With one fist still wrapped around the float, he used his other hand to tuck the lifesaver under his chest. Then kicked and pulled water with every ounce of reserve.

When the frigid water stole his strength—when his lungs could no longer keep up—when he thought for certain he was about to die, his hand struck bottom. Sensing he was only a few feet from saving himself, Travis used his last bit of energy to crawl onto the rocky beach.

Then he lay there, spent, trying to reclaim his breath, willing his body up the slope toward the fire. He started to tremble violently. No matter how hard he tried, he couldn't stop the shaking.

The fire—he had to get to the fire. Fading in and out, he managed to roll over. After pushing to his knees, he staggered to his feet. Then somehow, wobbling like a toddler taking its first steps, he stumbled to the fire ring. That's when the lights went out. His legs turned to rubber and Travis collapsed flat on the ground.

He came to an hour later, lying prone where he had fallen. But amazingly he was covered head to toe by an opened sleeping bag. To one side a smoky fire snapped and popped. The flames sounded alive as a bundle of green wood.

Travis turned his head and got another surprise. Snuggled alongside him, half under and half out of the sleeping bag, was his pal Seth.

"All right . . . so you're back among the living. Thought maybe you were gonna nap all day," Seth's baritone burrowed into a niche within Travis's fog-filled brain.

"From the looks of things, you must have taken an early

morning swim. What's up with that? It had to be one cold bath."

Like the curtain of an opening act, the fog began to lift. The death plunge slowly came into focus. Travis remembered the errant bobber, the big fish, the towed canoe, a sudden cold splash and his desperate struggle to reach land.

But that's all he could recall. He couldn't remember coming ashore. He couldn't picture crawling to the fire.

But yet here he was, alive—wet and cold—but alive. After a lull he finally found his voice. "It wasn't my idea. Like you said the other day. Sometimes stuff just happens."

"It sure does. But I thought we had a deal. You take care of me, not the other way around. Good thing for you I had to take a whiz. When I crawled out of my tent, I saw you lying here. You didn't answer me so I dragged myself over. You were breathing but looked kinda blue. I knew you must be really cold."

"Thanks, you probably saved my life," Travis mumbled through chattering teeth.

"So? You want to tell me about your water-world adventure now or later?"

"Later. I need to get to the tent, change into dry clothes. I'll tell you about my cruise after I warm up. In the meantime, why don't you start heading for the tent. You can rest in my sleeping bag as soon as I'm through changing clothes."

Travis draped the damp bag over Seth's tent before crawling into his own shelter. Stripping off his wet clothing, he slipped into dry underwear. That's when he remembered he'd have to use cutoffs. He'd only brought one pair of jeans—the ones he had on. But he did find an extra sweatshirt and pulled it over his head.

Still chilled to the bone, Travis gathered his soaked clothes and treaded barefoot to the fire. Now he was happy he'd stockpiled wood. Shivering, the youth stood as close to the flames as he dared, careful not to burn the flesh on his goose-pimpled legs.

In the meantime, Seth had made a one-legged slither to Travis's tent. "Trav, you sure it's okay if I use your stuff?"

Travis hugged himself and nodded. "Go ahead. I need to move around, get my blood flowing. Soon as I toast all four sides, I'll hang things up to dry. Work should make me warmer."

"Thanks. But you know what else? I'm starving. When you're finished with your clothes, maybe you can fix something to eat. Maybe use one of the freeze-dried meals. Try one the bear already opened. Once it's heated, I'm sure it'll be okay."

Travis nodded and turned his face to the fire. "Okay, but give me a few minutes. My body's so stiff it's gonna take a while to get motoring."

"One more question, Trav. Where's my canoe? I was getting sort of attached to it."

Travis turned toward the tents. He managed a hint of a smile. "Seth, I left it where all good boats belong."

"Yeah? Where would that be?"

"Where d'ya think? It's out in the water, my friend. Far out on the lake."

Travis hugged the fire until he'd warmed enough to tackle his chores. Clutching the hatchet, he trudged to a fallen aspen. Its branches spread fan-like on the sodden ground. Then he willed his hand to hold the ax firm enough to chop off several bundles of branches. These he trimmed and dragged to the fire ring.

He jammed the pointed ends into the soggy earth until they wouldn't tip. Over one bundle he spread his jeans, jacket and soggy sweatshirt. He used the second limb to keep the clammy sleeping bag from touching the ground.

The teen went about the work as if an icicle had touched his soul. He'd come close to dying. Close to being an article in the weekly paper. He pictured the headline, "Local Boy Drowns on Autumn Outing."

He kept making mistakes, so many poor choices. And that's exactly what they were—choices. He chose to go on this trip. He chose to not turn around at the first signs of trouble. He chose to push the canoe high over his head, and later, to lip the fish that hooked his hand.

And then there was today's miscue. It was his decision to take the canoe out, foolishly thinking he'd fix yesterday's blunder.

He'd made so many mistakes. What did his mother say? Trouble was like bananas—it usually came in bunches. She was right. She knew. Trouble could come in bunches. He'd made so many errors. He had to get his act together and start using his head.

Travis peeked inside his tent. Seth was huddled in the sleeping bag. An alarm bell began buzzing in Travis's brain. His friend's normally ruddy cheeks were now a pasty white.

"How are you doing in there?"

"I've been better. But I'll be all right once you get some grub rounded up. Are you even working on it?" Seth rasped.

"Easy, pal. It won't take long. I just need to get one of the food packs from your bag and boil some water. Fifteen or twenty minutes, tops. I'll bring you some when it's ready."

Travis rummaged through the remaining packets, choosing the one that the bear had ripped. The bag was divided into three sealed pouches. Two of the three were still full, their powdery mixtures untouched.

At the fire ring he exchanged the packet for the cooking pans, and walked them to the lake for filling. He was barefoot and decided he'd go out a couple of steps, past the debris floating near shore.

As he waded into the water, something snagged one of his toes. Looking down he saw nothing. But something was there. He could feel it. He bent to remove what he thought must be a weed. At first touch he was puzzled, but then suddenly excited. His toe had caught the fishing line.

Thrilled, he threw the pans on the bank and began pulling in the line. Hand over hand he brought it in— enough line that he could fish again! Then he came to the empty hook and realized the big fish was long gone.

Travis began pulling in the other end. He felt a slight resistance. His spirits raised another notch. The bobber was still attached. With a watery plop, the red-and-white ball broke free of the surface, nearly hitting him in the shin.

He raised a clenched fist and pumped the air as if he'd scored a winning goal. "All right! About time we had some good luck!"

The find fueled a shot of fresh optimism. At least they wouldn't starve. Travis felt better about using a food packet. With a pair of pans over hot flames, the meat and vegetables swelled and started to resemble real food.

After letting both pans steam for a moment, he declared them cooked. Then he transferred half of the meat into the vegetable pot and vice-versa. He left one pan resting on the rocks and took the other over to his tent.

He stopped just outside the door. "Hey, bud! Soup's on."

No reply.

"You in there, dude? Time to eat."

Again, no answer—only the noise of the breeze rattling branches in the background.

"Come on, buddy. Wake up. Your food will get cold,"

Travis barked in a bolder voice.

There was a return grunt—nothing more. Travis set the pan on the ground, zipped open the door and poked his head inside. Seth was curled so far into the sleeping bag, only the top of his head was visible.

"Seth, you want to eat or not?"

Seth's head slowly emerged. "Huh? Oh, okay."

"What's the matter? Are you feeling all right?"

Seth slowly shook his head. "No. First I had the chills and then I was hot. Now I got the chills again."

"Better eat something. You'll feel better."

"I'm not hungry anymore. I lost my appetite."

Travis crawled all the way in. "You gotta eat something. Here, I'll help you sit up."

Seth began to cough—a rasp that burbled up from deep down in his lungs.

Travis paused. The alarm bells were ringing again, louder. When the coughing jag ended, he said, "That doesn't sound good. When did you start with the hacking?"

"A little bit ago. But the hot-and-cold thing started yesterday. The ankle injury must be sapping all my get-up and go. With my bad ankle and all this lying around on the wet ground, I'm probably catching a cold."

Travis thought it sounded far worse than a cold. Chills, fever and a sudden loss of appetite—it had to be more than a garden variety cough. But he kept his fears to himself, saying, "You're going to hurt the chef's feelings if you don't even taste it."

Seth picked at the offering, finally finishing all of it. When he was through, he burrowed back in the bag and closed his eyes. Within minutes he nodded off.

It hadn't taken Travis long to wolf down his portion.

He'd eaten by the fire, pondering the latest concern. What if Seth was really sick? Could it be pneumonia?

Isn't that what his mother warned him about when he'd go ice fishing without a hat and gloves? She'd caution him about catching pneumonia. And he'd heard about old folks going to the doctor with a winter cough— only to die of the disease.

Needing something to do, Travis set the pan down and checked to see if his clothes were dry. Only the sides closest to the flames were toasty. He rotated the sweatshirt and sleeping bag, and then stood staring into space. What was he supposed to do about Seth?

For now . . . nothing. There wasn't much he could do. He wasn't a doctor.

Hunger pangs still gnawed at the edges of his stomach. The meager meal hadn't filled his tank. There was one thing he could do—fish. Kneeling alongside the fire, he rewound the reel. Several times smoke blew in his face, irritating his eyes and nose, making him sneeze.

Dodging smoke spawned a thought. Maybe there was way to preserve the fish.

A few neighbors on Poplar Lake had little buildings used to smoke fish. There was even a tiny smoke shack at the Kane's' Lodge. Maybe Seth knew how it was done. Seth seemed to know most of the things that went on around the resort.

But in order to preserve the fish, he'd have to catch some first. Rod and reel in hand, he headed for the lake.

Another nugget of luck was to find a few guts that hadn't been washed away. Luckily, critters hadn't made the same discovery or the remains would have vanished faster than free popcorn at a ball game.

His first cast went unanswered; the bobber lay lazily on the water. Travis let it float for a few minutes then reeled in. The hook was bare. Attaching more bait, he cast again—this time with almost instant results. Soon the corral took on the look of an overstocked aquarium.

Travis spent the entire day fishing, taking only a short break to fry a few fillets and look in on Seth. As dusk arrived he decided to give up. Thick clouds meant full dark would fall quickly. But he felt good knowing there'd be plenty of fish to fry in the morning. Nearing the fire ring he saw that the wood supply was low. Another job for tomorrow, he mused. Just like home, there were always chores waiting on him.

Next he checked Seth's sleeping bag. The fabric seemed dry, warm and ready for use. Folding the bag over his shoulder, Travis headed for the tent. Besides being famished, he was dog tired—totally worn out.

He slipped into the shelter and snuggled into Seth's sleeping bag. Once on the ground, resting, his entire body cried foul at being abused. It seemed impossible to find a comfortable position. No matter which way he flip-flopped, his shoulder whimpered for relief. At times the bruised hand joined the protest, announcing with throbs that it needed attention. The only aid was to keep flexing it, working the hurt away a bit at a time.

Finally, as darkness enclosed their camp, fatigue conquered pain. Travis dozed off.

He awoke during the deepest part of the night. He lay still, not moving a muscle, wondering what had interrupted his slumber. He poked his head out of the sleeping bag and strained his ears. A breeze shivered the tent fabric, meaning the wind had changed direction. But Travis didn't think that would have nudged him from sleep.

The soft splash of waves washing over rocks came from the beach. That was a common sound he often heard through the open window of his bedroom. It wouldn't have been cause for alarm. Travis felt around for his flashlight. Then he remembered it was in the other tent.

He lay back and held his breath, willing his ears to pick out any sound that didn't belong.

Then there it was—a deep, clunking thud—like the heel of a hand drumming the top of a barrel. Travis froze, concentrating on the strange thumping. He dismissed that it was an animal. And it didn't sound like something he should fear. Eventually, curiosity got the better of him. He worked his way out of the bag and felt for the door.

It was nearly as black outside as it was inside the tent. But by some trick of physics, the lake was able to reflect a little of the meager moonshine attempting to poke through the cloud cover. There was enough light that Travis could make out the shoreline. Turning left, he saw a single winking red eye. For a brief moment his heart stopped. Then he realized it was only the last glowing ember of the fire.

After standing perfectly still for a time, listening, he shuffled toward the fire ring. He scuffed the grass in an attempt to locate leftover wood. The toe of one shoe touched a limb, then another. After quickly stirring the ashes, Travis added both and waited for the fuel to catch.

Once flames began flickering, he used the firelight to guide himself to the lake. The thumping sounded close, down the shoreline just beyond camp. By now his eyes had adjusted to darkness, and it was little challenge to tread along the beach.

As he passed the fish corral he paused, hoping breakfast was still swimming around in the shallow water. All the rocks looked to be in place but it was too shadowy to make out individual fish. He'd have to assume they were all there, waiting to greet him after sunrise.

As Travis walked on, the clunking became more distinct.

He stopped to peer into the shadows along shore. Something large, whale-sized, was wallowing up and down in the water. Travis grinned. The mystery was solved.

The clunk came as the canoe bumped the rocky bottom. Air pockets under the seats had kept it from sinking below the surface. The shifting wind had released the craft from the tree's grip and it had returned home on its own.

Travis removed his shoes and waded into the water until he found the bow rope. Wrapping the cord around his waist, he tugged the canoe toward shore. When he was close to the beach, he tied the cord to a shrub.

Add another chore onto tomorrow's to-do list. The canoe could be turned over and bailed out in the morning. It's not like they needed it, there was no place to go. Still, it was good to have it back. He headed back to the tent, hoping sleep would quickly return to him.

But sleep didn't come easily the second time around. Twice, Travis had almost drifted off when he was jolted awake by whoops and hacks coming from his friend in the neighboring tent.

"Seth's sick," he whispered in the dark. "Really sick."

Then Travis forced himself to focus on good things—safe things—delicious things. Eventually he slipped into a dreamless slumber. The next sound he heard was Seth's voice asking if he was planning to stay in bed all day.

Chapter Thirteen

C H A P T E R   T H I R T E E N

Work crews didn't clear the Gunflint Trail until Sunday afternoon. The Larsens headed for town only moments after big, yellow machines removed debris from the end of their drive.

The twenty-five-mile trip to Grand Marais did nothing to bolster their mood. They passed miles of downed timber. Trees that hadn't been toppled stood bent and bare, stripped of their colorful foliage.

Tucked far down behind a huge hill, the town had escaped the full fury of the storm. Except for a few branches and some missing shingles, it was business as usual. The Larsens' first stop was the ranger station. A half-dozen pickups and cars sat in the paved parking lot. Several vehicles had government decals on their doors.

Once inside, Roger Larsen waited while the rangers talked to other Trail residents. When his turn finally came, the information he received wasn't heartening. They hadn't been able to locate another local aircraft. The small planes hangered at the local airstrip had been damaged. Besides, one of the rangers said, it was still unsafe for an air search. Until the clouds cleared, they wouldn't chance losing a pilot.

The only bit of good news was the governor was considering calling in the National Guard to help with cleanup. When, and if, he did, there might be a chance they could use a guard helicopter. But until somebody knew for certain the boys were in danger, the rangers had more than enough to do handling other storm-related issues.

Mr. Larsen inquired about the Caribou Trail, the road that wound its way from Lake Superior to Brule Lake. He learned most of the route had been opened but it was still blocked short of the boat landing. It would be take another day or two before the right-away would be cleared all the way to the lake.

The ranger assured Mr. Larsen that if any outfitters radioed in with news about the boys, they'd get a message to him. Until the weather decided to cooperate there wasn't much that could be done. Roger left the building without knowing much more than when he entered.

Back in the car he relayed the information, or the lack of it, to Linda and Beth. There was nothing more they could do but shop for supplies and head back home.

Few words were spoken on the return trip. No one said it, but the thought crossed their minds. It might already be too late for a rescue.

Linda paid no attention to the tear trickling down her cheek. She held her wet gaze to the passenger window, saying a mental prayer that somehow, some way, her firstborn was safe.

Roger drove on autopilot, lost in thought. He was thinking about ways they could get on with the search. He wracked his brain for a connection. There must be someone who could help them.

The Larsens were almost home when a name flashed. Robert "Bob" Ritzer, an old friend who had recently retired from the Department of Natural Resources. Bob was a veteran pilot. He even had his own airplane. Bob had often worked with Roger doing low-level moose counts, skimming the tree tops in his faithful old Cessna.

First thing in the morning Roger would drive into town and make a few calls, see if he could locate his old friend. He knew Bob had moved to a lake home somewhere in central Minnesota. If Bob still owned the plane, and if he hadn't already changed from floats to wheels, Bob would help. The man knew both the Larsen children and always asked about them.

Roger kept the thought to himself. He didn't want to build false hopes. He decided to continue up the road to the resort. They could let Lynn Springwood know what little they had learned.

A mammoth log skidder was clearing the Kanes' drive as the Larsens' SUV approached. Waiting while the thunderous rig pushed away the last of the logs, Roger thought about what he'd tell Seth's mother. There was really not much to say. Their boys were in real trouble—maybe more trouble than they could handle.

* * *

"Yeah, well, good morning to you, too!" Travis snapped sarcastically at Seth's dig about sleeping all day.

"You're still in the sack. What's the big deal if I get some extra rest? Who's doing all the work around here?"

"And so you are," Seth answered around a hacking cough. "I was just checking to see if you were still in the tent. I can't tell from in here."

Seth coughed again. "I thought maybe you were out exploring the countryside . . . finding a place to buy us breakfast."

"Not a chance. The closest grocery is quite a hike. Don't think I'd be back before dark.

Travis poked his head outside. "I guess I better get up. By the way, how are you feeling?"

"No change. I woke up with chills a couple of times.

My canteen's about empty. Can ya find some clean water? Or is the lake too full of leaves and junk?"

"It's not a problem. I'll wade out a ways to fill the pots, strain the water through my socks. That'll filter out any crud."

"Thanks, but no thanks. I think I'd prefer the crud before drinking stinky sock tea."

"Relax. I've got a clean hankie. I can use it as a filter.

Travis finished tying his Nikes. He crawled from the tent, stood and stretched. "Hey bud, I've got some good news."

"Yeah? What? That it's Monday morning and we're not in school?"

"Believe me, I'd rather be in class than here. The news is, your canoe came home last night."

Travis told Seth about the mysterious midnight sound. Seth said he hadn't heard a thing but was glad to have his boat back. Then with the next breath, he said he didn't know what good it would do. He wasn't up to any portaging, much less trying to push, paddle and pull around the dozens of blowdowns blocking the outlet streams.

Travis didn't reply. He stood with hands in pockets, looking out at the lake.

After a time, Seth asked, "What's the weather like?"

"Well . . . it looks about the same as yesterday. Lots of low, wet-looking scud. I can't even see the Misquah Hills. They're pretending to be real mountains by poking their little tops into the clouds."

"That means another day without an air search," Seth croaked between coughs.

"Seth, what did you say the other day—no rest for the weary? Guess that means me. Do you need water now or should I get the fire going first? I caught a real mess of fish yesterday. We've got plenty for breakfast."

"I can wait for the water. Do whatever you have to do. I'll hang out and listen to the sound of you working. Not every day I get to hear that."

After rounding up more wood, Travis rekindled the blaze. He trudged to the corral, scooped out a dozen of the tiny fish and cleaned them on a flat rock.

Once the thin slabs were browned, Travis carried a full pan to Seth's tent. He unzipped the door, and was shocked when he stuck his head inside. Seth's complexion had gone further south. His friend's naturally dark skin had vanished—replaced by a sick, yellowish white.

Travis kept mum about Seth's lack of color. Instead he forced a smile to his lips. "Once again, world famous chef, Travis De-Larsen, has prepared a nourishing, healthy mushy meal . . . low in fat, high in protein. Enjoy!"

Seth gurgled up a couple of coughs and gave a weak reply. "Thanks, but I really could use a drink. An aspirin or two might help. There are a few left in the first-aid kit, right?"

"No problem. I'll get right on it."

After closing the tent door, Travis brooded. Seth looked awful, about two steps from death's door. "We've got to get rescued today or I'm going to have to come up with another idea," he told himself. "My legs are fine. I can walk. I have the map and a compass. Besides, with all the trees pointing in one direction, it'd be pretty hard to get lost. I just can't panic. Gotta' keep telling myself not to panic. I can do it; there's got to be a way out of here."

For Travis, the day disappeared like fresh snow on warm pavement. After filtering some drinking water, he burnt several hours gathering wood. He didn't quit stacking until there was enough to last for several days.

The thought of smoking fish kept rattling around in his head like a loose marble. What he needed to build was some type of support—an apparatus that would hold the fillets over the fire without burning.

He got started by collecting an armful of green branches, which he patiently wove together. Then he stuck a series of forked sticks into the earth around the fire ring. To these, he attached the web of branches. When he was satisfied the web was secure, and high enough not to catch fire, he headed for the lake.

Cleaning the mess of fish took longer than anticipated. When he finally finished, Travis placed the little slabs on the branch netting. Then he added green wood to the fire. The damp fuel smoldered, sending up more plumes of smoke than flames. Travis wasn't certain if this was the right way to way to smoke fish, but it was worth a try.

Several times he abandoned his projects to check on his pal. Each time, after softly saying Seth's name, he received the same reply—silence. Travis assumed Seth was sleeping. Rest being a good thing, he didn't disturb him.

While the fillets were drying, Travis labored at restocking the fish corral. Strange, he mused, that he should be fishing for survival and not for fun. It reminded him of studying third world countries in social studies. At the time, Travis had not given a thought to how important catching a fish could be. He now held a different outlook. He understood that a few fish could mean the difference between life and death.

In the afternoon, Travis tugged the canoe to shore. Barefoot, and with his jeans rolled up, he wrestled it right side up. Then he bailed with a cook pot until he could drag the craft all the way up on land. Once he had it there, he tipped the canoe over, spilling out the remaining water.

The work kept his blood pumping. That morning,

when Travis went outside, every breath formed a white puff. Without sunshine, the temperature had refused to warm by more than a few degrees. And for the third straight day, the heavens hung low like a dirty sheet. Occasionally a cloud would act like a playground bully and spit, causing Travis to be thankful he'd packed his waterproof windbreaker.

As his body was busy, so was his brain. It argued back and forth, debating his next step, and the odds of survival. What were their chances of being rescued? Maybe he should go for help? Could he manage the canoe on his own? How choked with timber were the other streams?

Finally, Travis decided he'd had enough mental exercise. He knew what to do. He'd take the canoe across the lake and have a look. He'd go see just how badly the outlet had fared.

Seth was sleeping when Travis crept into the tent and eased the map from the pack. After giving his sick friend a concerned look, Travis quietly left the tent and plopped down on the grass near the fire to study the map. With a finger, he traced the remainder of the route. On the chart it looked like a no-brainer. A couple of streams, a couple little lakes and a short portage—and he'd be at Brule. From there it would be simple water work. In all, he decided, their campsite couldn't be more than five or six miles from the big lake.

He did some mental math. If he left at first light in the morning, and if the streams were open and running, he should get to Brule around noon. And with luck, be at the outfitters' base long before dark.

It was worth a try, he thought. It was something he could do. "If the clouds are hanging low tomorrow morning, I'm out of here," he whispered to the breeze.

He jumped to his feet and trotted to the tent to put the map away. Then he scurried to the canoe. It was time to explore.

His target was a stream that connected this lake to the next. Recalling how tippy the canoe had been when he almost drowned, he placed several large rocks in the bow. The weight settled the canoe deeper into water, making it far more user-friendly. Grasping the spare paddle that had been duct-taped to the thwarts, he stroked straight across the lake.

Travis beached the canoe as soon as it bumped land. The channel opening was only a short walk away. Reaching the spillage, Travis smiled. Lake water was gurgling into the creek. More than enough water, he saw, to float the canoe. He could wade ahead and use the rope to tug the craft over riffles and windfalls.

The storm had huffed straight down the channel. Trees were tipped parallel to the bank, but none completely crossed the creek. Travis was excited. The voyage out should prove easier than he could have hoped for—or at least on the portion he could see.

Except for the ache in his shoulder, the return trip was uneventful. Travis secured the canoe and checked the drying fish. The fillets had shrunk to the size of half dollars. He touched one. Not only was it small, it was hard as a month-old biscuit. He brought it to his mouth and bit off a piece. It was dry and smoky tasting. But to a starving teenager, it was edible. Better than eating wood, he figured. At least it had food value.

A chest-wrenching cough shattered his thoughts—Seth.

"How's it going in there?" Travis inquired as he neared their tents. "Feeling any better?" The answer was a sick-sounding series of hacks, followed by, "About the same, hot and cold, no energy. If this coughing didn't keep waking me up, I think I could sleep 'round the clock."

"Hey pal, I'm getting worried about you. Between that ankle and your cold, you're one sick puppy."

"Not a whole lot we can do about it. Someone will find us soon. We'll be all right."

Travis stared across the water, pondering the remark. For the first time since the storm, he saw birds winging over the forest. Large and black, they were ravens or crows, he thought. Whatever their species, they were lucky. They could fly over the mess of tangled trees.

Finally he said, "You really believe that we'll be rescued anytime soon?"

"Gotta think that way. Search and Rescue's gotta be looking for us right now."

"Hmmm. Maybe. But it could take days before they can get through the portages. Meantime, I came up with a different plan."

Travis explained his idea. How the outlet stream looked fairly clear of blowdowns. How the map showed that they weren't more than a few miles from the big lake. He told Seth that if it was still cloudy in the morning, he was going for help.

Between hacks and whoops, Seth tried to protest. He reminded Travis that most of the time, when people aren't rescued in wilderness emergencies, it's because they didn't stay in one spot. He argued that Travis had his own problems. He said it would be impossible for Travis to portage—especially with all the trees that had to be blocking the portage to Brule.

But Travis had made up his mind; he was going at first light the next day. He'd leave the majority of the smoked fish and a couple of freeze-dried meals. He'd place the food and both canteens inside the door where Seth could reach them.

The only things he'd carry would be the rod and a few of the dried fish. Travis assured Seth that by the next night he'd be eating a juicy burger back in Grand Marais.

Seth couldn't convince Travis otherwise. He told Travis that he was foolish to leave, but if he did go, to pack more gear. He talked him into taking his tent, sleeping bag, cooking pan and the meal packs. He made Travis promise he wouldn't go without them.

Travis gave Seth his word, then used the last of the quickly fading light to pack for an early departure.

Chapter Fourteen

C H A P T E R   F O U R T E E N

Travis tossed and turned in his bag as the first soft glow lit the horizon. Now that a new day had arrived, he was having second thoughts. He worried that if he got hurt there would be no one to help. Having slept on his decision to leave for Brule Lake, he wasn't at all certain that he could make the trip solo.

Earlier the night before, Seth had needed help crawling from the tent. Barely strong enough to stand on his good leg, Seth had become lightheaded. Travis had had to hold him up until he regained his balance.

The incident had convinced Travis that he had to go for help—ASAP. After they'd switched back their own tents, Travis had used the last of the light to sort out gear.

When he was done packing they had another talk. Travis reasoned that this trip was the right thing to do. If help arrived before he made it to the outfitters, Seth could tell the rescue team where Travis could be found. He shouldn't be hard to locate along the route to Brule. Besides, Travis thought, with any luck he'd be at the outfitters before dark the next day. He'd send a Search and Rescue team out to the campsite for Seth.

Before attempting sleep, they made a pact. If the weather improved, Travis would stay put. That was his hope now—that the clouds had given up and gone away. That they'd moved elsewhere, bringing gloom and doom to a new neighborhood, anywhere but here.

During the hours of darkness, doubt had crept into the shelter and stolen his courage. Before falling into a fitful sleep, all sorts of scary possibilities haunted him like Halloween ghosts. Now these thoughts lingered like a grease spot, washed but not gone, impossible to completely remove. He was starting to get scared. What if he couldn't make it out on his own?

Dreary light began seeping through the tent fabric. It was time. Travis knew he had to get up, check the sky and make a decision.

* * *

It wasn't until late Monday afternoon that Roger Larsen managed to contact his pilot friend Bob Ritzer. He was more than willing to help. And fortunately, the floats were still on the Cessna. They were not scheduled to be removed until the following week. Low clouds or no clouds, Ritzer would be there—pronto. He'd flown thousands of miles on instruments; a low ceiling wouldn't keep him away.

Roger was to let the local rangers know about the plane flying in to help with the search. They'd need permission for low-level flying over the restricted wilderness. Bob said he'd crank up the Cessna come Tuesday's first light. Winds permitting, the flight would have him at Poplar Lake before nine that morning.

Roger made a quick trip to town. Permission was granted to use the floatplane. The ranger in charge informed him that if the boys hadn't shown up by midday Tuesday, arrangements would be made for a National Guard helicopter. A little late, Roger thought, but he thanked the man anyway and headed for home.

Back at Poplar Lake, Roger reset the dock. There would be no waste of time getting into the plane when it arrived. He draped a blaze-orange parka over an end post as a marker for Bob to spot from the air.

Finished with his lakeside preparations, he went to visit the resort. He wanted to inform Lynn and Sarah that help was on its way. With luck, by this time the next day the boys would be home, ready for a good meal and a warm bed.

* * *

Travis left the security of the sleeping bag. Like a bear coming out its den, he poked his head out the tent door. Nothing had changed. Overhead, clouds draped low like dark, wet blankets on a clothesline. The gloom was still hanging around the neighborhood, unwilling to let a warm sun shine down from a blue autumn sky.

Travis crawled out on all fours. Then he got to his feet and stood in the morning stillness, thinking. He didn't see any other way to solve the dilemma. As soon he fried a few fillets for breakfast, he'd make like a magician and disappear.

"Think of it as a new adventure," he told himself, attempting to recharge his courage. If things got tough, he could always turn back and return to camp.

He rushed through the morning chores. In record time, the fire was crackling and fillets were sizzling in a pan. By the time the sun should have been showing a friendly face, the meager meal was ready. Travis wolfed down a few fillets before delivering the remainder to Seth.

"Good morning. You up?"

Seth was more than awake. He was fully alert, mulling over the fact that Travis was taking off—leaving him all alone. Seth knew he was in a fix, a real jam. He was barely able to take care of his most basic needs, and he was more than a little scared. This was serious stuff. What if Travis had an accident and couldn't reach help?

"Stay put," was what Rollie had drilled into the guides. "Don't panic and stay put. Help will come to you."

Seth had heard that message many times. And it made sense. But he also knew he couldn't talk Travis out of leaving. Travis was just as petrified, but felt he had try something. Staying put hadn't gotten them anywhere.

"Yo, Sethman. I fried up a few fillets. Feel up to eating before I take off?"

Seth cleared his throat and said, "I can't talk you into staying put, can I?"

Had Seth not had a coughing jag, he may well have heard a "yes." Unfortunately his body betrayed him, issuing forth a series of lung-wracking whoops. The prolonged hacking was enough to push Travis over the fence. He had no choice but to leave. Another day or two might be too late.

When Seth finally stopped coughing, when his lungs demanded a timeout, Travis's answer was firm. "No, you can't. The weather hasn't changed. Nobody would be crazy enough to fly this morning."

Seth cleared his throat again. "Are you sure?"

"Yup, positive. Eat the fish later if you like. I filled the canteens. I don't need one. I put the smoked fish in a plastic bag. And I'll leave the trail mix in case you get really hungry."

Travis unzipped the door and reached in to place the offerings on the floor. He quickly resealed the door and stood for a moment, hands in pockets. "I'm gonna go now. I'll see ya sometime tomorrow. Just get some rest. And Seth . . . don't worry about me. I'll be fine."

Travis was about to turn away when Seth answered. "Trav? You still out there?"

Travis froze. "Yeah, what?"

"Good luck. Be careful. And thanks. I know you're doing this for me."

Travis stared at the tent as if he could see inside. "What d'ya mean, for you? I'm stuck out here, too."

"Yeah, but you'd be okay until Search and Rescue came along. You've done a great job of taking care of us." Seth started coughing again, causing Travis to wince. He said another "goodbye" and walked away.

It took only a few minutes to roll up the sleeping bag, collapse the tent and stuff both in a packsack. He spent another moment looking at Seth's shelter. Then without saying a word, he picked up the pack and trudged to the canoe.

* * *

Shortly before nine Tuesday morning, the Larsen and Springwood households gathered on the Larsens' deck. All had ears trained toward the heavens, listening for the sound of an airplane engine. Doug Davis, Lynn Springwood's Saturday night friend, was in attendance. He insisted on being present when the plane arrived.

Doug was a veteran of many outdoor escapades. Magazine assignments had taken the journalist to all corners of the globe—to places far more remote than the Boundary Waters.

A stint with the military had included basic training in search and rescue, along with wilderness survival. But more than sharing knowledge, he needed to prove to the Springwoods he wanted to be part of their lives, part of their future.

Doug's lanky frame rested against the deck's top railing. He chatted quietly with Roger Larsen. The two had immediately hit it off. Roger could sense a quiet strength in this new acquaintance. When in a quandary, Doug was the type you wanted on your team.

The two men began gazing at the map laid out on the picnic table. Roger had used colored markers to highlight the search area; a red line indicated the boys' most likely path—a yellow line marked alternative routes. They were discussing what they should do if they spotted the boys from the airplane.

"I'd say we'll have to wait and see," Doug concluded, eyes glued on the chart. "If they're camped on any of the larger lakes, your friend should be able to set down and pick 'em up. But what if they're somewhere along here?" he continued, pointing to the Cone Lake Chain. "Those lakes are too small for a float plane to land and take off. We'd have to go in by canoe."

"Then let's hope they're on one of the bigger lakes," Roger replied. "Those narrow connecting streams have to be clogged with timber. It'd be tough going . . . real tough going."

"We'll just have to . . . say, do ya hear that? Sounds like your friend made it."

The snarl of a single-engine aircraft engine growled above the cloud cover.

"He's up there somewhere," Roger said, scanning the wooly blanket overhead.

As he spoke, a red-and-white floatplane broke through the haze. The engine's howl rose as the plane leveled off. Roaring toward the east, it banked sharply and returned to make a low pass along the shoreline. It continued down the lake for a mile or so, banked again and started back.

"What's he doing?" Roger asked. "He should be able to see us."

"I'm sure he does. But he's a smart pilot. I think he's checking for debris. He doesn't want to set down on any water-logged trees."

"Sure, that's what he's doing. That wily old codger doesn't miss a trick. If anyone can fly in these conditions, I'd bet on Bob."

The Cessna had reached the eastern end of the lake and was once again in a tight turn. When the plane was parallel to shore, the growl backed off. The aircraft began to sink toward the surface. Just as its pontoons were about to touch, the engine barked again, leveling the floats inches above the water.

The plane flew this way, defying gravity, until it was several hundred yards from the dock. Then the pilot chopped a bit of throttle, and as expertly as an old duck landing on a familiar pond, the pontoons pushed spray.

Once again the engine revved, pulling the plane past the line of spectators. Finally, when he thought the wind was right, when it would drift the aircraft to the dock, the pilot swung the plane around and cut the engine.

"Very impressive. He knows what he's doing with that water bird," Doug praised. "It wasn't his first landing, that's for sure."

"Right. Bob's had that airplane for years. He told me once that every landing is new, that conditions are never quite the same. That's why he likes to fly his own equipment. He knows exactly what to expect."

Moments later the airplane drifted close, forcing the men to stoop under the wing. Roger grabbed a wing strut and pulled, snugging a pontoon tight to the dock.

The pilot's door popped open. "Hello, Roger. Soon as I stretch a mite we'll go find that kid of yours. Gotta say, though, you folks sure did get hit by a whopper up here. Couldn't tell much 'til I dropped through the clouds, but what I did manage to see doesn't look good. Trees are down in every direction from here."

Robert "Bob" Ritzer was a compact, wiry fellow in his early seventies. His head sported thick gray hair that framed a pleasant, weathered-creased face. He slipped out of the pilot's seat and onto the pontoon as if he were years younger, then grabbed Roger's right hand and shook it firmly before jumping onto the dock.

"Bob, old friend, you are indeed a welcome sight!" Roger exclaimed.

"Sorry it's under such uncertain conditions. But I know that kid of yours. He's a chip off the old block. If anyone his age can make out there, my money's on Trav. We'll find him. We won't quit 'til we do."

After introductions, the group began discussing the immediate plan.

"Can three of us go up? Will the plane manage that?" Roger asked.

"Sure, no problem. By air we can cover in minutes what it'd take days to travel in a canoe. If we need to lighten the load I can always run back here and drop one of you off. Besides, the more eyes, the better. With this low ceiling, I'll be busy at the controls. We don't want to snag a float on one of the few trees still standing."

"Okay, then. We're ready when you are," Doug said, stepping up on the float and crawling into the back seat.

Roger waved crossed fingers to the women and climbed up into the copilot's seat.

"Remember how to start this old bird?" Bob asked Roger.

"I think so. Want me to fire it up?"

"Go ahead, I'll hold tight until the engine catches and then shove off. If it pulls away without me, give it a little gas and right rudder before shutting it down. It'll drift back and we'll try again."

Roger wasn't certain Bob was serious, but he leaned over and made certain the throttle was in the closed position. He flipped the master switch and turned the key. When the engine made its first cough, Bob gave a hardy shove on the strut. Quicker than someone half his age, he stepped on the float and hopped up behind the yoke. With a couple of extra pops, the engine roared to life.

Bob fed the cylinders fuel. The prop came alive with enough oomph to pull the aircraft away from the pier. Seconds later the floats were skimming whitecaps. The veteran airman tugged back on the wheel. The Cessna shuddered as it broke free of the water, then pointed its nose in the air. The search was on.

Through his headset Doug had to ask. "How in the world did you manage to find Poplar Lake through the clouds? Weren't you afraid of getting lost?"

"Nope. Got an electronic gizmo with me, a new GPS unit," he answered. "I programmed the location of the lake into its memory. Darn thing is accurate to a couple hundred feet anywhere on the planet. Go figure. Oh, by the way, the cloud cover really isn't very thick, not more than a few hundred feet. Wouldn't be surprised to see it burn off before long."

Chapter Fifteen

"This is sweet," Travis mused as he tugged the canoe through shallow water. Unlike the narrow, boulder-strewn creek that had crippled his friend, this stream was wide and flowed through a low, flat area.

Both banks were filled with downed and battered trees, as if some monster had flicked its tail, flattening everything in its wake. But the broad channel meant that windfalls couldn't span completely across. And he was making great progress.

A rush of air made him look up. A small flock of ducks—probably mallards, he thought—was winging south. "Now that's the way to go, fly right over this tangle," Travis muttered to the wind. "I should be so lucky."

He'd gotten a good start on the day. After saying his final goodbye, he hadn't wasted a second. After a quick paddle across the lake, he beached the canoe. Wanting to lighten his pull, and to keep the canoe floating as high as possible, he pulled the rocks out of the bow.

Then he removed his tennis shoes, rolled up his jeans and waded into the water. With the line around his waist, Travis didn't stop until he was halfway to the next lake. The shoulder had pained him while paddling, but now, with the rope around his middle, it seemed fine.

But before long he discovered he was working too fast. His chest was heaving; his breath was coming in short gasps. It was time for a break.

He secured the canoe alongside the bank and climbed into the stern. His stomach was already asking to be fed. The few little fillets he'd eaten this morning were history. Like a racecar running flat out on its last drops of gas, his engine needed refueling.

Unfortunately, that wouldn't be easy. The trail mix was back at camp with Seth. He'd brought the fishing rod along instead, reckoning he could always catch a meal. But even though he was famished, Travis didn't have time to fish. He regretted not pilfering at least part of the trail mix.

A crow's cawing caught his ear. Travis called back, in a perfect imitation of the big black bird. As if prompted by a stage manager, more crows called in.

Some of Mother Nature's critters that don't have to do any grunt work, Travis thought. The ungainly flyers seemed to find grub everywhere. They reminded him of a riddle his little sister had shared once at the supper table. She'd asked her dad if he ever noticed that crows often ate road kill, but very few ever got hit. Did he know why?

"No, but I'll bite," he'd answered. "Why is that, do you suppose?"

Beth had to stifle a laugh. "Because they work in pairs. There's always another crow watching from a power line or tree branch."

"Yeah, I've noticed. So what?"

"Well," Beth giggled. "When traffic gets close, the one perched up in the tree calls out to its mate on the blacktop . . . *Cawr* . . . *Cawr!*"

They had all had groaned at the simple joke. But right now he wished he were sitting at that table; his plate filled with warm, tasty food. He'd gladly chuckle at a ridiculous riddle. It'd be a small price to pay for a hot meal.

Recess was over. Travis stepped out of the canoe and into the water. His feet and calves were ice. They hadn't warmed during the brief stop. But if he were going to reach his goal, he'd have to ignore the ache.

After twenty minutes of chilly sloshing, Travis was staring at open water. At least for a time he could crawl into the canoe and paddle. His feet would get a chance to thaw out.

He checked the chart to pinpoint the exact site of the outlet. He found his present position, the west end of this second small lake. To reach the next stream he would have to paddle along the south shore.

He tucked away the map, pushed the canoe into deeper water and hopped in. Without warning a pair of mallards took wing with a noisy flutter of feathers.

Travis positioned the paddle as if it were a gun. "Kaboom! Kaboom! Dead ducks!" He boomed, wishing the oar was the real thing. Roast duck would certainly help fill the hole in his middle.

But the paddle was just a paddle, and he stroked on, wondering what time it was getting to be. He figured he'd broke camp before seven, so by now it must be between eight-thirty and nine-thirty. If he could keep up the pace, he'd be sure to finish before dark. But he knew full well that "if" was a tiny word with big possibilities. He continued paddling, eyes alert for the outlet.

He didn't find it at first. All he saw were broken trees splayed along the beach. Finally spotting a narrow opening between a pair of windfalls, he ran the canoe aground. He'd explore on foot.

Travis let out a long groan. The channel wasn't nearly as broad as the one he had just slogged through. To make matters worse, windfalls crisscrossed the opening like giant pick-up sticks. Navigating this stream was going to be a challenge. He could only hope he was up to it.

For a moment he just stared. Could he do it? Did he dare push on? Maybe he should turn around and head back to camp. Maybe spend the remainder of the day fishing, taking care of his pal. An image of Seth pushed its way to the front of his brain. His friend needed more help than a few fish for dinner. Regardless how hard it was going to be, Travis knew he had to try to get out.

He struggled to lug the canoe over the first blowdown, then the next—and the seemingly endless series after that. Lifting and pulling was grueling work, the hardest labor Travis had ever encountered. His forward progress slowed to a crawl. When he could no longer look back and see open water, he took a break. It was time to check the chart.

Perched on the butt end of a blowdown, his feet dangling above the water, Travis perused the map. If he was reading it right, he was only about a quarter-mile from the third lake.

He was folding the map when his ears caught the drone of a distant aircraft. His heart rate soared. Someone was looking for them! But a long, skyward stare revealed only the familiar gray clouds. His hopes plummeted. The aircraft had to be above the overcast ceiling. It couldn't possibly be search and rescue. It was probably some guy heading for Canada on a fishing trip. Without the slightest inkling the plane was headed to Poplar Lake, Travis returned to his task.

He slid off the log into the knee-deep water. Then he grabbed the bow rope and began wading. He hadn't gone far when his calves began cramping. Yet he didn't quit. He slogged on despite the discomfort—pulling the canoe over, under and around tree trunks, broken branches and lost limbs.

Thankfully, in time the heroic effort was rewarded. Through the jumbled forest he caught glimmers of shiny light—open water! Finding the pot at the end of the rainbow couldn't have thrilled him more. He was closing in on the last of the little lakes.

Energized, he paused only long enough to catch his breath. The map indicated a portage trail directly across the bay. But then he wondered—why there was a portage trail at all? The chain of lakes spilled its excess water into Brule. So why wasn't the stream used for the portage? A waterway should have been an easier passage than carrying a canoe overland.

The lake wasn't large. It was more of a giant pond than one of Minnesota's famed ten thousand waterways. Travis paddled without pause, knowing he could recoup his energy on land.

He pulled in between a pair of tipped aspens, their uprooted bases imitating miniature mountains. The forest extended right to the water's edge. Rather than snapping off at the base, dozens of trees chose instead to tilt, yanking out their roots and clumps of soggy soil as they fell. As a result, the shoreline was a series of hill-like mounds—as if a fleet of gravel trucks had backed up, raised their boxes and dumped their loads.

It was impossible to walk along shore. Root mounds and tree trunks created an obstacle course. A better choice was to wade in the water. Using the paddle as a hiking stick, Travis slogged along in search of the stream.

Unlike the rocky, gravelly beach where they'd camped, the lakefront was mucky underfoot. Each step was an effort as the mushy bottom tugged at his feet like quicksand.

As he sloshed alongside the jumbled forest, Travis realized there would be little likelihood of land travel. Even if he located the trailhead, the tangle of downed timber would put a stop to portaging.

That meant the creek was his only option. He'd find the outlet, and then push, pull and splash his way through like he did on the last stream.

He slogged the waterfront for several hundred yards but came up empty. Discouraged, he did a one-eighty. The outlet had to be on the other side of the boat.

The effort of returning to the canoe required a rest stop. Perched on a tree trunk, rubbing his cold, prune-skinned feet, he thought about building a fire. No, that would eat up time. Fire building wasn't part of the schedule.

When his toes began to tingle, he splashed off in the other direction. He didn't have to go far. He'd paddled right past it. The entrance was concealed by a sprawling spruce, its thick-needled branches forming a billboard-sized barricade.

Travis trudged to the fallen giant, hoping to find an easy way around. His lips formed a satisfied smirk. There was enough space between the spruce and an uprooted aspen to slip through with the canoe.

But first he had to deal with hunger pains. Travis waded back to the boat and dug in the pack. His fingers grasped the package of smoked fillets wrapped in an old freeze-dried pouch.

The chip-sized fish bits didn't look at all appetizing. But he was running on fumes. He needed energy. Maybe they would help take his hunger meter off "E."

Pinching his nose, he popped one into his mouth and chewed. It tasted like a smoky fire. But he swallowed anyway. He repeated the process. Then while the fish bits were heading south, he used his hands to cup water from the lake. Maybe a little liquid would make the fish fillets swell, and fool his stomach into thinking it had received a real meal.

"Yeah, sure," he grinned across the empty lake. "And pigs can fly."

Travis received an unwelcome surprise when he began towing the canoe toward the outlet. Water sloshed about in the bottom of the boat. Some of it, Travis knew, came from getting in and out with dripping wet feet. But not this much. Something else was happening.

As he pulled the bow on land, buckets of water sloshed to the stern. Travis dug into the pack for the pan he'd brought along. Water meant weight; it'd have to be bailed.

The leak was getting worse.

* * *

Flying like a big bird that was all business, the Cessna made the first of several low passes over Meeds Lake. Bob lowered the aircraft until it was kiting only a couple hundred feet above a slate-gray floor. Roger and Doug craned their necks every which way, hoping to catch a glimpse of the boys or their camp.

Except for the buzz of the engine, the cockpit was silent. After the third pass Bob's baritone echoed in the headsets. "Let's check the next lake. They probably passed through here long before the storm struck."

"Good idea," Doug responded.

"Agreed," Roger added. "I think they'd be at least two or three lakes into the trip, maybe more, if everything had gone well."

As the plane neared the end of the waterway, Bob pushed the throttle knob and then gently pulled back on the yoke. The aircraft responded by pointing its nose above the horizon.

Seconds later Bob backed off the power. The Cessna dipped its nose as it traced the sliver of water connecting Meeds and Henson. Even with the plane slowed to a few knots above stall speed, the snarl of twisted timber flashed by in a blink.

"Bob, d'ya think we'd be better off a little higher up? You know, get a wider picture?" Roger questioned.

"Roger, Roger," Bob replied, remembering how he used to joke with his friend about the aviation term meaning "understood and will do."

But unlike other flights, Roger Larsen didn't offer his standard comeback, "Betcha' boots, Bob,"—his mood was far too serious for word play. Instead, he replied, "Pretty tough to spot a green canoe in all the downed evergreens. The darn thing will blend right in."

"Lynn told me Seth brought along his blaze-orange hunting jacket. Let's hope he's wearing it," Doug added.

Bob pushed in a bit of power and pulled up the nose, leveling off just under the clouds. The ground no longer blurred by in a flash. Instead, objects looked smaller, and the narrow waterway appeared more like a stream than a long, skinny lake.

Bob spoke through the intercom. "After another pass or two, I'll need to put down on Devils Track, see about getting fuel. It took more gas than I'd planned getting here this morning. I have to feed this old bird every four hours to keep it in the air. It's been almost three and a half since the last fill. We don't have a whole lot of flight time left."

"Ah, let's hope that's not a problem," Doug said from the rear.

"Shouldn't be . . . by air Devils Track can't be more than a few minutes from here," Bob returned.

"The gas pumps . . . " Roger began.

"What about the pumps?" Bob interrupted.

"The pumps are run by electricity. That's a luxury we haven't had since the storm. Let's hope the airport has a Plan B."

"We'll figure out something, my friend, even if we have to dump in some high-octane outboard motor gas to mix with the fuel still left in the tanks. I'm going keep this old bird in the air 'til those kids are found," Bob promised.

"I like your attitude," Doug extolled. "We all should be so lucky to have a friend like you."

* * *

Seth struggled to stay awake. He could always sleep during the long, dark, dreary hours. He wanted to listen for help. And he wanted to go home. Never had he felt so alone, so frightened—or so miserable. His ankle ached and his chest felt as if it had been invaded by aliens.

His temperature rose and fell like a busy elevator. One minute he would be chilled and shivering, as if he'd just stepped out of a cold shower. All he could do was burrow into the bag, tuck his head under the cover and wait for the shakes to cease. Just minutes later, he'd start perspiring. Sweat would trickle off his forehead, forcing him seek cooler air.

And then there was the coughing. Long, deep wrenches that made him feel as if his insides were coming apart. When the coughing stopped, he felt weak and wished he had the luxury to just nod off and wake up somewhere else.

But no matter how hard he fought to keep his eyelids open, he did doze. The bouts of sleep were filled with vivid dreams. One of which had images of predators surrounding the tent; all waiting for him to pass to the other side, hoping they'd soon have a feast.

Seth awoke from that dream drenched in sweat. It was still morning. Bright light reflected off the lake flooded the tent. But shivers suddenly shook his body as fear washed over him. What if . . . what if help didn't arrive in time? Would the creatures claim him first?

He reached for the canteen and swallowed several

gulps. "I gotta think positive, can't panic. Gotta keep calm. Sooner or later somebody's bound to find me."

To keep his mind demons at bay, Seth tried to think of all the songs he'd ever sung. He thought of an old sixties tape his Mom sometimes played on the stereo. What did the song ask? *"How many roads must a man walk down?"*

Seth wasn't certain, but he did know the main chorus; *"the answer my friend, is blowing in the wind . . . the answer is blowing in the wind."*

What did that mean? What kind of answer comes with the wind? Not a good answer around these parts, he thought. There'd be no trails you could walk around here.

Humming the tune in his head, Seth dozed off again. This time he dreamed he heard an engine, like that of an airplane. Then, lifting like a morning fog, the drone faded.

* * *

Fueling the airplane took longer than the men would have liked. Lacking electricity, the aviation gas had to be hand-pumped from the holding tank into five-gallon cans. The containers were then carried to the dock and poured through a funnel into the plane's wing tanks. When the left tank was full they repeated the process with the right wing.

The good news was that the cloud deck continued to thin. Here and there hints of blue gave promise to the most pleasant afternoon since the storm's passing.

Roger made use of the airport's battery-powered radio. He was able to talk to the ranger station on the status of search and rescue. Weather permitting, a chopper would be available first thing the next morning.

He was happy to hear they also were organizing a small fleet of powerboats to search the shoreline and islands of Brule Lake.

155

In the meantime, they should continue to search with the Cessna. At present it was the best chance they had of finding the young campers.

Roger passed along the information to Bob and Doug as the three prepared to depart.

"We'll find them on this flight," Bob encouraged. "We just didn't get far enough into their trip to spot them. I bet they're camped along one of the lakes, fishing for their lunch, enjoying every minute of their excuse to miss school."

"Bob, I hope you're right on the mark. Let's go find out," Roger said with more cheerfulness then he felt.

It was approaching mid-day when the plane's pontoons pulled free of the lake's grip. Bob put the plane in a climbing turn and headed back to the search area.

* * *

Travis was as thrilled as a little kid at a carnival. Despite the low water, the channel was wider than he'd first thought. Once past the clogged outlet, towing the canoe was easy.

It was still on the morning side of noon. Travis figured he was already halfway to the big lake. He began to daydream. What would he have to eat when he reached civilization? Maybe he'd chow down on a double cheeseburger. That would help fill the hollow hole where his stomach used to be.

After a time, Travis realized the streambed was changing. He'd been slogging pretty much through level land. But now the ground was starting to fall away, beginning to slope toward Brule.

The creek tightened its banks, forcing the water higher and faster as it began its race downhill. The frothy liquid dashed and danced over boulders and rocks. From farther downstream came the gurgle of whitewater, giving warning to stay back.

The incline meant one good thing—fewer trees had been knocked over. The crest of the hill had shielded them from most from the wind's full fury.

The channel continued to narrow, pushing the water higher and faster. Travis struggled to keep the canoe in his grasp. Things had quickly reversed. Instead of being towed, the canoe was now pulling him.

At the outlet the water had only been ankle deep. Now it was up to his knees. All around the canoe, wisps of white soapy foam bounced and jiggled before dashing away downstream.

Travis sensed he couldn't hold on much longer. Clutching the gunnel in one hand, he grasped the pack-frame with the other. The frame had just cleared the side when a powerful surge made him lose his grip. Then, like a horse out of the starting gate, the canoe raced ahead.

Travis could only watch.

Once back on land he dug in the pack for his socks and shoes. Much more comfortable, he shouldered the pack-frame before trudging downhill. He'd discovered the hard way why the creek wasn't used as a portage route—it was extremely rough on equipment.

Travis came upon the errant watercraft several hundred yards down-slope. The canoe had lodged tight against a windfall. The lively current splashed and frolicked against the boat as if it were a new plaything.

Somehow he had to lift the canoe over the tree trunk. Travis surveyed the situation. He came up with only one solution. He'd have to remove his clothes, wade in the water and muscle the boat over the top.

Wading waist-deep in chilly water almost took his breath away. Travis knew he'd have to work fast before he ran out of body heat. A mistake like that could prove fatal.

His first attempt failed. He hadn't lifted the boat high enough to clear the trunk.

On the second try, Travis grabbed the bow and with a mighty heave broke it free of the current. Then, as if fighting for his life, he thrust upward.

The bow now rested on the log. He had to battle to keep the canoe straight with the channel. Slowly he worked his hands along the gunnel until he was at the stern. Using the last of his energy reserve, he shoved the stern in the air while pushing forward. Grudgingly, the canoe slipped over the tree and splashed down on the other side.

Travis climbed up the bank and lay down on the ground, shivering and sucking air. The canoe didn't wait. It sprinted on without him.

Once his breath returned, Travis used his hand to brush water off his goose-dimpled skin. He slithered quickly into his clothes, and then dug into the pack for his windbreaker.

After looping a pack strap over his good shoulder he began shuffling downhill. Several times he had to abandon the stream's bank because blowdowns blocked the way. But thankfully most trees had survived the storm surge. Despite not having a path, he was making good time.

The walking warmed him. At first he had been tramping in a trance. But as his body temperature rose, his brain began to clear. And then he realized . . . he was almost there!

Just ahead, he recognized the flat, white reflection of light coming off water. Travis quickened his pace, jogging joyfully around downed trees and tattered forest debris.

He arrived at the lake a few yards south of the stream.

All he had to do was find his transportation, climb in and paddle across to the landing.

Finally he broke out in a full-blown smile. Because there it was, sitting in the shallows, looking much like some strange, prehistoric reptile.

As quickly as he'd smiled, he frowned. Something seemed askew, but he wasn't sure what. For one thing, the canoe was resting in the shallows, half filled with water.

For the umpteenth time he stripped off his jeans. He was going to have to wade out and try tugging the boat closer to shore before bailing. Nevertheless, Travis was excited. Both he and the canoe had finished the hardest part. Now all he had to do was paddle, make the call and he'd soon be home.

Wading in, Travis bent down and snatched the rope swimming near his wrinkled feet. He gave a tug that turned the bow toward shore. With the cord wrapped around his waist, he plodded for land. This was going to be the shortest and sweetest pull of the day.

He released the line and grabbed the bow plate. He gave a mighty heave, tugging the canoe far enough toward shore that the gunnels were above the surface.

He'd bail it out and head straight across the lake. Heck, he'd probably have to go to school tomorrow. The ordeal would be over. He grinned at that thought. What a tale they'd have to tell.

Travis was about to slosh to land for the bailing pot when he made a dreadful discovery. Through the root beer-tinted water filling the canoe, he spotted something terribly wrong. Ignoring the cold, he splashed to the stern. A dark, menacing streak ran parallel to the bottom of the hull.

"Oh God, please don't let it be what it looks like . . . let it be a stick, anything but what it looks like!"

Travis pushed up jacket sleeve but was hesitant to put his hand into the water. If what he thought he was seeing was true, it was a disaster. There'd be no more use of this canoe. He'd have no choice but to walk. His legs would be his only way out.

The youth stood staring at the dark line for a good minute. Gritting his teeth, Travis plunged his hand into the water, needing to touch it. Instantly fingers sent the message to his brain. His mind passed along the message to his vocal chords.

"No, no, no!" he howled. "Why, God? Why?"

Pulling back his hand, he turned and began sloshing toward shore, tears blurring his vision. The wild whitewater ride had been too much for the already dinged and damaged watercraft. A narrow strip of fiberglass was missing—completely gone, leaving a jagged gash in the bottom.

There'd be no paddling this old canoe ever again. It was as useless as a fish with a bicycle.

He'd made the trip to the big lake as hoped. But there was no pot at the end of this rainbow. Instead he found himself alone, hungry and cold.

Travis slogged to dry land. In a daze he pulled on his jeans, socks and shoes. Then he found a log and plopped down. Uncontrolled shudders wracked his chilled body. He began sobbing, large tears streaming down his cheeks.

What choices were left?

* * *

In a matter of minutes the Cessna was back over the search site. Roger directed Bob to the more popular of the several routes into Brule. All eyes looked down.

Meanwhile, seven miles to the southwest, Seth woke to a ray of sunshine. He took a sip from the canteen and then realized the need to go out. He had some basic business that needed tending. But that was easier said than accomplished. The slightest wiggling caused his bad ankle to protest. It took time and effort to slither through the door.

Once outside, Seth got his first look at the day. Clouds still filled the sky. But they weren't threatening, and for brief bursts, bits of blue were exposed.

Seth's spirits raised a notch. There might be an air search yet today. Encouraged, he reached in and tugged the orange shell through the tent door.

By the time he finished his bathroom break, Seth was bushed. But he had enough oomph to spread the colorful jacket open alongside the tent. The bright garment should be an easy mark to see from above.

Once back in his sleeping bag, Seth tried to think positive. A Search and Rescue team would find him soon. They had to be looking. He closed his eyes and sucked in a deep breath—a mistake. The rush of cool air caused him to cough.

He hacked so hard his ribs hurt. Then the chills returned for a turn at his torment. The only escape was sleep. Seth tucked his head under the cover, curled up as much as his ankle would allow and nodded off.

* * *

For the first half hour of flight, Roger and Doug's eyes scoured the shores of Horseshoe, Gaskin and Winchell Lakes. No evidence of a campsite was seen. Instead the men only viewed miles of storm damage.

Roger consulted the map. "Maybe they took the long way, through the Cone Lake Chain. Let's check the west end of Winchell one more time and then make a pass around each of these little lakes."

"Gotcha. Makes the most sense to me," Bob replied,

banking the aircraft to the west. "One thing's for sure . . . no way anyone could walk through that maze under our wings. It's hard to believe the size of the storm path. It must be hundreds of thousands of acres."

The plane swooped low and slow over Winchell, targeting the lake's far end.

"See anything?" Bob asked.

"Nothing," both men answered in unison.

"Up ahead," Roger said, pointing through the windscreen. "Look at the end of the long bay. It's connected to this lake and then flows to the Cone Lake Chain toward Brule."

"We'll take a pass over all of 'em. Keep your fingers crossed." Bob replied.

The plane was passing over the first connecting stream when Roger hollered. "All right!"

"Where?" Both Bob and Doug asked.

"Look . . . near where the creek spills into the first lake. I see blaze-orange by what looks like a blue tent."

Bob put the plane into a climb. Then he banked and circled back. "Yeah! I see it! That's gotta be them."

Like air out of a broken balloon, Roger's joy whooshed away. Travis had a green tent, not a blue one. So where was it? And where was Seth? Wouldn't he have heard the engine noise? Why wasn't he out waving at them?

Bob cut through his thoughts. "Gentlemen, we have a problem. I can land on that little lake, but there's no way I could get this bird out of there. It's just not big enough. Any suggestions?"

They discussed their options while Bob circled. There was still no sign of life coming from the blue tent. That bothered each of them, but no one mentioned it.

Their decision was to fly straight back to Poplar. There they would lash an aluminum canoe to the struts, grab Roger's chainsaw, then wing back to Winchell. Roger and Doug would use the saw to cut their way down the channel. Without complications they'd reach the blue tent in a couple of hours.

* * *

Seth had fallen into a deep, coma-like sleep—the slumber of the ill and exhausted. Sometime during the deepest part of the rest, he had a dream that seemed real. He dreamt he heard an airplane . . . that it was circling above . . . peering down at his shelter. Then the dream turned sour. Seeing only a lonely tent, the pilot flew on, looking elsewhere for activity, hoping to spot two boys in a green canoe.

The image faded and went blank. He continued to doze. Only an occasional cough and nasal snores came from the tiny cloth house.

Chapter Sixteen

C H A P T E R S I X T E E N

Travis sat slumped on the log, tears staining his ruddy cheeks. Long moments passed. In time the cool wind touched him. He began to shudder, some of the shaking caused by fear and frustration, some by the breeze.

Travis knew he ought to get moving. He couldn't sit and mope all day. But how and where would he go?

He didn't have an answer. He wracked his brain for a backup plan, one that would still get him home. Chilled, he jumped to his feet and began pacing, pumping blood to stiff limbs.

Warmer—and thinking more clearly—his brain conjured three possibilities. The first was to camp right here and wait for search and rescue to find him. But that could mean that Seth wouldn't be rescued until after Travis had been found.

Hiking out was another choice. But after a few minutes of mulling over the pros and cons, he dismissed it. Brule Lake had miles and miles of shoreline. With all the blowdowns, it would take forever to hike around to the other side.

His third option was to head back to camp. What would it be, a four- or five-mile trek? He could continue to take care of Seth. At least they'd be together until they were rescued. This choice seemed to make the most sense. It was something he could manage. And since it was only early afternoon, there should be enough daylight left to reach their camp before dark.

By not having to pull the canoe he should make good time. The only problem would be walking the shorelines. Travis tried to recall how each looked. The image was fuzzy. He had focused his attention on paddling straight across. He hadn't paid attention to the lakes' edges.

Still, returning to camp felt like the right choice. He made the decision to head back to Seth. First though, he'd take care of his stomach. Tucked in the packsack were the last two freeze-dried pouches. Before taking off he'd start a fire and have a hot lunch—refill his tank.

His mind set, Travis gathered twigs for a fire. When he had enough to start a modest blaze, he reached into a pocket for his lighter. His pulse quickened when the hand came out empty. He slipped his hand into the other pocket. Nothing. He patted the back pockets. Empty.

He felt in his windbreaker. Still nothing. Travis stood like a deer caught in headlights; a pained expression contorted his facial features.

When had he last used the lighter? He could only think of that first fire following the storm. After that, he'd always stirred hot ashes from the previous fire and then added tinder. He hadn't needed the lighter since they'd set up camp.

Travis thought about his jeans. They'd been off and on a couple of times already today. And the day he nearly drowned . . . he'd hung them upside down to dry. The lighter could have fallen out almost anywhere. There'd be no hot lunch today—only a few dry, quarter-sized chunks of smoked fish.

Resolved to put something in his belly, Travis gagged

down the fish fragments. Then he scooped up several handfuls of water to wash away the taste.

If he was going to rejoin his pal before dark, he needed to get his rear in gear. Travis took one last look at the canoe. It hadn't moved much. It was still bumping bottom near shore. He turned away and began trudging up the slope.

The uphill hike warmed him. His jeans were drying and he was thankful for small favors. Through an opening in the forest canopy, Travis caught brief glimmers of blue.

It occurred to him that the sky was changing. There was still a gray ceiling, but it seemed higher, less hostile than before. At least one good thing's happening today, he mused as he plodded around a windfall.

The upslope walk went well until he reached the hill's crest. There, the wind had landed a knockout punch. Trees were tipped and tangled with each other in an almost impenetrable mass. Though he could fight his way through, Travis was occasionally forced to detour well away from the stream.

Finally he arrived at the spot where the channel widened, the current slowed and the water became shallower. Another decision—wading in the stream might be faster than combating the maze on land.

Travis settled on a log. He was removing his shoes when his ears perked up. Was the faint sound he heard that of an outboard motor? Or was it an airplane? He wasn't certain. The sound was too distant. After a time, the buzz faded to nothing. Had he imagined it? Or was it simply wishful thinking? Maybe his ears were playing tricks on him.

Whatever the case, he had to get moving.

Travis stowed the footgear in his pack. Not wanting soaked jeans, he pulled them off, too. He rolled them up and stuck them into the pack alongside his battered jacket and tired shoes.

An image of how he must look filled his mind. Despite the worries, Travis couldn't help but crack a wry grin. A tall, nearly naked kid . . . clad in white briefs . . . wading knee-deep in water with a half-filled pack on his back. The scene wasn't exactly cover material for his favorite outdoor magazines.

As Travis began wading, he quickly discovered that the water route proved much faster than dodging debris on dry land. After a few minutes of slogging, he spotted the opening of the little lake—the plump, fallen spruce still guarding the gate.

He waded forward, mindful not to trip, not wanting to become thoroughly sopped. Without the ability to build a fire, he didn't dare take an unplanned bath.

* * *

After setting down on Poplar Lake, Bob taxied directly to the resort dock. Much like autos strung across a parking lot, scores of silver canoes lined the beach.

"Take any one you want. And don't worry about banging it up. You've got to find those boys," was Rollie's reply when Roger asked to borrow a canoe.

"Grab my new chainsaw, too. It'll cut through the thickest of logs quick as a hot knife through warm butter. It's a professional model with a big fuel tank. You can work steady for the best part of an hour before it needs gas. A full tank should be more than you'll need to cut a few trees out of the channel. I'll go get it while you're fixing a canoe to the floats."

As Rollie hobbled up the steps to the tool shed, Lynn and Sarah Springwood trotted down to the beach. Occupied with a canoe, Roger and Bob merely nodded a greeting. Doug remained by the dock.

"What did you find out? Was there any sign of the kids?" Lynn asked anxiously when she was within earshot.

With carefully chosen words, Doug informed the women about the discovery.

"You saw Seth's tent but not the boys? What does that mean? Are they all right?"

"We don't know. We'll know more in an hour or two. We have to cut our way to the lake. We won't have the answer 'til we get there."

Lynn suddenly felt lightheaded. Her legs went rubbery and her knees began to buckle. Doug stepped forward and embraced her before she fell. Lynn clung tight, burying her face against Doug's chest, tears leaking from closed eyelids.

Sarah stood silently off to the side. She began to understand. Her mom did need someone her age to confide in. The remarks spat out earlier now seemed so unfair. If only she could take them back. But she couldn't. Instead, when her brother returned, she'd make him understand, too. Their mother deserved that much. Besides, this Doug seemed to be a cool guy. He had a lot going for him.

Sarah's thoughts were interrupted by the clanking of metal on metal. She turned to watch as the agile, elderly pilot wrapped a cord around the canoe and tied it tight to one of the plane's pontoons. Satisfied that the cargo was secure, the man spoke. "Doug, as soon as Rollie comes back with the saw, I'm ready to fly."

Just then the resort owner came scurrying down the steps. He clutched a chainsaw in one hand, two paddles in the other. "I think you better take these. A canoe generally works better if you paddle it."

Blushing, Roger took the paddles. "Thanks, Rollie. I'm thinking so much about the boys I'm not totally with it. You're right. It'd be darn hard to canoe without these."

Before returning to the men, Doug whispered in Lynn's ear. Then he walked over and took the power saw from

Rollie. Bob climbed up to his pilot's position. Roger and Doug shoved the gear in the cargo door, closed it, then scrambled into own their seats.

Rollie pushed the plane away from the pier and watched it taxi away. If only he were twenty years younger. He'd paddle every lake in the Boundary Waters until he found the boys.

He was the one who had given Seth the canoe. He felt equally to blame for the boys' absence. He just wished there was more he could do.

* * *

At one hundred miles per hour, the flight back to Winchell Lake took only minutes. Bob put the plane down on the narrow arm of water connecting it to Meeds Lake. Then he taxied toward shore until the floats nearly bumped bottom.

Roger and Doug climbed out on a pontoon. They quickly had the canoe untied and bobbing alongside the float. Bob passed down the paddles and power saw. After lowering the gear into the boat, both men jumped into knee-deep water.

"Turn me around," Bob requested. "I'll taxi out, shut down and listen. When I can't hear the saw anymore, I'll pop up to check your progress."

Doug grabbed a wing strut and began turning the plane. The engine coughed to life and he gave a hard shove. Satisfied Bob could taxi out, he followed Roger to shore.

Each holding onto a gunnel, the men tugged the canoe to the outlet. There they discovered the stream was too shallow for paddling.

"Okay, so we use our legs instead of our arms," Roger said, "Probably works out better anyway. We can take turns, one of us going ahead cutting, the other pulling the canoe. When the saw man gets tired, we'll switch."

The trunks and tree branches jamming the stream were no match for two determined men. Rollie had been right. The new saw cut like magic. In seconds, it sliced through the thickest of tree trunks. Some stubborn windfalls had to be severed in two places, so the middle dropped into the water where it could be pushed aside. Others only had to be cut once. Working nonstop, the men reached the lake in no time at all.

Doug swung the bow of the canoe onto the bank. After checking to make sure it would stay put, he scrambled after Roger.

Would the campsite be occupied or abandoned? Neither man spoke as they jogged across the clearing, afraid of what they might not find.

* * *

By the time Travis had slogged along the entire shore of South Cone Lake, his feet were ready to quit. They were cold, bruised and nicked from rocks and sticks. The rest of his body ached in agreement. Travis promised himself a break when he reached the next stream. The inlet was only yards ahead, and a fat stump offered a resting place. Exhausted, he sloshed from the water and stumbled up on land.

Shrugging off the pack, Travis plunked on the rotting stump. He glanced down at his feet—not a pretty sight. Both were bluish-white and so puckered they looked like a badly wrinkled shirt forgotten in a washing machine.

Digging into his pack, he dug out the windbreaker. Then he wrapped it around his lower legs, completely covering his calves and feet.

For the time being he was content to sit, letting the jacket thaw out his frigid limbs. The distant buzz of an airplane begged his attention.

"All right! It's about time," he cheered. "That's gotta be close to camp! The pilot will probably spot Seth's tent.

We'll both be home tonight."

With renewed energy, Travis repacked the jacket, slipped into the pack straps and waded into the next stream. He made great progress until he reached a new challenge. With so many thoughts filling his head, he'd put aside a unique feature of this waterway. Halfway between the lakes, it widened into a marshy pond.

About the size of a grade school playground, it hadn't been a problem coming downstream. He had simply climbed in the canoe and paddled. But now on foot, he was faced with a new dilemma. The pond was too deep, the bottom much too mucky, to attempt to wade. The only alternative was to hike around on land.

Travis studied both shorelines, trying to decide which would be the easiest to navigate. Neither looked inviting. Where marshy wetland ended, hundreds of split trees lay on their sides.

* * *

Roger's fingers trembled as he unzipped the tent flap. What he saw inside conjured up mixed emotions. He was delighted to see Seth. The lad was sound asleep. But the raspy breathing and a pallid complexion said they'd arrived none to soon.

But where was Travis?

Had his son been killed in the storm? Had he been crushed by falling timber or swept into the lake? Roger would have to get those answers from the young man in the sleeping bag. But for a moment, Roger did nothing. He was hesitant to wake Seth—afraid of what he'd learn.

Pulling his head back from the tent's doorway, Roger looked at Doug. "Well, we got here in time to save one of the kids. He's sound asleep."

"Who is it? Seth or Travis?"

"Seth's in the tent. There's no sign of Trav."

"Oh Roger, I'm sorry. But let's not jump to conclusions. Maybe Travis went for help . . . left Seth behind."

"Hmm . . . maybe. I hope. I guess we better wake Seth and find out."

It took several seconds for the ailing youth to come out of his fog. Sleep and sickness had him in a firm grip. Once he recognized Roger Larsen, Seth spoke, his voice slurred and scratchy. "Did Travis get home already? He just left this morning."

"What? Are you saying Travis is okay? He's alive?" Roger blurted, his voice threatening to fail him at any second.

"Yeah. No one came to get us so he went for help. Isn't that how you knew where to find me?" Seth croaked before starting a coughing spell.

When the hacking halted, a new voice filtered through the fabric. "Were you too sick to travel with him?" Doug queried.

"Well, yeah. But it's not on account of this cold. We think my ankle is broken. I can't walk so good."

"It's all right. You won't have to take a step. Roger and I'll carry you to the canoe and float you to the plane. You'll be back at the resort in an hour," the deep voice replied.

"But what about Travis?" Seth wheezed, squirming toward the entrance. "Shouldn't you be looking for him first?"

"Soon as we have you back home we'll search for Trav. If he was healthy enough to take off on his own, we should find him without much trouble. You can tell us his plans as we float you up the flowage."

The men slid Seth from the tent, still tucked in his sleeping bag. Doug bent over and scooped Seth into his arms as if he were a rag doll, then began walking toward the canoe.

While Doug was getting Seth settled in the bottom of the boat, Roger broke camp. He stuffed everything but the tent into the boy's packsack. He noticed the holes and rips in the nylon. Obviously there was a story behind the tears that the boys could tell later, when both were safe and sound.

Roger rolled the tent around its poles, grabbed the pack-frame in his free hand and took off for the creek. The sooner they got Seth home, the sooner they could track down his son.

* * *

Rage was rising in Travis like hot lava in a volcano. He wanted to scream and yell, curse and swear, kick out at something. The route he'd chosen to bypass the pond was practically impassable.

The ground was boggy and soft—treacherous to step on without taking a tumble. Nearly all of the spruce and tamaracks had tipped with their bottoms still attached, creating a tightly packed maze of muddy root clumps.

The stricken trees' needles and branches reached out to claw and scratch every inch of exposed skin. Others grabbed at his sweatshirt and pack-frame, holding him prisoner until he could back up and negotiate his release. Only his jeans escaped their clutching, but like his Nikes, they were changing color. The root clusters of moist earth slapped a fresh coat of mud-brown to everything they touched.

So many sharp-needled branches encircled Travis he wasn't sure which way to go. Frustrated, he stopped and reminded himself for about the ninety-ninth time not to panic. He'd get through this.

On firmer ground, the trees had fallen mostly in one direction. But here, in the boggy soil, the conifers tumbled helter-skelter. Wherever there had once been a small opening, a spruce or tamarack had tipped to fill the space.

The only view was up. But that didn't help. The sun

wasn't out. So he stopped moving altogether and just stood in place. Before moving on, he had to figure out which direction was the way back to camp.

Then, for some reason, Travis recalled the gifts from his mother. The multi-tool was in its case attached to his belt. Its pliers, clippers and blades couldn't help him now, but something else could—the compass. It'd been hanging around his neck like a piece of jewelry since he left home. Up until now he hadn't needed a compass. But now, trapped in this tangle of fallen trees, he could use it to take a bearing.

First he needed a bit of open space. Ignoring his aching shoulder, he shrugged off the pack. Then he broke the branches around him until he could turn in a circle with arms extended.

Next he pulled out the map. Northeast. If he just kept working his way northeast, he was bound to meander back to the stream. Travis tucked the map away. Then he tugged on the soft cotton cord securing the compass.

He hadn't paid much attention to this gift. At the time, all his interest had been on the multi-tool. Now he noticed there was something unusual about this particular pathfinder. Travis held it flat in his palm and stared. Then he thought he knew. This compass was fatter, thicker, than others he had used.

Why, he wondered? But he didn't dwell on it. There were more important things to think about. Holding the compass level at chest height, Travis slowly rotated. He stopped when the red needle and the "N" aligned. Then he shuffled his feet a few degrees to the right. Bingo! That was the direction he needed to travel.

Slipping the pack on his shoulders, Travis started forward. The chances of making it to their campsite before dark were quickly shrinking from slim to none. Unless a miracle happened and a path opened up, the afternoon would be long gone before he escaped this prickly prison.

* * *

Even in his groggy state, Seth was impressed at how easily the men were able to coax the canoe through the channel. Seth sat on the bottom with his back resting against the rear seat.

Roger guided the bow. The stranger pushed the stern. Despite the load, the duo easily slipped the boat over shallow riffles. Several times they even hefted the canoe airborne as if it were nothing more than a piece of carry-on luggage.

Seth had no clue to the identity of the stranger. Roger hadn't introduced him, and Seth wasn't about to ask. Probably one of Roger's friends, he thought. Whoever he was, the man's quiet confidence made Seth sense that he was in good hands.

For a time no one spoke. Then Roger broke the impasse. "So what you're telling us, Seth, is that Travis hoped to cross Brule before dark today? Is that the long and short of it?"

"Yeah, pretty much. That's what Trav told me. Mr. Larsen, I didn't want him to leave. But I really didn't feel strong enough to stop him. Besides, the plan sounded okay. He thought there might be boats out on Brule looking for us. That would have saved him lots of time. Then they could send someone to find me."

"Don't be hard on yourself," the stranger said. "It sounds like a good plan."

"Yeah . . . except Travis has a couple of problems, too."

"What kind of problems?" Roger asked with interest.

"Ah, he got sorta banged up on our first day out. The canoe fell, hit his shoulder and hand."

"How bad?"

"I can't really say, but the shoulder hurt every time he lifted or carried something."

Roger directed the next question to Doug. "What do you think?"

"Sounds like a deep bruise . . . maybe a cracked collar bone. Painful, but certainly not life threatening."

Seth could already see into the opening of the bigger lake. Looking like a huge multi-colored goose, a red-and-white aircraft bobbed on its surface.

"Mr. Larsen, I thought it was against the law to use private airplanes in the Boundary Waters. You won't get in trouble or anything will you?"

"No," Roger chuckled. "You guys are far more important than a simple rule. Rules can be worked around. I bet once we return to blue skies we'll see lots of air traffic around here. This storm damage goes on for miles. The Forest Service will be taking lots of photos."

"How are things at the resort? Are Mom and Sarah okay?" Seth rasped between coughing jags.

"Everyone's fine. But your mom's worried sick about you."

"I suppose . . . what with the storm and all."

Bob had spotted the crew coming up the outlet. He cranked the engine over. Then he used just enough throttle to swing the plane toward shore and taxi close. Coming to shallow water, he shut down and waited for Roger to grab a pontoon. Bob sat in his pilot's seat, puzzled. The young man in the canoe wasn't Travis. But he recognized the boy's handsome dark features. He had met the lad at the Larsens' several years earlier. This was Travis's best friend, Seth.

So where was Travis?

It took the men only minutes to load up. In little time they had Seth strapped in, and the saw, paddles and pack stowed in the storage bay.

"The canoe has to stay," Bob informed the others. "With four of us in here, we better play it safe."

"Not a problem. The guides can pick it up next summer. Rollie won't miss it." Roger replied.

Roger walked the canoe to shore. He pulled it up on the beach, rolled it over and tied the bow rope to a shrub.

Returning to the aircraft, he pushed out into deeper water, then hopped up on a pontoon. Bob cranked the engine. Moments later the floats were skimming the surface, eager to return one injured young camper to the care and comfort of his family.

To Seth it seemed they had just become airborne when he felt the pilot slow for landing. Was it possible that what had taken two days to paddle and portage could be covered in minutes by air? Apparently it was, because through the side window he recognized the familiar shape of Poplar Lake.

The landscape below looked foreign, strange. Here and there he noticed splashes of green where spruces and pines clung tight to their needles. The remainder of the terrain was the shade of oatmeal—pallid gray with streaks of dark and light.

To Seth it looked like Goliath's comb had stroked over the land, forcing the forest to bow down in one direction. He was worried. If Travis had to travel through a mess like that, he'd never make it out. His buddy would need a bulldozer get through.

Bob banked for their final approach. Then he backed off the power and dropped the pontoons on the water. Roger advised him to taxi to the Larsen dock. Linda should be home. His wife was a nurse. Who better to do a quick check of Seth's injury?

The Suburban's rear seat folded down to make a long bed. Doug hefted Seth directly to the garage. The men slid Seth out of the sleeping bag and lay the youth flat on the carpeting.

Linda and Beth had watched the plane pull up to the

dock. Uncertainty set in when only Seth was removed from the aircraft. What did that mean? Where was Travis? Was there only room for one of the kids? But wouldn't one of the men stay behind with the other boy?

Roger embraced both his wife and daughter. With a reassuring smile he began. "We didn't find Trav, but he's fine. He left camp at first light this morning heading for Brule. Seth says he has a couple of bruises but is basically okay. You and Beth can take Seth over to the resort and pick up Lynn. Seth needs to get to the hospital. His ankle is either broken or sprained. But worse, it sounds like he has the early stages of pneumonia. His color's awful. He's coughing a lot, and he says he's been on a roller coaster between fever and chills."

Linda's eyes widened. "Oh Roger, are you sure Travis is okay? They've been out there alone for over five days."

"Seth says that Trav has been taking care of him since the storm struck. That sounds like he's fine to me. Go ahead now, pick up Lynn and get Seth to the hospital."

"Oh, of course. But I won't stop worrying until Trav's back home."

"Me neither. But there's a good chance we'll have him home before you're back from town."

As the Suburban pulled away, the men sat at the kitchen table munching cookies and gulping coffee. Roger had the map spread out and was using a marker to highlight the remaining search area.

"Heck, Rog. It can't be more than six or seven miles between where we found the Springwood kid and the outlet to Brule," Bob mumbled around a mouthful of cookie crumbs. "We shouldn't have any trouble spotting Travis along that route. Especially if he's on the big lake."

"How's the fuel situation?" Doug asked.

"Fine, we put less than an hour on the engine since we filled up. There should be plenty for the rest of the day."

"What do you guys say we go get him?" Roger asked.

Bob and Doug headed for the dock. Roger was closing the garage door when a Chevy Blazer pulled up the drive. On the driver's door was a Cook County Sheriff's Department star. A worried-looking woman sat behind the wheel. She slowed the vehicle to a stop and opened her door.

Roger walked over and waited while the woman got out. The nameplate on her uniform read "J. Reynolds."

"Officer Reynolds, what can I do for you?"

"Larsen, right? Roger Larsen?" the deputy inquired.

"Yes, that's me. What is it?"

"We should go inside. I have some news for you and your wife."

"My wife just left with the Springwood boy. With the help of my friend's floatplane, we found him this afternoon."

"Really? That's great to hear. I'll get it out on the radio."

"Officer Reynolds, if you have something to tell me, please get on with it. We're about to take off to locate my son."

"Well, yes. It's about your son. The rangers sent a couple of powerboats out on Brule Lake this afternoon. They were hoping to spot your son and his friend."

"Great! Have they seen any sign of my boy?"

The deputy looked down, avoiding eye contact. "I'm sorry, but that's the bad news. They found his canoe a few minutes ago. It was nearly submerged, only the float tanks keeping it from sinking. The ranger who radioed me said there was a long gash in the bottom, as if it had hit something right below the surface."

Roger felt his stomach lurch. "How far offshore did they find the boat?"

"I'm not certain, Mr. Larsen. But the men did a search of the shoreline. There was no sign of your son."

Roger felt the blood drain from his face. How could Travis, with all his experience on the water, become victim to it? There had to be another explanation. There was no way he could accept this news.

Down on the dock, Bob and Doug witnessed the conversation. They couldn't hear the words. But the look on Roger's face said it wasn't a good report. They waited until the Blazer drove away before joining Roger on the deck.

"Want to share the news?" Bob asked.

"It's bad. A search boat just found the boys' canoe. It was offshore on Brule, a hole in the bottom, no sign of Travis."

"Have faith, Rog. That kid of yours grew up on the water. He's probably hiking around the big lake right now. Let's go find him," Bob encouraged, staring at his Cessna.

"He's right," Doug added. "Trav survived the storm. He's probably waiting for us as we speak."

"Come on, Rog. Let's go have a look." Bob directed, and without waiting for a reply, started down the steps.

Only a few hours of daylight remained. Out of sight, but just over the horizon, clouds were gathering, getting ready to once again blanket the BWCA.

Chapter Seventeen

CHAPTER SEVENTEEN

When he first heard it, the engine's growl was faint and far away. At the time, Travis was ensnared in tangled brush and broken limbs. He was battling his way back to the stream.

The drone grew louder.

Travis fought frantically to free himself. Moments later the aircraft roared overhead. Through boughs and branches, Travis was only able to catch a glimpse of its silver pontoons and red tail feathers. As quickly as it had come, the aircraft was gone, the pitch of the exhaust fading.

"Gotta get out of here, gotta get out of here," Travis mumbled on the razor edge of hysteria. Single-minded, he struggled forward. Minutes later he managed a meek smile of relief. He'd reached the end of the pond.

Cold, clear creek water quenched his thirst. But the liquid didn't help ease the ache in his stomach. He flashed on the freeze-dried packets. An airplane meant a hunt was underway, that Search and Rescue would arrive soon. He could afford to use one of the emergency rations. The dry powder had to have some food value. Why not make a cold soup?

After taking out the tiny cooking pot, he filled it with several inches of water. Then he slit the bag and emptied the complete contents into the pan.

Using a small stick, he stirred until everything swirled together. The runny mixture looked similar to split-pea soup, not one of his favorites. He brought the pan to his lips and sipped—surprise. Except for a slightly salty taste, the mixture was bland. It was flavorless as the paste he had once eaten in kindergarten. Removing the stir stick, he took a full swallow.

When the pot was empty, he used a forefinger to glean the gooey sop stuck to the bottom. He didn't pause until the pan was polished and his finger licked clean as a Saturday wash.

His stomach didn't feel quite so hollow.

* * *

The passengers saw only snarled trees along an empty shoreline. To get a better look at the outlet area, Bob put the Cessna into every flight angle he knew. He climbed and dipped, rolled and swooped, tried level passes at different altitudes. Still, they saw nothing. Except for islands, rocks and shallows, there wasn't a trace of Travis.

A powerboat was visible off to the east, heading for the far shore miles away. Bob flew over the lake to get a better look. The men were bothered by what they witnessed.

The large aluminum fishing craft held two people. Resting between them, upside down across the gunnels, was a green canoe. Even from several hundred feet up, the long gash in its bottom was visible.

The men remained mute. It looked like the sheriff's deputy had heard it right. Travis was somewhere down below, under the cold, dark water.

Bob banked to the west and broke the silence. "Let's have another look at those channels. Maybe Travis decided to head back to the camp."

"Okay," was all Roger could say, wondering why Travis would turn back. All he'd have to do was build a fire. It was something searchers would be bound to see. The man fought back tears. He needed clear vision to see any sign of his son.

"I'm gonna fly a little higher. Give you guys a wider view," Bob said. He added a hint of power and pulled into a slow climb.

* * *

Wading in the water was taking its toll. Travis was chilled to the bone. He slogged to the bank and slipped off the pack-frame. He wanted the windbreaker.

On the move again, he came to an area of evergreens. Some were bent; others were broken with boughs drooping into the water. Travis recalled the difficulty pulling the canoe through their branches. This time he didn't have the canoe to think about. He climbed the bank, looking for a way around.

There was a better route. Nearby, a huge Norway pine had refused to surrender to the wind. Even with half a dozen immature trees leaning against its giant trunk, it had stood tall, refusing to fall. The boughs formed a tunnel under which Travis could walk. But first he clambered over a pair of aspens toppled near the water's edge.

Needles and twigs poked and pricked at his bare feet, adding to his discomfort. Travis paused to look up at the massive evergreen. It was a tree with enough strength to put up with its neighbors butting into its space. From its size, it had to be old growth timber. Possibly a tree too young a hundred years earlier, which had been passed over by loggers.

Awed by its mass, he stood quietly, staring up, wondering just how old it was. At first, in a weary trance, his mind didn't register the noise. Suddenly he came to life. The plane was returning, flying back in his direction.

He needed to get to an opening, pronto! He was standing in a terrible place to be spotted. The creek was his best chance. Travis spun back the way he had just come, scrambled over the aspens and fell flat on his face.

From overhead came the roar of the aircraft. Travis pushed himself up and stumbled toward the bank. He broke into the opening just in time to see the plane howl overhead.

There was no way anyone could have seen him. Not in a green jacket under a canopy of pine boughs. Add another huge disappointment to the list of recent woes. His best chance would be at camp, out in the open. Set up the tent, spread out some clothes. He needed to move on.

Who knows? Maybe they've already found Seth. Maybe there's a warm meal waiting back at camp. Travis turned and for the third time, crept over the blowdowns.

Looking up at the ancient pine, he yelled, "Thanks for nothing, old man. You just cost me a ride out of here."

* * *

The second pass over the channel held the same results as the first flight. The men saw the same rocks, water and torn forest. None saw a clue to indicate Travis was anywhere along the route.

Roger was certain his son would have started a fire, smoked up a message; especially once he knew there was a plane overhead. It made even more sense that Travis would have done the same on the shore of Brule. Even if Trav hadn't planned on staying put, he would have left some evidence that he was alive.

Roger's heart was a cold stone. He shuddered, thinking of the loss. These kinds of tragedies fill the news every day. But it's always someone else's kid that drowns, crashes or gets a rare disease—never your own child.

"Roger, you with us?"

"Yup, Bob, what?"

"What do you want to do, keep looking or turn it over to the authorities?"

"Oh, right. I suppose they'll bring a team over to drag the lake." The thought of his son being snagged on some huge hook sickened the man further.

"It's your call, Roger. I'll fly 'til dark if you want, if you think there's the slightest chance of us finding him."

"Thanks, but it doesn't look good. If Travis was okay, he'd have built a fire or left a message somehow. My God, Bob. He's gone. My wonderful son is dead, and it's as much my fault as his."

"Don't blame yourself. The Maker works in mysterious ways. If Travis is gone, God must have had another plan for the lad."

"Thanks for trying, but I've never believed that line. If God was fair, Trav would be alive. To say he was hand-picked for a higher purpose is bull, and you know it."

"No, my friend, I don't. Even at my age there are lots of things I don't understand."

* * *

Travis realized he would not reach the campsite before dark. Going around the bog had eaten up too much time. He didn't want to camp by himself, but he wouldn't have a choice.

Nearing exhaustion, he was wading along the edge of Middle Cone Lake. The bottom was mucky. Progress was slow. At least it wasn't as frightening as the bog slog.

That experience had been a preview of hell without flames. Travis hated tight, close places. He was musing about the experience when he noticed that the day's light was leaving.

Overhead, clouds had regrouped. They had closed

ranks and were wearing scowls. Travis hoped they wouldn't choose to spit. With no way of making a fire, he didn't want get soaked.

Most of the shoreline walk was behind him when Travis decided he'd had enough. It wasn't all that far to the next connecting stream. But he knew he couldn't possibly travel in the dark. There were too many obstacles. Plus, he had already pushed his body to its limit and beyond.

Far better to pitch the tent, finish the trip in the morning.

Travis stumbled up the shrub-covered bank and blinked. He couldn't believe his luck. Here was another grassy area, much like the one where Seth and he had spent the past few days.

Weird, he thought. Most of this country was nothing but volcanic bedrock or forest. Then, when he needed an open campsite, it was there, just waiting to be used.

He wrestled into every stitch of clothing he'd brought on the trip. Then he decided to do a little exploring. A short hike from the lake helped explain the clearing. Nestled in weeds and small shrubs were remnants of two small cabins. Walls and roofs had collapsed years earlier, no doubt crushed under heavy winter snows.

A mound of rotting boards and beams was centered in one of the rock foundations. A few rusted metal straps and large, crude spikes still clung to several timbers— evidence of how the cabins had been held together.

Shuffling back to his pack, Travis pulled out the map. In the fading light his young eyes were able to decipher the small print. Just to the left of the lake it read "old logging camp."

That would explain it. Loggers had probably used this spot—and the one like it on North Cone—as storage yards for cut timber. Years of horse and foot traffic packed the soil, making it difficult for trees to take root.

Well, so much for the history lesson, Travis mused. Best to pitch the tent while there was a little light left.

He chose to set up the shelter on a flat area near the lake. The first time he had ever slept in a tent had been on a pack trip with his dad. He was still amazed that a package the size of a bread loaf could become a bedroom in mere minutes. It was magical the way the thin tubes and elastic cords worked together to form an egg-shaped dome.

His dad had made him practice in the yard. Before their first trip, Travis must have set up the tent and taken it down a dozen times. He had even practiced in the dark, without a flashlight, snapping the tubes together by feel.

Weary as he was, he was thankful for all that practice. He labored on autopilot as he checked the ground for sticks and stones. He was too tired to search out pine needles to place under the floor; weeds would have to be cushion enough.

When the tent was ready, he tugged the sleeping bag from its small sack. It was another marvel of modern science. How could something so fluffy and warm pack into such a small space? Then it struck him—he should be thanking Seth. It was Seth who insisted he bring the survival gear. Travis had been so sure he'd be at the outfitter's resort for supper he had planned on leaving almost empty-handed.

Before long, night crept into the campsite. Places that had been in shadows were now dark. Soft light still lay over the lake, reflecting off its rippled surface—with some of the radiance spilling into the clearing.

Travis pondered using the last package of powdered food. No, not yet. They might need it tomorrow. Seth might still be alone. It made sense to save it—just in case.

Before pushing his pack into the tent, Travis pulled out the flashlight. He switched it on and was relieved. The batteries still clung to life. He sighed, took a last look at the lake and then followed his gear into the shelter. Once inside he zipped the door, and in the dark, snuggled into his sleeping bag.

Despite being covered in warm cloth, Travis trembled. This might prove to be the longest night of his life.

* * *

The Suburban pulled into the Larsens' drive just as night was closing the curtain. Light, spilled from a Coleman lantern, cast shadows through the kitchen window. Down at the dock the Cessna gently bumped against a pair of worn tires.

Linda Larsen paused before turning off the engine. She wasn't certain what to make of the scene. Was Travis inside—warm, safe, secure? Or was he still out there somewhere—alone and frightened?

The return trip from Grand Marais seemed to take forever. She'd used a telephone at the hospital to call the ranger station. No one would give her an answer. "Check with your husband," was the best they would do.

Wouldn't they have told her if they had good news? But maybe they didn't know, what with the phones not working over the hill. That must be it, she prayed. They didn't have an answer to give her.

"Mom, you okay?" Beth asked, freeing herself from the seat belt.

"Sure, sweetheart. Are you ready to go in? It looks like Dad's home."

"Think they found Travis?"

"I guess we won't know until we go see."

Mother and daughter stepped out of the car. They went up the short set of stairs leading to the side porch. Through the window, Linda spotted her husband and Bob Ritzer sitting opposite each other near the far wall.

Because the room was in shadows she couldn't read their faces.

Sucking in a deep breath, Linda opened the door. On pins and needles, she stepped into the kitchen entry. Startled, Roger looked up, stood and hurried toward her.

Linda's heart clenched. Her husband had wet eyes. Only two things made her husband cry. One was extreme joy, such as when the children had been born. The other was over a great loss, like when his father suddenly passed away.

Roger's face was a mask of pain. Linda knew in an instant these were not tears of joy.

"Roger, what is it? Travis, is he? Oh, dear God! No!"

He went to her then, pulling her tight. A long wail rose in Linda's throat. "Nooooo, Roger, nooooo! He can't be. There must be a mistake."

Tears flowed. Beth stood frozen in place, mouth agape. Then she, too, understood. She ran to them, squeezed in between and clutched their waists.

Bob sat quietly in the shadows, tears glazing his vision. He knew the worst tragedy a parent can face is the loss of a child. He and his wife had experienced that pain. Their only son had been killed in an auto accident.

The boy had been eighteen, had just graduated from high school, and was preparing to attend college. The year following the accident had been the hardest of Bob's life. He knew many sad days lay ahead for this family.

Long moments passed. Except for the sound of sobbing and the ticking of a wall clock, the room was silent. Eventually the Larsens ran out of sobs. They parted, and then still holding hands, walked slowly to the sofa.

"Roger? Bob? Are you certain? How? What happened? Did you find him . . . his body, I mean?" Linda asked in a voice hardly more than a whisper.

"No. No one found him. But a search party found the canoe offshore on Brule Lake. A section of the keel was missing. There was no sign of Trav," Roger choked.

Beth had cuddled close, trying to put together the pieces. "Dad, that doesn't mean he's dead. Maybe he's just lost in the woods."

"That's what Bob and I were just talking about. But there doesn't seem much reason for hope. Seth told us what Travis had planned for today. There's no reason to believe he wasn't in the canoe."

Roger took a deep breath and then continued. "The canoe couldn't have gotten to the big lake without him. Besides, we checked the route between Seth's campsite and Brule several times. There was no sign of Travis."

Roger paused to blow his nose. "We should know more tomorrow. Search and Rescue will round up more help, look again in the morning."

"I don't believe it! I won't believe it! I won't believe it until they find his body!" Linda sobbed, clenching her fists to her cheeks."

"Travis knows about boats. He wouldn't have tried crossing big water if he wasn't sure he would make it. He's alive, Roger. I know it. He's out there somewhere right now, wondering why someone hasn't found him."

Roger pulled his wife tight and gently stroked her hair. "Let's pray that's the case," he whispered. "Let's hope it's true."

* * *

Lynn and Sarah Springwood remained at the clinic in Grand Marais. The doctors weren't too concerned about Seth's cough. Although pneumonia hadn't been ruled out, their best guess was bronchitis. Test results would tell them more. In the meantime, they prescribed several medications to clear up his lungs.

It was the doctors' opinion that a good night's rest, along with the medication, would have Seth ready for the trip to Duluth by morning. X-rays had shown a fracture on a flange of the ankle joint. There had also been some tearing of ligaments. A bone specialist had been consulted by telephone, and surgery was scheduled for midmorning the next day.

Doug would drive them to the hospital in Duluth. He had joined Sarah and Lynn at the clinic but had not gone in to see Seth.

Before meeting the Springwoods, Doug had checked in with his daughter. Telephone lines were working in his brother's neighborhood. The call had gone through. Cindy was fine. The girl loved staying with her aunt and uncle. When would she see him? After more small talk they said their goodbyes and hung up.

Sarah took to Doug like cream to coffee. She had made a secret vow about letting her mother live her own life. She meant to keep it.

Sarah met Doug at the Larsens' home while they were waiting for the floatplane. He seemed like a gentleman, yet not a sissy. She liked the way he looked right at her when he spoke, like she was an equal, not just some flaky kid.

Doug's worry about Seth seemed genuine. Also, her mom had told her that Doug had canceled a very important project in order to help. He must really care.

Sarah had to admit he was also a very good-looking guy. She could see why her mother was attracted to him. Sarah's next challenge was to get Seth up to speed.

* * *

Seth had figured out on his own who this stranger must be. He must be the one his mother was dressing up for on Saturday nights. Seth was all right with it. He liked the dude.

So Sarah thinks she knows something I don't. That's okay, he thought. The guy cared enough to come looking for me and he hadn't even met me yet. That was worth more than pocket change.

Seth flashed back to his time alone in the tent. How he had thought about the lie. The "lousy lie," he had called it. He remembered how he had laid there, hurt and scared. How he told himself he'd butt out of his mother's business. The time had come, he thought.

Mom's right. Remember Dad, but it's time to move on.

Seth's next thoughts were about Travis. Had they found him yet? Probably. Trav should have been easy to see. Maybe they'll bring him to the hospital for a visit.

Next Seth wondered about Travis' shoulder. Did it need surgery? Nah, he couldn't have been doing all that work with a broken bone. Could he?

Through a medicated fog Seth recognized the voices of Sarah and his mother. Then a man's voice joined the conversation. Was his mom crying? Why would she do that? Was she that happy to have him back?

He'd have to remember to ask her in the morning, tease her about it. The meds took hold, and soon the fog became a quilt. Seth slipped into a soothing sleep.

Chapter Eighteen

CHAPTER EIGHTEEN

Night came on quickly, wrapping the lonely tent in a black robe. Travis lay awake, seeking a comfortable position. He was hoping to find one where he could sleep without pain.

He had never known such total darkness. The sliver of moon wouldn't rise until well past midnight. But even that wouldn't be much help. With the sky filled with woolly clouds, Travis sensed lunar light wouldn't make a discernable difference.

This was the night he had imagined after the bear had ransacked their supplies. This was the night all alone in the wilderness.

Travis had predicted he'd be terrified, and he was.

He cowered inside the sleeping bag. How would he make it through so many dark hours? He'd run out of options. He'd used them up, had made too many poor choices.

From somewhere far across the lake a coyote began to yip. Intruding on the night's silence, the bark was high and sharp. From far away a second little wild dog answered, its voice faint but clear. Then the night became as quiet as an empty church.

The call of the coyotes, or brush wolves as they were sometimes referred to, hadn't added to his terror. Travis knew coyotes weren't dangerous. They mainly ate small rodents, rabbits and things already dead.

But when real wolves started howling, Travis quivered in his sleeping bag.

Knowing that timber wolves avoided humans wasn't much comfort. That was easier said in a classroom. But being on your own, far from friends and family, brought new meaning to the word fear.

The first howl came from behind the tent, somewhere nearby in the snarled forest. Starting with a thick, deep bass note, the call climbed an octave before sliding down and fading away. Off to the southeast came an answering call—the howl rising eerily over woods and water.

As if coached by a ghostly director, a chorus of wolves crooned from all points of the compass, usually one at a time—each adding its own verse.

Travis knew a few things about the wild canines. His father was an expert on the subject, and had shared much. He'd learned that howling was the wolves' way of staying in touch, like neighbors hollering a hello across a street. But knowing such a thing didn't matter much now. Each howl sent fear shivers up and down the teen's spine.

Once, while trekking with his dad on Isle Royale, Travis had seen the work of a wolf pack. They had stumbled across a fresh kill, a huge cow moose. Her thick coat of heavy hair had been ripped open, slashed as if by razor-edged knives. Huge hunks of muscle were missing.

Travis had seen firsthand that a wolf was an expert killing machine. And killing was what it did for a living.

With trembling fingers he felt for the tool case hooked to his belt. He unsnapped the catch and opened the tool to the longest blade. If any wolves come a calling,

I'll be ready, he thought, knowing in his heart that a knife would offer little help.

As abruptly as they'd begun, the wolves stopped talking. Sudden silence draped over the tent like a coroner's sheet over the deceased. It was so quiet Travis could hear the rush of blood pulsing past his eardrums.

He lay on his back, eyes saucer-sized, staring up at the black hole overhead. His brain became a jar of jumbled thoughts and scary images.

He'd be thinking of one thing and suddenly another problem would pop up to replace it. Travis couldn't help wondering if he was losing it, going crazy.

That he could be so tired, and yet not sleep, made no sense. Time slowed to crawl. Several long hours passed. All the while, bad thoughts kept bouncing back and forth like a tennis ball in a nonstop match.

Sometime before midnight a light drizzle began to fall. At first Travis was upset. He'd been soaked enough on this trip. But the continuous pitter-patter of raindrops filled the silence, making him drowsy. He was dry in the shelter, warm in his bag, and finally nodded off.

Travis awoke to the tent fly snapping. Startled, he cried out. "Seth, Seth, you awake?"

Then recall came. Seth wasn't here. Travis was alone. There was no one nearby to answer. Travis curled up in the bag, hoping to fall back to sleep. But that wish wasn't to be.

Instead of slumber, his worries returned. Then when his empty stomach growled like an angry animal, Travis knew he wouldn't be getting any more sleep. He might as well get up and face the new day.

As his mind came alive, so did his body, protesting with aches and pains. It felt like he was lying on a bed of sticks and stones. The nicked soles of his feet hurt, his sore hand ached, and the injured shoulder felt like it had been struck with an ax.

While willing himself to move, he stared straight up. The tent fabric was dancing, its rhythm forced by a wind blowing in off the lake. In the murky predawn of early morning, it occurred to Travis there had been a weather change.

Stretching his long legs, he yawned, rubbed his eyes and then forced his muscles to budge. He crawled out of the bag the way he had crawled in—fully clothed except for shoes.

He picked up the survival tool and returned it to its case. After unzipping the flap, he slithered forward and then stood with his lanky frame poking up through the entry door. Slipping on the left shoe and then the right, he took a few tottering steps. He wanted a look at the weather.

The sky looked so close Travis thought he might be able to touch it with a long stick. Tattered ribbons of misty clouds raced below a gray ceiling. A damp wind chased off the water nipping his nose and cheeks.

He focused on the far shore. It was a miracle, he mused again. Miles and miles of timber had been twisted and snapped—yet he and Seth hadn't suffered so much as a scratch. Most of their ills had been self-inflicted.

He had so hoped that the morning would arrive clear and sunny. That it would be filled with blue sky and brilliant light. It would be so nice to stay put for a few hours, give a search plane a chance to spot his tent. But with a thick, low cloud cover, that wasn't going to happen.

The only bright spot—he'd survived the dark hours without being any the worse for wear. Thank goodness he had finally fallen asleep.

Travis thought of his buddy. Was Seth still at the camp? If so, he'd need help. There was enough murky light to break camp. Best get to it.

Pulling his pack out of the tent, Travis considered using

the last food packet. Why not? His stomach was demanding attention. He'd be back at camp before noon. And there would be plenty of daylight left to catch fish and start a cooking fire with his pal's lighter.

After adding water, Travis stirred until the mixture turned goopy. He closed his eyes, tipped the pan and let the gooey mess drain into his mouth. Ahhh!

It was so much better than it looked. Like the day before, he licked the pan spotless. He carried it to the lake, used it as a cup and then rinsed it out. Despite sore feet and aching joints, he was ready as he'd ever be.

Soon after packing up, Travis waded into the water. Rested and refueled, he made excellent progress. Soon he could see the opening of the last lake, the one where they'd camped. Ignoring his cold, pain-filled feet, he slogged forward. Suddenly he was startled by the sounds of crunching brush and branches.

Without pausing, Travis splashed to a blowdown, grabbed a limb and hauled himself out of the water. Using a branch for support, he stood, craning his neck. Ahead, near the opening, a huge, dark shape lumbered toward the lake.

For a moment Travis was uncertain what he'd seen. But a gigantic set of antlers bobbing above the downed timber gave up the answer. It was a moose, a huge bull, six feet at the shoulder; its wide, palmed antlers fanned air higher than a basketball hoop.

Travis stood wide-eyed, petrified, holding his breath.

The big bull turned away, ambling out of the boy's sightline. Travis didn't know what to do. The moose had gone the same way he'd have to travel.

Finally he went back into the water. As quietly as possible, he slogged forward. While still some yards away from the lake, he again pulled himself up the bank. Then he crept behind a windfall. After a moment of indecision,

Travis stood tall and peered through its branches.

"Great!" he muttered, catching hints of dark-brown hair. "What now?"

After a brief wait, he began threading his way along the bank. He took a dozen well-placed steps and stopped. Careful not to make noise, he climbed on the trunk of a downed tree.

Looking as large as a moving van, the moose was casually plodding the shallows. Every now and then the animal would dip its horse-like snout into the water. When it lifted its head, there'd be vegetation dangling from its mouth.

Travis knew moose weren't to be messed with. He had heard tales about how ornery the bulls become during the breeding season. Travis thought that was about this time of year. He'd read the accounts of loggers being chased into trees by love-crazed moose. A person needed to keep their distance.

The moose's presence meant the shoreline was temporarily off limits. Instead, Travis realized, he'd have to struggle through the tangled maze of timber. It quickly became clear that land travel in this part of the BWCA was nearly impossible. After a time, Travis chose to sneak back to the shoreline and check to see if the coast was clear.

It wasn't. The bull hadn't gone far. While Travis had been struggling in the forest, the moose had lollygagged along the lakefront, unaware of the teen's travel troubles.

Travis wanted to shout at the brute, throw a rock, hit it with a stick—a really big stick. And he almost did throw a rock. He even picked one up. But then, recalling the chase tales, he decided that pegging a moose on the rear probably wasn't a good idea. He saw no other option but to head back into tangle-town.

The next hour passed like the one before. Despite the chill

in the air, hard work soon had Travis sweating and sucking air. He'd had enough. Certain that by now the moose had gone elsewhere, the teen angled toward shore.

No such luck.

The giant critter was still there, munching away without a care in the world. Only this time, the moose had heard Travis's brush-crunching footfalls. Perhaps thinking it was a rival bull, and with astounding speed, the moose raced from the shallows.

Travis spun around, searching for an escape route. There wasn't one. After a moment of indecision, he scurried over a twisted maple and then glanced over his shoulder. The bull had put on the brakes. It stood staring; raking the beach with a front hoof, angry puffs of vapor streaming from its long muzzle.

Travis gulped. Then he did what he'd been trying to avoid—climbing. The teenager scrambled onto a tilted aspen. Scared stiff, he clutched its lower limbs, and despite the cumbersome pack, shimmied up like a nervous monkey.

Catching movement, the bull charged. It stopped at the base of the tipped tree. Large, brown eyes studied the strange creature clinging to the branches above its head. Following a moment of uncertainty, the brute lowered its antlers. Then it plowed forward to give the blowdown a thrashing.

Satisfied that the display was enough warning, the moose slowly turned and lumbered to the lake. A sigh of relief escaped Travis's trembling lips. He watched as the monstrous mammal splashed out of sight. With nervous hands he slowly slid back to earth. Both his palm and shoulder throbbed. Ignoring the pain, he tiptoed toward the water.

Finally! Looking totally unconcerned about the incident, the bull was ambling in the opposite direction. Travis took a deep breath and realized his knees were knocking.

From his vantage point, Travis couldn't get a sightline on the camp. Once again he removed his shoes and pants. Slogging along shore was definitely less effort than breaking brush.

Fifteen more minutes of treading water brought Travis to the fish corral. Relieved to be back, and eager to see his friend, he clambered up the slope. But unhappily for the tired teen, and much like the fish-pen, the campsite was void of life. Seth's tent was nowhere to be seen.

"No! No! No! This can't be!"

Flattened weeds and clumps of pine needles were the only clues that tents had once stood on the flat ground above the lake. Fighting a wave of despair, Travis dashed to the fire ring. He knelt and felt—only cold, damp ashes.

There'd be no fire to warm him today.

The teenager stood in a trance. Moments passed before he realized he was shivering. He was still nearly naked from the waist down. What he needed to do first was get dressed.

After pulling on his jeans, Travis rushed to set up the shelter. It was something for a plane to see. That's how they probably spotted Seth, he thought. Once the tent was pitched, he unrolled the bag and crawled in.

He needed to warm up. He needed to think.

But what should he do? He had been making all these decisions and none of them panned out. If he had only stayed put like Seth had said—he'd be home now—safe and sound.

The morning's labor had tired him. And the hole in his middle was knocking on the door, asking to be filled. But he couldn't do a thing about it. There was nothing left to eat.

Probably best to take a nap, try to forget about his

hunger pains. Maybe when he woke, Search and Rescue would have arrived.

Wiping at his eyes, Travis tucked his head into the sleeping bag. Surprisingly, within minutes he dozed off.

* * *

Early that same morning, a variety of watercraft bounced and pitched on the choppy waters of Brule Lake. A fleet of boats gathered near the outlet where the canoe had been found. A navy of searchers had had come to look for one of their own.

Doug and Roger sat grim-faced in two of the boats. Upon hearing the news, Doug had canceled his Duluth trip. Lynn and Sarah would transport Seth to surgery without his company.

The men had met hours earlier in Grand Marais. Then they'd made the drive along Lake Superior and up the Caribou Trail to the boat landing. Each was teamed with a fishing guide. Both guides were members of the local Search and Rescue squad. Like so many others, they had volunteered time and equipment to help locate the Larsen boy.

Bob remained at Poplar Lake in the event the weather improved. Maybe he'd be able to take another look from the air. Chances of that happening weren't great, however. The forecast called for falling temperatures and the possibility of a cold rain, turning to wet snow.

If the temperature dropped near freezing, it would be too dangerous to fly. Small planes don't do well with snow and ice. Small planes with large pontoons under their wings do worse. It was doubtful that he'd be doing any piloting today.

At the lake, volunteers received instructions from the officer in charge. With orders given, the operation got under way. Most of the boats were equipped with modern fish-finding sonar units. But today they wouldn't be searching for walleyes or bass.

Their target was something larger.

The fleet would zigzag back and forth in front of the stream outlet. If an indication of a bulky object showed up on their sonar screens, divers would go down for a look. It was a slow process. A sad process. And one pursuit nobody wanted to win.

Roger huddled in the front seat. Hands in the pockets of a parka, he stared at the sonar. His mind was a cheerless merry-go-round of emotions. Part of him hoped that the search was a waste of time. Another voice said that if his boy was resting below, his body should be recovered.

This was the most difficult task he'd ever faced. Deep down Roger held onto a faint glimmer that the search was needless. Maybe Travis was camped somewhere else, waiting for a ride out, waiting to be found.

* * *

Later that same morning, Travis suddenly sat up. Something had roused him awake. At first all he heard was the wind whipping the tent fly. He remained perfectly still and concentrated. His ears caught the faint "whump-whump-whump" of helicopter blades thumping the air. Hope soared. They were looking for him. Good thing the tent was up. He was sure to be seen.

Travis slipped deep into the warm sleeping bag to wait. He began daydreaming of what he would eat when he got home. He pictured his mother serving roast beef and mashed potatoes. There'd be a big glass of cold milk, maybe a piece of cake and a scoop of ice cream for dessert.

Nah, she'd be too upset to cook. Maybe the family would go somewhere, order a pizza with all the toppings. Pizza's supposed to contain all the food groups, right? That's what he'd ask for, a pizza. Keep it simple. Beth would like that, too.

Nothing to do now but pass the time, he mused—and before long, daydreamed himself back to sleep.

* * *

For most of midday the fleet worked the waters near the outlet. Twice there was a rush of excitement as several boats' sonar units showed something big on the bottom.

The divers had been brought over to check. In one case it proved to be an old fish house. Abandoned years earlier, its rotting plywood frame now littered the floor of the lake. The second signal had bounced off a sunken log, a large hunk of water-soaked wood unable to stay afloat.

At two o'clock the sheriff called the boat captains in for a conference. He thanked them for their time and efforts. He was canceling the search. They'd covered the entire area several times. It was time to quit. Out over the lake, the camouflaged National Guard chopper made one more pass, banked to the south, and was soon just a noise in the distance.

One of the few female boat pilots started to protest. Some years before she'd almost lost a child in the same manner. When it was explained that even the high tech gear of the helicopter showed nothing but rocks and boulders below, she had to concede. No body would be found today.

The sheriff asked, weather permitting, if they'd be willing to return in a week or so. By then the boy's body may have floated to the surface, as drowning victims tend to do.

Roger sat sullen in the front of the craft, aware all eyes looking his way. What was he going to tell Linda? The guilt he felt for giving the trip's okay weighed heavily on his shoulders.

* * *

In a cluttered cubicle at the local newspaper, a lone reporter sat staring at her computer monitor. She had just completed an article for the weekly publication. A mother of three, she shuddered at the headline glowing on the bright screen.

Local Teen Missing. Little Hope Left.

* * *

Travis opened his eyes about the time the helicopter was leaving. It took a moment to come fully awake. His mind flashed on the chopper. He was going to be rescued soon. But why hadn't that happened yet? Couldn't they see his tent popped up in this big, fat opening?

Suddenly alert, Travis strained to hear. Nothing. Not a bird, not a squirrel—there was only the rustle of tent cloth.

What was going on? Why hadn't they found him? Then like the moon appearing from behind a cloud, the reason started to glow around the edges of his brain.

"No!" he screamed. "They wouldn't, they couldn't, impossible! No, no, no! Please, God, don't let them think that!"

He remembered that he'd left the canoe in the water. What if it had washed away from shore? What if someone found it? They'd probably think he was in the lake.

Did everyone think he was so stupid he'd try using a boat without a bottom?

My God! They thought he was dead! The helicopter wasn't searching for him; it was looking for his body!

Dread and fear bore into the boy like a drill through soft wood—quick and clear. Panicked, Travis began screaming, "I'm alive! I'm alive! Come and get me! I'm alive!"

But even as he bellowed, Travis knew no one could hear him. There would be no rescue today. They thought he was gone, resting somewhere deep in the cold water of Brule Lake.

Chapter Nineteen

CHAPTER NINETEEN

Travis lost track of time. He had no idea how long he'd burrowed into the bag, feeling sorry for himself. But later that afternoon he faced the reality that no one would come for him.

If he wanted to live to tell the tale, he'd have to do it on his own. He inched out of the bag and began taking inventory. The first step was a thorough search of his packsack. He pulled out his extra sweatshirt and put it on. He did the same with a spare pair of socks.

He appraised the objects scattered on the tent floor. There was the pan, flashlight, the pocket-sized tackle box and the pack rod. Except for the map, that was it. No, he thought, he also had the survival tool and a compass.

His stomach growled, demanding to be fed. But it wouldn't be getting any pizza today. Instead he'd have to do some fishing, only without fire, he'd have to eat his catch raw. Yuck!

Moments later Travis trudged to the rotting log. Then by using the blade of the survival tool, he chipped away a bit of soft wood. Fortune smiled. Clutching two grubs in one hand, the rod in the other, he shuffled to the shoreline.

Luckily, small perch and sunfish were still hanging out in shallow water. Within the hour a dozen or more were swimming about in the fish pen.

If fish had to be swallowed raw, Travis wanted the fillets to be bone-free. Using a chunk of split wood for a cutting board, he carefully carved the flesh from four fish. When finished, he had eight tiny slabs.

Next he washed off all traces of bloody slime. He pinched his nose, tipped his head and popped a fillet into his mouth. With eyes squeezed tight, he gulped. The bite-sized morsel slid down his throat without protest.

Seven little fillets chased after the first. Then Travis was at the corral again, scooping fish up on the bank. An hour of cleaning and swallowing followed. Finally his stomach felt fed. It wasn't full, but it had something to work with and, for the moment, seemed satisfied.

Travis turned his gaze to the heavens. The sky had remained dreary, threatening. The clouds looked like they could leak any minute. Unless Search and Rescue used a helicopter, there wouldn't be any air traffic. Best he got ready for another session with the long hours of darkness.

Travis pictured the previous night, and how frightened he'd been. He needed a weapon. But what kind of weapon could he make, a bow and arrow? No, too hard.

Wait a minute! The survival tool had a knife. He could carve a spear.

He hobbled to the aspen windfall where he'd cut boughs for the smoked fish experiment. This time he selected a straight limb, one about half as thick as his wrist. He worked it up and down until it broke free of the trunk.

Then he sat on the log, whittling. The knife was razor sharp, the wood fresh and supple. It didn't take long to shape a tapered point. He finished up by nipping off the branch buds along the shaft.

Satisfied, he stood, thrusting his arm at imaginary targets. Holding the primitive weapon made him feel safer. He just hoped he never had to use it.

As he trudged to the tent, he realized dusk was falling. Night was already saying hello to the forest behind camp. Without light there wasn't much he could do except burrow into his sleeping bag.

Rest would be welcome. His whole body was bone weary.

At least he wasn't starving.

* * *

A somber mood filled the Larsens' lakeside home. Upon hearing the tragic news, friends and neighbors had gathered—each hoping to lend support.

Linda had been a nervous wreck ever since the storm had passed. Nevertheless, she remained stoic in front of Beth and their guests. It was Roger who walked around in a fog, uncertain what to say or do.

Bewildered, confused and frightened, Beth occasionally broke into tears. She couldn't accept that she'd never see her big brother again.

Bob was still there, hoping the ceiling would lift. He wanted one last look at the entire portage route. "Just in case," as he put it. But, according to the latest forecast, that wasn't going to happen anytime soon. If the weather didn't look any better by morning, he'd have to take off or risk getting wintered in.

He needed to get the Cessna back to its lakeside hangar. It was time to trade the floats for winter wheels. If Roger wanted, Bob would fly back in a couple of days. He'd land at the local airstrip. Then they could search some more.

Roger saw no need for it. Bob had already given so much. Besides, there was nothing more to be done. Even though Roger clung to a thin strand of hope, all the evidence said it was hopeless. Travis was gone.

Eventually the friends and neighbors departed. There had been enough grief sharing for one day.

The Larsens prepared for bed.

* * *

Travis had trouble dozing. His earlier naps were part of the problem. But it was greater than that; he was more frightened than tired. Like soup on a hot stove, his brain kept bubbling up bits and pieces of the survival stew he was in.

Early in the day he'd been so sure he was going to be rescued—flown out—sleeping in his own bed tonight. But now he was just as certain that wasn't going to happen.

"Don't panic. Don't panic," he kept telling himself. "Plan, plan, plan—make a plan. No one's going to save you but yourself."

Maybe an answer would come to him in the morning. Didn't things always look better in the daylight? Maybe that red-and-white floatplane would wing by for another look. Maybe they'd spot his tent . . . maybe, maybe, maybe.

To take his mind off his situation, Travis forced his brain to think about other things . . . good things . . . fun things. He thought about how he enjoyed teasing girls, yet how awkward he felt around Katie. He pictured sitting across from her in first hour. All around him friends could be yakking up a storm—yet his tongue felt twisted in a knot. Why was that? Did he have that much of a crush on her?

After a time he began thinking out loud. "Wonder if the kids in school know I'm missing? Yeah . . . it's probably around the whole town by now, probably even in the paper."

To help clam his jittery nerves, Travis began counting

backward from one hundred. The activity seemed to help. As he neared zero, his eyes grew heavy and his breathing slowed.

"Things will be better in the morning," he mumbled, and then dozed off.

Amazingly, Travis slept through the night. Once asleep, his battered body had craved rest. When he did awake, gauzy light was trickling through the tent fabric above him. Crawling out the door, he stood, stretched and let eyes survey the surroundings.

The air held a sharp bite. Tiny white clouds formed with every breath he exhaled. That was new. He hadn't been able to see his breath so easily other mornings. Travis was suddenly reminded he had no way to make a fire. That thought sent a secondary chill through his bones.

He tied his shoes and headed for the lake. A thin skin of ice had formed near shore, trapping leaves and bits of debris. Farther out a thin vapor hung close to the surface, rising here and there like puffs of steam from a boiling kettle.

Freeze-up time! Could it be here already? Travis stood pondering that autumn was changing to winter right before his eyes. When he realized he was shivering, he turned and let his feet lead him back to the shelter.

He snuggled in his sleeping bag until the shaking stopped. Once warmed, he stretched out, building the courage to go outside again. The compass cord was chafing his neck. Looking for any excuse to stay put, he tugged the string, pulling the compass free.

Propped on an elbow, Travis studied the compass lid, again puzzled by its bulk. The device seemed twice as thick as others he had seen. The back appeared to come off, curious. He held the compass tight in both hands and twisted. Nothing moved. Using the survival tool, he gently tapped around the edge and tried again.

This time the cover began to turn. With a couple of full twists, the compass and the cover came apart. The inside of the lid contained a flat, rock-like material. Really weird, he thought. Why would a rock be glued inside a compass cover?

It made no sense.

For several minutes Travis studied the strange stone. It somehow seemed familiar but he was uncertain of what. Aware that his stomach was growling, Travis replaced the lid, slipped the cord around his neck and slid from the bag.

He needed to catch breakfast.

Fish guts were right where he had left them. Travis cut slivers of intestine for bait, then cast far as he could over the rim of ice. Cold began nipping at his ears so he tucked his head into the hood of the windbreaker. Then he stood that way, staring vacantly, waiting for a bite.

The exhaust of a distant engine drifted over the lake, intruding into morning stillness. The growl grew louder. Travis recognized the sound—an airplane! The noise was coming from behind him, somewhere near Winchell Lake. But because of the foggy vapor, Travis couldn't see the horizon. And then he realized if he couldn't see the sky, how could a pilot possibly see him?

The yowl grew closer. The aircraft was passing directly over the Cone Lake chain. Through the haze, Travis could barely make out the floatplane's white fuselage and silver pontoons. Travis jumped up and down, flailing his arms in the air. Then he began screaming, "Down here! Down here!!"

The airplane flew straight ahead. As quickly as it had come, it was gone, the engine howl fading like a distant train in the night.

"No! No! No! Come back!"

Travis stood with shoulders slumped; a tear trickled down

his cheek. Weren't they ever going to see him? Dabbing at his eyes, Travis returned his focus to the bobber, tugged on the line and reeled in.

At least the fish were willing to help.

* * *

That morning, some miles distant, the Larsen household awakened to the same gloomy sky. Bob peered through window glass at the outside thermometer. The big, red needle pointed at thirty degrees. Then his gaze drifted to the thin white layer of frost coating the deck boards and grass.

Cradling his coffee cup, he strolled through the living area to the unbroken set of patio doors. Looking like gray smoke, a sheet of fog lay over the lake's dark-gray water. Only the top of the Cessna was on display. Its pontoons were hiding in the haze.

The forecast hadn't change—freezing drizzle turning to snow by the weekend. He hated to leave. But if he didn't, there was the real possibility of getting weathered in. It was probably best to depart while he could. Besides, it was past time to take off the floats and put wheels on for the winter.

Roger carefully carried his coffee into the room. He joined his friend at the double doors. "What d'ya think, Bob? You gonna fly out today?"

"I hate to leave, Rog . . . but I think I better go soon."

"What about the fog?" Roger asked, nodding at the lake.

"Not a big problem. It's only a thin layer. I couldn't land, but I can take off okay. Once I climb out, I'll be fine."

Roger continued peering through the glass. After a quiet lull, he said, "Bob, I can't thank you enough for all your help. You're a true friend. I owe you."

The gray-haired pilot shook his head. "Nonsense, you don't owe me anything. I'm just sick about the outcome.

I don't know how you and Linda are holding up."

"I'm sure we have lots of long, sad days ahead of us."

The two men stood for a time, staring out at the lake, each lost in their thoughts. Bob broke the silence. "Have you thought about a service for Travis? Betty and I would like to attend."

"We were thinking about next Thursday. The sheriff's going to have another try at locating the body. Jeez! I hate to say that. It makes me sick."

Roger paused, fighting back a snuffle. "Anyway, Travis loved the water. We thought we'd have an outdoor prayer gathering where they found the canoe. Lots of our friends and neighbors have boats already on trailers. We'll meet in the church parking lot. Those that want can share rides across Brule."

Bob turned and looked directly at Roger. "I think that sounds appropriate. If the weather clears, Betty and I would like to be there. I should have the plane on wheels by then. We can fly up to the airstrip Wednesday afternoon or early Thursday morning. Maybe we can borrow a car or catch a ride with one of your neighbors."

"No you won't. We'll pick you up. You'll stay with us, no argument."

"Okay, no argument."

Wearing pajamas and a long face, Beth shuffled into the room. Seeing her father, she ran to him and hugged at his waist.

"How did you sleep, buttercup?"

Beth looked up with sleep-filled eyes. "Lousy. I kept having dreams about Trav."

"Dreams? What kind of dreams?"

"I dreamed he was still on a camping trip . . . but he was

getting lonely and wanted to come home. Dad, the dream seemed so real. He even called me 'Little Booger' and I teased him back."

"It's okay, honey. We must never forget what he was like."

After a quick breakfast of rolls and juice, Bob got ready to go. The Larsens walked him to the dock. It was apparent Linda hadn't slept well, if at all. Her face was drawn. Dark circles underscored her red eyes. She gave Bob a quick hug, said thank you more than necessary, and then headed up to the house.

Beth stood quietly as she watched the men preflight the plane. Once all the lines were removed, Roger held a strut as Bob readied the engine for start-up. Before latching the door, he said, "Rog, once I'm above the fog, I'll make a pass over the boy's route. Who knows, stranger things have happened."

"Thanks, Bob. We'll see you next week."

The engine caught and the plane taxied from the dock. After a few minutes of warming, the pilot pushed in full power. Seconds later the pontoons skimmed water.

From the deck, all Roger and Beth could see was the tail cutting through the haze. Then suddenly, as if tugged by a string, the wings found lift and pulled the pontoons into clear air. For a minute the Cessna climbed straight forward, then banked and headed southeast.

Bob hated to leave. It would be better to have found the body—better to have closure. He knew this flight would make no discoveries. He was between layers. A thousand feet above was a cloak of scud, probably full of ice-forming moisture.

Ahead and below, the air was clear. He could see for miles. The problem was with lake water. The thin fog layer made it impossible to see to the surface. No way would he be able to spot a boy near a beach, or a body in the water. The safe thing was to point directly toward

Superior and follow its rugged coast south.

Bob was occupied controlling the aircraft as it passed over North Cone Lake. Except for a sporadic glimpse of green where spruce and pines lay along the shore, the shoreline was mostly a blur of silver-gray. He flew straight ahead—lost in sad thoughts—unaware of the young man below, waving his arms frantically to be seen.

* * *

Travis was gutting a fish when the light came on. He was excited by the possibility. His mother had made a remark when she handed him the present. But he'd been so eager check out the tool he'd paid little attention. The comment had to do with the compass.

What did she say was inside? That it was a flute? Or did she say it was a flake? Neither made any sense. The material looked like rock. But why was it there? There had to be a reason. It had to serve a purpose.

The answer came like a jolt of electricity, sudden and sharp. Pioneers, explorers and mountain men—all had started fires with steel and stone. Travis felt his pulse quicken as the picture cleared.

Excited, he let both the knife and fish fall. Flint! The rock was flint. He knew flint was what made a lighter spark. And primitive muskets, they were called flintlocks. Flint was used to ignite the powder.

And for crying out loud—even more stupid not to remember—he lived along the rock's namesake—the Gunflint Trail! How could he be so dense?

He whipped out the compass and unscrewed the cover. Then he stood like a dressmaker's dummy, staring at the mineral fastened to the inside.

He was uncertain what to do with this new knowledge. An idea took shape. He trotted to the beach and started looking at rocks. Maybe he could find one that would spark when rubbed across the cover. He picked up several small stones, and then chipped each one against the grey material.

Not a hint of spark.

This was crazy. Why include flint with a compass if there wasn't a way to make a spark? Then suddenly, like knowing the right response on a quiz, the answer popped to the front.

The survival tool! It was made of fine steel—the best money could buy. The answer was the tool itself.

Travis hurried to the fish-cleaning area where he had been working. He picked up the tool and pulled the blades open one at a time. There were two types of screwdriver heads, a file, a blade that looked like a miniature saw, a skinny blade that looked suitable for poking holes, and one rough, stubby blade he didn't recognize.

But that had to be it. One side the blade was hatched with fine ridges; the opposite side was a file. With shaky fingers Travis dragged the blade across the stone.

Nothing. He tried a second time—again, no luck. The third time he smacked the steel against stone with a swift, almost angry swipe.

Sparks! Miniature fireworks shot into the air. They reminded Travis of the day they were following a logging truck down the road. One end of a chain had come loose from the truck's bed, and several links were bouncing against the pavement. A stream of bright yellow sparkles chased after the vehicle. These sparks could be like those from the chain. They could chase some of the darkness away.

Travis had to endure a learning curve before he produced fire. It was one thing to strike sparks, another to make something burn. He formed a small pile of the driest twigs and bits of birch bark he could find. Time after time he struck steel to flint. It wasn't to be. The pile refused to ignite. About ready to give up and eat the fish raw, he altered his approach.

He gathered several handfuls of paper-like birch shreds. Then he sat patiently pulling the outer layer into thin little strips. He didn't pause until he had a pan full of the fluffy material.

Next, using the knife blade, he began whittling slivers off a dry limb.

That done, he walked to the edge of the woods in search of a dead spruce. He found one that was just perfect. He stripped the brown needles from several boughs—enough to fill two pockets. Finally, breaking off a couple of branches, he dragged both to the fire ring.

After moving the rocks into a smaller circle, he placed the birch bark fluff in the center. Over this he dribbled slivers of whittled wood. Taking the needles from his pocket, he scattered them on the pile like cheese bits on a salad.

He was ready to try again.

Bending low, he struck steel to flint. Sparks shot past the intended target. He moved closer yet and struck a second time. Dribbles of light landed on the nest but quickly faded.

The third time a big spark made a direct hit—smack in the center of the fluff. Only this time the spark clung to life. Taking care not to disturb the nest, Travis bent close and blew. The glow grew, followed by a wisp of smoke.

Travis puffed a bit harder. As if he had turned up a dimmer switch, the tiny flames flickered light, and then suddenly the whole nest burst into orange flames.

Travis felt as if he'd just won the lottery. He hustled to gather more fuel, and fed the hungry blaze until the flames were waist high.

The flickering fire offered warmth. Equally comforting, much like someone had turned on a light in a dark attic, some of Travis's fear faded.

Chapter Twenty

C H A P T E R   T W E N T Y

Throughout the day, the temperature refused to rise.
Now with sunlight fading fast, the air held a sharp chill.
Both achy and weary, Travis chose to turn in.

It had been a busy afternoon. He'd gathered wood,
restocked the fish corral and cooked a mess of fillets.

Each trip to collect dry fuel took him farther from camp.
Several hours had disappeared dragging and stacking.
Travis didn't want the fire to grow cold—ever!

Now he wished he had a clock, one with an alarm bell.
He'd set it every few hours—get up—add wood to the
fire. But he didn't have a clock, just as he didn't have a
lot of things. He'd have to badger his brain for another
way to wake up.

Although dusk had dropped, it was too early for sleep.
All he could do was stretch out, listen to the pop-crackle
of the fire and ponder his plight.

After lengthy consideration, Travis came up with three
new options. One, he could stay put—grow skinny on
a fish diet—hope Search and Rescue would eventually
find him. But that was scary. What if they'd already
stopped looking? He'd get wintered in, locked tight in a
frozen prison.

Or, maybe he could stock up on smoked fish and head cross-country over the Misquah Hills. The map showed a logging trail that direction about a dozen miles distant. But travel through a storm-damaged forest would be difficult at best. Plus, there was the risk he could get lost and run out of food.

The third option would be to stay put for a few more days—while prepping to take off. If no one showed up, he could head back to Brule Lake. With the steel and flint he could build a bonfire, hope it would be noticed from the other side of the lake.

In the meantime he wouldn't think about the muck and tangle the Brule trip would imply. But at least there wouldn't be any surprises. He'd know what to expect. He flexed his shoulder. Although it still ached, it seemed a little better. In a day or two the pack shouldn't be such a pain.

That's what he would do; wait here a few days. Then, if he had to, he'd trek through the chain of lakes once again. With that decision settled, Travis found it easier to think about sleep. Exhausted from fresh air and heavy work, he slept without waking.

But sleeping through the night meant no glowing coals would be greeting him when he awoke. When he stumbled out at first light, the fire appeared to be dead. Panicky, he picked up a stick and poked around in the ashes. He was about to give up when he uncovered a single tiny, hot, surviving ember. Stacking twigs and bark around it, he knelt and blew. He huffed so hard that after a time he began to feel dizzy.

Moving the bark slivers tighter to the coal, he sucked in a lungful or air and blew with gusto. Ashes scattered in all directions, even on his face. But it worked—the bark began to glow. Then after a second encouraging puff, the fluff flared into fire. Travis vowed he would not let the fire grow cold again. It was too much hassle to have to start from scratch.

Shortly before noon the sun broke through the clouds. As the sky cleared, it painted the lake's surface a pleasant blue. Working as a team, sunshine and wave action eroded the rim of ice along shore. When the thin layer had all but disappeared, Travis trudged to the beach. It was time to restock the cupboard.

He didn't quit fishing until the corral was full. He wanted enough fish for several days of one-course dining. He fried up a few fillets for a late lunch. Then he cleaned and dried the remainder by the fire. For Travis the day seemed to pass like a school recess—in the blink of an eye. Almost before he realized it, dusk was falling.

The big star was about to settle in for the night. And for the first time in days, there would be a sunset. As if in tribute, a smattering of high cirrus clouds became stained with pinks and purples. Further to the west, the horizon collected shades of fire. Hues of oranges and reds melded together like melted crayons. And unlike other evenings, this one would have twilight.

Just before full dark Travis plodded to the lake. Shucking his shoes, he waded out to fill the pot. That chore finished, he sat tight to the fire, savoring its warmth and light. The teen was thinking about how to wake up during the night.

He didn't want to repeat the morning's huffing and puffing exercise. Besides, he might not be so lucky a second time. It'd be so much easier to if he could just get up, add fuel to the fire and go back to bed without worry.

Travis swallowed a sip of water. The drink sparked an idea. One way to interrupt his slumber was to overload on liquid. A full bladder would be his alarm clock. He could kill two birds with one stone—tend the fire and drain his kidneys with one fell swoop. So, before he turned in, he drank his fill, and more, until he couldn't swallow another drop.

The teenager was feeling pretty proud of the plan until

he crawled into the sack. Things didn't go quite the way he planned.

First he got a bellyache—cramps so bad they made him curl like a rolled-up rug. He made though the tent door. He crawled a few feet and began vomiting putrid streams time and time again. He remained outside for nearly an hour. Waves of queasy nausea alternated with terrible cramps. Eventually, sharp chills forced him back inside.

Travis shivered in his sleeping bag, knowing he'd done it again. He'd made another stupid decision. Jeez! He knew better. He'd read about it in survival books. After many days of being empty, a stomach can't tolerate suddenly being stuffed.

From now on he'd have to eat and drink in moderation.

Even after the waves of nausea subsided, sleep eluded him. His stomach was sore, his throat raw. A full bladder soon forced him to go out again. But with twilight long gone, and the moon not yet up, the tent was bathed in black. Travis felt around for the flashlight.

He was about to pass through the door when he jerked to a halt. What was that strange noise? There it was again, along with the sound of splashing water.

Alarmed yet curious, Travis poked his torso through the door, and at the same time, flicked on the light. The sound was coming from the lake. He aimed the beam toward the beach.

He didn't see it at first, its black fur coat blending with night. But then, as if it dropped from the sky, it was there—caught in the shaft of light. Although not nearly as large as the one that had raided their camp, the bear was big enough to set Travis's teeth to chattering.

The creature's snout had scented fish innards. It was harmlessly savoring a free meal. The bear should have been denning up this time of year—about to hibernate the cold winter months away. But unfortunately for

Travis, this bruin had selected to hole-up in the hollow trunk of a large pine. The old tree had snapped in the storm, demolishing the animal's winter quarters. And now, while wandering around in search of a new hide-away, the bear had scented food.

Travis switched the light off, not sure what to do. Maybe nothing, maybe it would just go away. But what Travis didn't realize was that all the handling of fish parts had left a strong scent on his clothes. The bear finished cleaning up the leftovers, then started following its nose.

Though he couldn't tell in the dark, Travis sensed the bear had moved. He switched the flashlight on again. Just a few yards away the beam bounced off a pair of pupils. Way too close! Travis shrieked, grabbed the spear and dashed toward the cliff.

Thinking about it later, Travis couldn't decide who had been more frightened—the bear or himself. As Travis fled, he'd screeched out a second blood-curdling curse. Surprised that a human was near, the bear also panicked. It spun around, bumping the fish rack.

The rack toppled into the fire. It landed with enough force to throw up a shower of hot sparks. Dozens went shooting into the air like miniature rockets. Several landed on the bear's muzzle, adding to the critter's confusion. Terrified, the bruin took off as if it had been struck by buckshot.

As he crouched by the cliff, Travis heard distant splashing. In search of a more peaceful place to spend the night, the bear had already crossed the creek.

"Stupid, stupid, stupid!" he scolded himself. He knew better than to leave garbage near camp. He'd just been too lazy to clean up. From now on he'd make sure he threw the fish parts far away from the tent.

For a time the bear scare masked Travis's stomach pain. Once his nerves settled, cramps returned—though not as severe. But at least one part of the wakeup plan worked. The fire was tended through the night.

Daylight was a promise when Travis finally dozed off. As he slumbered, the new forecast held true. Travis discovered the change when he awoke to a cold rain pelting the tent shell.

The first moisture had been more mist than real rain. The temperature had dropped to below freezing. That meant the mist formed ice on every surface it touched. By the time fat drops started falling, the tent shell wore a cold, crystal coating.

The tent dome began to look like an igloo. The frozen shelter wasn't certain whether it should collapse from the weight or stand stiff like a soldier. So it did a bit of both. Rising warm air from Travis's breath caused the ice over his head to melt. Awakening to rain pattering, he sat up, bumping his head on the sagging ceiling. It responded by sagging even more, its cold, wet fabric brushing his skin.

In a sleep-filled fog, the teen's first thought was that an animal was outside. He dropped flat to the floor and remained motionless, waiting for an attack. When none came, he poked his head out of the bag.

Mental cobwebs had to be cleared before he figured out what was happening. The first hint was the drumming of rain. Instead of pinging, it sounded more like a slap. Travis reached out to touch the sidewall. It was stiff and cold.

What now? The whole tent might collapse and freeze him inside. He commanded himself to stay calm, to take deep breaths. It would take patience but he could knock the ice off a little at a time.

And for the next hour, that's what he did. He'd tap a small section of fabric until the cold layer cracked. Then he'd push up until the broken pieces slid off. By the time he'd finished, the rain had stopped falling.

Pulling on the windbreaker, Travis ventured out.

He was greeted by an incredible alteration to the landscape. It was if a King Midas who loved silver, not gold, had laid a hand on everything. Weeds, brush, rocks, trees—everything glittered like costume jewelry. Even the pile of firewood wore a cellophane wrapper.

Although beautiful, Travis knew this was not good. He would need to stay close to the fire. He didn't dare become soaked; the temperature was well below the freezing mark.

Taking little steps, he slid over slick ground to the fire circle. With a stick, he poked around until he found a few hot coals. That was a morsel of hope. At least he could get the fire burning.

The snow started around midday. Travis had cleaned and cooked a meal. He was rebuilding the fish rack when a soft drizzle changed over to white flakes. At first they were scattered and light—nothing to worry about.

But later, while he was filleting fish, the flakes thickened. Within minutes the silvery landscape put on a white coat. Travis didn't want his jeans and shoes to get sopped. He fed the hungry blaze and then slipped into the tent.

Heavy, wet snow tumbled down all afternoon. Travis kept busy clearing slush from the tent top. Not until three to four inches fell did the butterfly-sized flakes ease off.

Meanwhile, Travis hadn't accomplished much. He'd dashed about for a couple loads of wood. And when the flakes finally slackened, he'd pan-fried a few more fish.

Cold, wet, and weary, the teen turned in. There would be no sensational sunset to end this dismal day.

After another fitful night, morning broke cold and clear. When Travis peeked outside, his eyes were dazzled by a postcard winter wonderland. The rising sun lit the landscape with such zeal he was forced to squint.

He was tromping toward the bluff to do his morning business when he spotted them. Tracks—lots of tracks—dozens imprinted in the snow. Travis recognized them immediately—wolf tracks!

More than one had crept around camp overnight. They came in all sizes, small to super-size large. His heart raced and it seemed as if his stomach was somersaulting. Instantly terrorized, he ran to the tent and clutched up the spear. Then, with weapon in hand, he stood frozen, eyes narrowed, trying to pick out movement.

Seeing no immediate danger, his pulse slowed, his brain focused. Wolves don't attack people. How many times had he heard that? Still, weren't there always exceptions to the rule?

Wait a minute! Wolves typically prey on the sick and weak. At this point and place in time, he probably fit that bill of fare.

"Okay! I'm over here!" he hollered, masking his fear with shouts of bravado. "Come get me now or go away, I've got too many things to do without worrying about you hairballs!"

Then he stood as if actually waiting for an answer. After a long moment, he yelled again. "Okay! You had your chance. It's too late now!"

After a time, the spear at his side, Travis went about his morning's work. But he kept looking over his shoulder—just in case.

The October sun still held a smidgen of its summer strength. Sunday lived up to its name. The higher the big star rose, the more its rays eroded the wintry mantle. By midmorning the white quilt had shrunk to a watery sheet. And in time, that too would disappear.

Travis busied himself breaking branches. He realized limbs from freshly fallen trees were too green to burn clean and hot. But when placed over dry fuel, they sent up thick clouds of smoke. And heavy gray plumes were just what he wanted. A clear sky meant someone might see the signal. And then maybe, just maybe, a plane would be sent up to investigate.

Sadly, Travis was too far off the beaten path. Needing to rid the roadside of brush piles, bonfires were burning all along the Gunflint Trail. Dozens of smoggy smoke plumes spiraled skyward like so many vertical jet trails. Even if someone did notice, there was no reason for anyone to think much of his small smoke signal.

And as it turned out, nobody did.

But never had sunshine felt so wonderful. The snow around the fire pit was the first to evaporate. With the sun's rays and the heat of the fire joining forces, it became possible to lie in the grass and actually enjoy the day.

Travis was tired, and like a stone-cold battery, totally out of energy. His all-fish intake wasn't providing a balanced diet. The teenager tipped his face toward the sky and basked in the rays.

Then he began fantasizing about food. Red meat—his body craved red meat. He wished he had gun, had shot that big moose—used the knife to cut steaks from its plump rear end. The meat would roast over hot coals, scent the air and make his mouth water.

Redirecting the daydream, Travis deliberated if there was a way to get red meat. He pictured different animals that called this area home. He made a mental list. Squirrels, chipmunks, foxes, coyotes, wolves, bears, deer and moose lived in the forest.

Then there were muskrats, beavers, raccoons, mink and a few otters in and around the lakes. He quickly dismissed mice and birds. Mice were too small. Birds weren't red meat.

Then he wondered what kind of an animal could be killed with a spear.

He could possibly get up close and personal to bear and moose. But no way did he want to. He'd be the one getting hurt. Then he wondered about beaver. Were they considered red meat? If he could find a beaver lodge, maybe he could spear one. Then he could roast it and find out for certain.

Venison would be best. But deer wouldn't let you get that close. Besides, this wasn't the best region for white-tails. Anyway, most deer had probably already migrated closer to Lake Superior for the winter. The snow wouldn't be so deep there.

In the meantime, the sunshine felt delicious. He continued to rest, half asleep, fantasies of food skipping about his addled brain.

The raucous call of a crow startled Travis. The sound of wings beating the air came from directly overhead. Suddenly wide-eyed, he took note to the cawing of other crows. The ungainly black birds seemed to be having a party somewhere near Winchell Lake.

"Wait a minute!" Travis exclaimed. "Crows—the finders of food—Mother Nature's clean-up committee. Those garbage collectors must have found something big. Why else would they be gathering in such a large group? It could even be a moose or deer."

First thing in the morning, he'd have a look.

* * *

Seth was driven home from the hospital wearing both a frown and a thick plaster ankle cast. Despite the success of the surgery, he was in a foul mood. The youth stared out the car window the whole trip, willing the snow to stop. He couldn't accept that Travis had drowned.

No way could he buy that! Especially after seeing how Travis had saved himself after flipping the canoe.

And then there was the pack. Search and Rescue should

have least found that much of Travis's passing. But they hadn't. Seth needed to convince somebody to make a second search. Maybe he could talk Doug Davis into looking again.

It was worth a try.

The principal made the grim announcement over the loudspeaker Monday morning. While his classmates were hearing the news, Travis was preparing for a hike. The unwilling camper had risen early—at the first blush on the horizon. Once up and fully dressed, he rushed through his morning chores.

Tasks completed, he headed to the creek. An empty pack-sack hung over one shoulder. The spear was clutched tight in his good hand. He hadn't gone far before making the first find. Someone had used a chainsaw to slash a path through the tree-clogged waterway.

That answered one nagging question. This was the way they took Seth out.

He pondered that before taking off his shoes. Then he rolled up his jeans and stepped into the stream. The water felt frigid—colder than he recalled. For a brief moment he considered returning to the tent. Then the image of red meat and real food sashayed across his brain.

He sloshed on.

Picking his way over rocks and boulders, Travis pushed ahead as fast as he dared. He didn't want to trip and get soaked. The morning had yet to warm. The water was ice-cube cold. Twice, the butt end of the spear kept him from taking a bath. But with a path already cut, and by blocking out the cries of his chilled feet, he was able to slog nonstop to the bigger lake.

He stepped out on the west side, plopped on a log and put on dry socks and shoes. His feet and ankles still felt colder than a pair of popsicles. He stomped in place until a bit of blood began circulating, causing a tingly feeling in his toes.

Nearby, dozens of crows were holding a noisy convention. Although their cawing filled the air, Travis didn't see any flapping of feathers. Using the shoreline as his marker, he closed in on the racket.

After a hundred yards of stalking, he paused to strain his ears. The squawking was coming from the woods. He was getting close.

Travis didn't relish sneaking through tattered windfalls. But if he wanted to learn more, he had to. Quietly as he could, he scrambled over trunks and tree limbs. Travel was slow but as it turned out, well worth the effort.

There was one last blowdown blocking the way. He climbed up and jumped down. His feet hit the ground with a thud. The sudden thump startled the flock of feasting birds. With wild wing flapping and a chorus of caws, the scavengers took to the sky.

Travis watched them become airborne, then moved forward. Not certain what to expect, he held the spear overhead, ready to poke or plunge. He stepped into an opening. About the size of a cottage, the space was the result of trees having been tipped in different directions.

But that wasn't what made the boy's heart sing. Collapsed on the forest floor were the lifeless hulks of two moose. All that remained of the smaller carcass were the head and legs. Most of the meaty body had been picked clean as a paper plate.

The larger carcass was that of a huge cow. Much of the middle and the front shoulder were missing. But except for several slashing cuts on the upper leg, heavy fur on the rear quarter was untouched. Enough rump roasts remained to feed a construction crew.

Rich crimson blood glistened on wet leaves. The wolf pack! Wolves must have done this—killing both animals when they'd been trapped in the opening.

Fresh food was staring him in the face and Travis didn't hesitate. Once he managed to skin back some hide, he carved out a huge hunk of muscle. He placed clumps of leaves on the bottom of the packsack, hoping they'd absorb blood seepage.

After the treasure was placed in the pack, Travis hoisted it high in the air. It was as heavy as three-dozen Big Macs—and all clean, fresh red meat.

One lonesome camper would eat well tonight.

Thrilled, he wished he could take all of it. But that, he knew, was impossible. Instead, he cut several thick steaks from the gory opening. He forced these into the side pockets. When he was sure not another ounce could be tucked into the bag, he turned to leave. He stopped to yell at the crows still cawing at him from far overhead.

"Hey you stupid birds! If you'd kept your big beaks shut, I wouldn't have bothered you. But thanks for the invitation. I really appreciate it!"

Travis didn't seem nearly as tired and frightened now. His situation didn't seem quite so bleak. Even the full pack seemed weightless as he retraced his steps. When he reached the creek, he chose to take a breather before wading back to camp.

He looked around for a comfy spot, one where he could rest and catch a few rays. Two trees had fallen side by side—one higher than the other—forming a shoulder rest like a tall stool. Travis climbed up on the lower limb and leaned back. He turned his head toward the sky, hoping to drink in some of the luscious sunlight.

The previous day's sunshine had melted nearly all of the snow. Only where shade prevented its warm rays from touching did any snow or ice linger.

Later—when he thought it over—Travis determined that the snowy patches had kept him from recognizing the next fantastic find. Instead of an aluminum canoe, his brain registered "big, old icy log."

Luckily, a birch branch losing its snow load alerted him. Travis was just climbing down from his perch when a lump lost its grip. Luckily the icy glob clunked the canoe with a loud metallic clink.

What? Rocks don't clang. Wood doesn't clank. The clatter needed to be checked out.

What a marvelous morning—the slashed path in the waterway—finding food—and now, transportation! This was a great day, one filled with new beginnings. Travis wasn't certain how he'd use the canoe. But he knew finding it was a good thing, and his spirits soared.

Now he'd get a second opportunity. He'd get one last chance to head home on his own.

* * *

The old adage about having "eyes bigger than your stomach" applied to Travis and the ambitious amount of steak he roasted. He'd weaved thin, green branch ends into a makeshift grill and could hardly wait for the meat to cook. Soon juices oozed out, dripping on the coals, scenting the air—making the teen's mouth water. Travis grew impatient. Once both sides of the steak had a chance to char, he plopped it into the pan. Then he cut off a piece, plucked it up with his fingers and brought it to his mouth.

Never—ever—had meat tasted so delectable! Travis chewed a few times and swallowed. Wonderful!

Fantastic! It was by far the tastiest thing to ever cross his lips. Like a hungry pup at a big, full bowl, he began to rush. He was soon cutting off chunks as fast as he could gorge them down.

Most of the huge slab had disappeared when his stomach said, "stop—enough already!" Travis dropped the pan and stretched out. Life was never so good, at least for a short time. For a week, he had eaten little more than mushy fish. His stomach was now stuffed full of heavy red protein. No way was it prepared for the overload.

First to arrive was the bellyache. It doubled him over as if he'd been punched in the middle. Next on the agenda were the heaves. Travis started throwing up chunks of partly digested moose.

As he lay on the grass he couldn't help thinking about the expression "sick as a dog." He had wolfed down the meal. And now he was paying for it. It wasn't until late in the day that he felt good enough to feed the fire and mull over his next move.

One thing was certain; Travis didn't want any critters sharing this delicacy. He shouldered the pack and hiked to where the woods began. Here the bluff had buffered the wind, and many trees remained upright. Travis searched for a branch on which to hang the prize.

He wandered around until he found one that would serve the purpose. Using a forked limb, he hoisted the packsack high above his head. On the third try he was able to snag a shoulder strap. Stepping back, he examined his work. Unless there was a Michael Jordan of bears in the area, the meat should be safe.

Just before sunset Travis tried eating again. He reheated the steak, and then nibbled tentatively, chewing each piece into little bits before swallowing. He was careful not to consume too much. He'd already upchucked enough to last him a lifetime.

Long shadows crept across the camp. Soon darkness would be in charge. Travis prepared to call it quits. Despite getting sick, it had been a delightful day. The sun had stayed with him all afternoon, smiling down from a cloudless, robin-egg sky. Spurred by the sunshine, the temperature had continued to rise. All traces of snow and ice had disappeared.

Propped on his elbows, Travis lay on the grass and used the last light to study the map. He was planning his escape route—his one last chance. He had food and a canoe, and that meant another a choice. It had to be a good one.

But the more he considered the old Alumacraft, the more confused he became. It hadn't been there when he and Seth had arrived at the dry creek bed. So than how did it get there? Were the portage trails open between here and home? If that was true, why leave the canoe behind?

He had another perplexing thought. He didn't recall seeing a paddle. You couldn't canoe without a paddle. He'd have to make one. But how would he do that?

That was something to think about while falling asleep. It was probably best to spend all of tomorrow getting ready to leave. Besides, the weather had finally turned sociable. Having food, and with fair weather in his favor, he could survive for a few more days.

With the last glimmer of twilight, Travis banked the fire and crawled into bed. He was feeling good about his chances. His stock seemed to be rising.

With a full belly, and new hope his head, Travis was soon fast asleep. Later a yellow curl of moon lifted above the horizon—doubling its image off the placid water. But as one contented camper dozed, other creatures began to stir. The stranded teenager hadn't been the only storm survivor.

The aroma of the steak grilling over an open fire had traveled far and wide. Many animals still prowled the wind-tossed woods. Most were famished. Since the storm had wrung its havoc, only wolves dined at their leisure. Large and powerful, they used the tangle to aid their hunting; their prey found it difficult to escape.

Smaller predators weren't so lucky. Hunting patterns had been upset. Finding food was not easy. The sweet scent of sizzling meat drew to them to camp like flies to honey.

They began arriving shortly after moonrise. The first was a scruffy coyote. It slunk about the edge of the campsite, sniffing out danger. The small brush wolf was extra cautious. Human scent lingered in the air.

A skunk was next in line. Unlike the coyote, the white-striped forager was bold. It waddled in with its tail held high. Almost immediately the skunk found a scrap of meat. Without pause, it snatched the delicacy and toddled back into the blackness.

A weasel came next, its brown coat molting to winter white. Saucy and confident, the rapacious little predator marched right up to the tent as if it had ticket. Circling to the rear, it came to where chunks of vomit littered the grass. Filching a bit of meat between its needle-sharp teeth, it scurried into the inky shadows.

The coyote observed the smaller animals finding free food. She finally decided it must be safe. But just as she padded close, two smaller coyotes appeared on the scene. They weren't so shy. Both trotted directly to the tent and began snatching up secondhand treats.

There had been enough sharing. The female growled. Then with a throaty snarl she sprang—teeth bared and hackles on end. The assault took the others by surprise. But realizing they were under attack by one of their own, the latecomers fought back.

Like most canine quarrels, there were more growls,

snarls and yelps than actual injuries. The first snarls awakened Travis with a start. Petrified at what was taking place on the other side of the fabric, he lay in fear, unmoving. To the terrorized teenager it sounded like wolves were quarreling over who would get the first bite of him. Twice the shelter shook as angry animals battered the tent cloth. Inside, Travis was scared stiff—thinking an attack was near.

The next time they hit the tent, he screamed, "Eeeeaaaaaah!"

The shriek was the loudest Travis had ever heard. He couldn't believe it came from his own vocal cords. But it worked. As quickly as the fight erupted, it ceased. All three coyotes backed away, each staring at the big round bump.

Travis continued to yell. "Get out of here! Go on!"

Cowards at heart, they did as they were told. They weren't afraid of each other, but they wanted nothing to do with a human. The coyotes turned and disappeared into the night. But the female didn't go far. She had been wounded. Limping, she crossed the clearing and found a spot to lie down.

The campsite went quiet. Travis quivered. He couldn't stop shaking. Every few seconds, he would yell at the top of his lungs.

More spooky silence. Quiet so thick it could be carved with a blade. Travis wished he had the spear. It was just outside the door. After what seemed like forever, he sucked up his courage. Trembling fingers undid the tent flap. Then he reached out and grabbed the pointed stick.

He lay still for the longest time, his fingers wrapped around the wooden spear, his pulse pounding like a freight train. As his heart rate slowed, his curiosity grew. He wouldn't get back to sleep until he was certain—certain the predators were long gone. On nervous knees he poked his head outside for a look around.

A pale crescent moon looked down at the lake. It yielded just enough light for Travis to survey the surroundings. His wide eyes didn't note anything unusual. Only glowing embers from the fire winked back. He rose on rubbery legs and stood, clutching the pointed stick.

"Go away!" he yelled. "Leave me alone!" Except for an echo, nothing stirred.

Had it been a nightmare? Or was his imagination running wild?

Travis knelt in the door and felt around for the flashlight. He flicked the fading beam on both sides of the tent. No, it hadn't been a dream. Tufts of tattered gray fur littered the ground. Flecks of blood stained the grass. The fight had been real. It hadn't been a nightmare.

He stalked to the fire and using the butt of the spear, stirred the ashes. Then with one hand grasping the weapon, he used the other to add wood. Hopefully a bright blaze would keep the meat-eaters away.

Taking a last scan, Travis returned to the tent and snuggled into his sleeping bag. He lay with nervous shakes, anxious that the wolves would return. He held as still he could, straining his ears to pick up any unusual sounds.

He heard only the breeze playing tag with the tent flap.

Relaxing a bit, he gulped a breath and began going over the events of the past week. He was still way too wired to doze off. After a time, he decided to go back out and sit by the fire.

Staring blankly across the flames, he began scheduling the next day. After the morning meal he'd get to work on a paddle. But he wasn't certain how that could be done.

Could he chop one from a limb? He didn't think so. The knife blade wasn't the right tool. He'd need a hatchet to do the job. But he didn't have a hatchet. It had vanished along with his buddy.

What would Native Americans have done? They didn't have steel axes. And how did Eskimos paddle kayaks? There were no trees in the arctic. What did they use . . . whale bones?

Bones—could he use moose bones? Why not? The shoulder blades on the cow were large and flat—probably too big. But the calf should be about the right size. He could attach a shoulder blade to a shaft. That might work. It'd be the first project of the morning.

At the first blush of dawn, Travis slipped inside. He needed to nap. After full daylight arrived, and topped-off with moose meat, he returned to the kill site.

Knowing where to look, it didn't take long to get there. The crows, along with other hungry animals, had been feasting on the leftovers. Most of the flesh had been consumed. The smaller carcass had been picked bare to the bone.

Using a rock for a hammer, he was able to free both shoulder blades. They seemed the right size. Yet Travis worried. How was he going to attach a flat bone to a round wooden pole?

Before leaving he cut long strips of hide from the cow's coat. Then, after stuffing everything into the packsack, he slogged to camp.

Stopping only for a quick bite, Travis spent the entire day laboring over the paddle project. First he had to find a sturdy, straight limb the thickness of his wrist. The better part of an hour was spent whittling one end smooth.

Next he attempted attaching a shoulder blade to the shaft. Tying strips of fatty hide to the bone wasn't the answer. The blade wiggled with the slightest touch. It was so loose it could easily slip off.

After several trying hours, Travis took a break. The simple project was beyond frustration. The solution came while he was getting a drink at the lake. A thin rock on shore rang a bell. It resembled a prehistoric ax blade.

He hefted the stone in his hand and pondered how early people made tools. That thought reminded him about a museum he had visited in sixth grade. One display was a collection of stone tools. How were they held together?

Travis was turning the rock over in his hands when the answer came—a split shaft. He'd have to split the lower end of the shaft, and then slide the blade into the opening. If the gap was longer than the bone, he could tie off the bottom, trapping the blade in place.

The idea filled Travis with renewed vigor. He dropped the rock and ran back to the task. The survival tool became his new best friend. Without it, making a paddle wouldn't have been possible.

Hours later, Travis held the paddle up for inspection. No piece of art, he mused, but it should do the job.

Long shadows of night began settling over camp. It was too late to make another run to the canoe. First thing in the morning he'd pack, paddle up Winchell Lake and check out the portage at the far end. With luck, Search and Rescue had opened it up. And if they hadn't, he'd turn around and head back to Brule Lake, just as he had done with Seth's ill-fated canoe.

* * *

This was the first time Sarah had been alone with Seth since coming home from the hospital. The siblings were in the cottage's living room, reading by lantern light. Crews were working overtime on the power lines, but still had miles of downed wire to repair.

Seth was on the sofa, eyes closed, his cast propped on a footstool. Sarah slouched in a recliner, a book in her lap. She was staring at the glowing embers in the fireplace.

Sarah broke the silence. "When are ya going back to school? Lots of kids have been asking about you."

Without lifting his eyelids, Seth mumbled, "Really, who?"

"Well . . . Maria for one."

Seth opened his eyes. "Oh yeah? What'd she say?"

"She was just being friendly . . . wanted to know how you were doing."

"What'd you tell her?" Seth asked, sitting up.

"That you were doin' okay. You are . . . aren't you?"

"Yeah, sure . . . I guess," Seth muttered.

"What do you mean, 'I guess?'"

"You can't expect me to happy about the way things turned out. I'm probably the reason Trav won't be coming back."

"Come on, you can't blame yourself. It was an accident. You didn't tell him to go off by himself."

"You're wrong. He'd never have left if I hadn't let him. I could have convinced him to stay . . . but I didn't. I won't forgive myself for that."

After a pause, Sarah spoke. "Does Mom know how you feel about this?"

Seth shook his head. "Why should she? She can't fix things. It's a little late for that."

Sarah pondered Seth's answer, then asked, "What do you think about Mom's friend?"

"Who? Oh, you mean Doug? He seems okay."

Sarah hesitated and then said, "He's asked Mom to marry him."

"Really? Well if that's what she wants, then that's what she should do. She has a life of her own."

Sarah sat up straight, her mouth agape. "What? You're okay with it?"

"Yeah, I am. I had a lot of time to think when I was by

myself. I think Mom should do what makes her the happiest. If I learned anything, no matter what you plan, things can change. Look at Dad. He was here one day, gone the next. If Mom wants to marry this guy, who am I to say no?"

Sarah gulped in disbelief. This had been too easy. "I agree. Should we tell her we approve?"

Seth lowered his eyelids again. "She doesn't need our okay, but if you want, you can."

"So you like Doug, then?" Sarah asked.

"Yeah, he seems like a nice guy. How about you?'

Sarah slouched in the chair. "I like him, too. More important, Mom seems happy. I think that's the most important thing. I'm glad we agree."

* * *

While Travis was away, a pair of eyes kept watch over camp. The coyote's leg had stiffened. She'd stayed put, patiently waiting for dark. Maybe then she'd have a better chance at sneaking a meal.

Travis was trekking to the meat tree. The coyote was half-asleep. As he approached, the crunch of footsteps put the predator on full alert. The wild dog awoke with a snarl, startling Travis, stopping him in his tracks.

The teen remained glued to the ground, staring. The coyote stared back, a growl rising in her throat. But something Travis saw in the animal's eyes told him there was nothing to fear. The critter looked as frightened as he felt. It just wanted to be left alone.

Travis shuffled backward. The coyote struggled to her feet. It was obvious the animal was hurting. Travis drew a quick conclusion. This had to be one of the fighters—part of the group that had terrorized him. So they hadn't been real wolves after all. They'd been brush wolves, no larger than the average dog.

Although the coyote appeared alarmed, it seemed unwilling to run. More relaxed, Travis found his vocal cords. "Ah-ha . . . so you were one of the critters that woke me up. Do you have any idea how worried I was?"

The coyote stopped growling. She tipped her head as if she was curious about something.

"Jeez! You scared me. But you don't look all that tough in the daylight. Matter of fact . . . it looks like you've been missing a few meals."

The creature stood perfectly still, her eyes locked on him.

"Hungry, huh? I can relate to that. Tell you what. You stay here. I'll get both of us a bite to eat. There's plenty to go around."

Travis made a wide loop around the coyote. With the forked limb, he unhooked the pack. After slicing a steak for himself, he trimmed off a second chunk. He hung the pack back up, and then circled into the open—talking all the while.

"Okay, I'm gonna share," he said, holding the meat out in an open palm.

Like an over-the-hill pitcher, Travis lobbed it in a slow underhanded effort. It arched into the air then landed with a plop. Uneasy, the animal retreated several steps.

"Here's the deal," Travis said. "You can have supper on me. But you've gotta promise not to wake me up tonight. I need my sleep. Okay?"

With those words he turned and jogged toward the tent.

Travis used the last of the light to restock the woodpile. Later he lay by the fire, staring at the sky in awe. Looking like pinholes in black canvas, thousands of stars twinkled. More than he'd ever seen. The Milky Way was so bright it stained the heavens with a strip of cream-colored light.

Although weary from the day's work, he remained alert, his ears tuned for visitors. When at last a slice of pastel lemon moon cleared the horizon, Travis stumbled into the shelter. In minutes he fell into deep slumber. He didn't awaken until sunbeams warmed the tent cloth.

Realizing the day had started without him, Travis rushed through his chores. He needed to eat, pack up and be on his way.

The first task was to reclaim the meat pouch. He was surprised to find the coyote still bedded where she'd been the night before. Only this time she let the youth pass without warning.

Travis continued to the fire ring, stirred the ashes and then added tinder. Once flames flared, he used a pair of pointed sticks to impale the meat. Then he set both sticks over the fire. While they were charring, he rolled up the sleeping bag and took down the tent.

Next Travis carried the branch with the smaller steak to the woodline. There he pushed the butt end into the ground and hollered. "Hey, skinny! If ya want to eat, you'll have to come and get it."

He listened for a reply that didn't come. After a moment he did a one-eighty and hiked back to his own meal.

Squatting near the fire, Travis thoroughly chewed each piece. He'd had it with bellyaches. Meanwhile, across the clearing, the coyote stood still as a lawn ornament. Finally hunger overcame fear. She dropped to her stomach and began slinking forward. Reaching the stick, she lifted her head and with amazing speed, snatched the offering. For a moment the coyote froze, as if studying the creature that had shared its food. Then, without a thank you, she turned and limped into the woods.

* * *

Making memorial arrangements without a working telephone was a problem. Lynn Springwood offered to help. Doug lived in town. His phone was in service. From that location, she was able to make the contacts.

Doug and Roger would make a trip across Brule Lake one day early. Borrowing a neighbor's boat, they'd take along chainsaws to clear an area near the stream. The following day, family and friends would be ferried across for the memorial service.

A rustic cross was being constructed in the school's wood shop. Sarah was to help secure the symbol. Seth would represent his classmates by saying a few words of farewell.

Those who helped with the search again volunteered their boats. This time they'd carry mourners to and from the service. After the ceremony, a few would stay behind. They'd scan the depths with sonar. They'd take one last look before winter winds blustered down from Canada, locking the landscape in arctic-like ice.

Chapter Twenty-Two

C H A P T E R   T W E N T Y - T W O

To lighten the load, Travis chose to leave a portion of the moose meat behind. He trimmed slabs from the big roast. Next, he placed two large, flat rocks into the center of the fire circle. Then he laid the meat strips on the stones.

Finally, he added the last of the firewood. Should he have to come back this way, he wouldn't have to stop long to eat. Wilderness fast food, he gloated—pretty darn clever. And if he didn't return, once the fire cooled, the coyote would have something to chew on.

Eager to be on his way, Travis scarcely took note of the cold water. He sloshed to Winchell Lake in a new record time.

After toting Seth's fiberglass *Titanic* around, handling the lightweight Alumacraft was a walk in the park. With little effort, he flipped the canoe over and slid it to the water's edge. He added two rocks in the bow for ballast. Then he set his gear on top.

His destination was the portage trail at the far end of the waterway. It was the route most campers used during the summer months. There'd be several miles of paddling before he learned whether the trail was cleared.

Maybe, he thought—maybe the storm didn't do any

damage at that end of the lake. Wouldn't that be great news? Maybe the portages were open all the way to Poplar—open all the way home!

With spirits soaring higher than a free-flying kite, he pushed the canoe into the water and hopped in.

Problems started with the first stroke. The paddle didn't work as planned. Its blade was fat—awkward—and at first kept banging the boat. He had to make sure his strokes were wide and well away from the gunnels. It was exhausting, muscle-straining labor.

He'd hoped to make four or five miles per hour. That wasn't going to happen. The paddle was ungainly, and the breeze was blowing head-on. The trip would take much longer than he'd hoped.

Despite these minor technical difficulties, Travis was content. He had a glorious day to return. The sky had been scrubbed clear of clouds. It was clean and pure; the rich blue of painted wall maps.

It didn't take long before strenuous paddling and warming rays made him overheat. For the first time in days, Travis shrugged off his windbreaker. Not long after, one of the sweatshirts followed. But he savored the feeling. This was the warmest he had been in days.

As he drew closer to the portage, hopes of leaving storm damage behind plunged. The trees were tipped, broken and bent, much like at North Cone Lake. The hills bordering the bay resembled a bad haircut. Most of the forest had been trimmed, but here and there saplings stood up like hairs missed by a careless barber.

Adding to his woes, his sore shoulder started aching again. With the constant strain of paddling, it reminded Travis that it hadn't fully healed. He found himself stroking more on the right side than the left.

That caused the canoe to turn off course. To swing the bow back in line, he had to use the blade as a rudder.

That slowed his forward progress even more. Travis surmised he wouldn't reach the trailhead until midmorning.

When he finally paddled into the bay he was no longer smiling. The wind had done damage here as elsewhere. The shoreline was a tangle of spruce, pine and poplar—pushed, snapped or twisted. If the portage trail had been opened, he didn't see it. The better part of an hour was spent paddling along shore, looking for a hint of human activity. There wasn't any.

Frustrated, he couldn't hold back his disappointment. Shaking the paddle in the air, he stared straight up and bellowed. "Why? Why are you testing me this way?"

This was not going to be an escape route. His only option was to turn around and head out the other way.

Travis received a helping hand on the return trip. The wind that had been blowing in his face now gave him a free pass. His arms and shoulders were able to rest. Using the clumsy oar mostly to steer, he sailed directly toward the outlet.

He reached the campsite in the middle of the day. Tugging the canoe down the creek hadn't been a problem. The camping equipment had stayed snug and dry in the bottom of the boat. Only his feet got cold and wet.

All that remained of the fire were rose-colored coals. The meat, dried of its juices, rested in the middle on the rocks. Travis sampled a piece. Although chewy, the strips were definitely edible.

He pulled on his windbreaker and plopped onto the grass. Now he had a new choice to make. Pitch the tent now and head for Brule Lake early the next day? Or leave now, and make camp along the way?

Travis pictured the campsite just one lake down. If he used part of this day to travel, he wouldn't have so far to go tomorrow. There'd be lots of daylight to float the canoe through the rapids. That's what he'd do—use this sunny afternoon to reach Middle Cone Lake.

Rustling leaves snapped him to attention. Alarmed, he sat up and then smiled. It was the coyote. For a time they just looked at each other. Travis broke the impasse. "Still hungry, huh?"

The coyote hobbled a step closer.

"Okay, okay, I'll share. But man, you scared me. You're gonna have stop being so sneaky."

Travis picked up a meat strip and broke it in half. He held it high and then threw it in the coyote's direction. The pitch fell short. Never taking her eyes off the boy, the animal inched forward. With a quick snap, she picked up the treat, turned and limped away.

Travis put the remaining strips in the jacket's big pocket pouch. He wasn't about to leave them behind. They might be supper tonight. He took a last look at the encampment, walked to the lake and slid the canoe into the water.

The difference was like night and day. The Alumacraft was so much easier to pull and lift. Although wet and weary, Travis worked without resting, reaching the old logging camp clearing in sunlight.

Soon after he beached the canoe, fatigue set in. He was both tired and hungry. The shoulder was a dull pain and his arms felt like two dead sticks. But hope had returned. He pitched the tent and started collecting fire material.

By the time Travis readied the fire-nest, the sun was a flaming globe in the western sky. But he now knew what to expect from the flint and steel, and went right at it. After catching a spark on the second try, friendly flames quickly followed.

Smears of red and pink painted the horizon; a fleeting reminder of what a beautiful day it had been. Long shadows had already crept into the forest behind camp.

Travis sat cross-legged next to the fire. He studied the flames, thinking about home.

A twig snapped. Travis jumped to his feet, turned and felt for the tool. Did he imagine a glimpse of gray in the long meadow grass?

The teen fumbled with the gadget, finally prying open the knife blade with shaky fingers.

Another twig snapped, closer.

He groped in a pocket for the flashlight. Squeezing tight, he switched it on.

Two eyes, like wet black olives, reflected in the yellow beam. Trembling, Travis raised the light over his head.

He sucked in a gulp of air, unaware he had been holding his breath. It was only the coyote. Apparently it liked the meat treats and had followed him. Travis switched the light off. Then he backed toward the fire and sat down alongside it. He reached into the pouch pocket and retrieved a meat strip.

He broke off a chunk and held it up for the animal to see. In soft tones he began talking. "Tell ya what . . . if you want a piece, you'll have to come to me."

The wild dog let out a low whine but crept closer. Travis continued coaxing. Then he flipped the treat forward. Like she'd done in the morning, the coyote grabbed and gulped in one quick flash.

"You still hungry?" Travis repeated the process until the coyote was within reaching distance. He pulled a second strip from his pocket and broke it in half. Then he dangled the scrap at arm's length. Never taking its eyes off Travis, the coyote snaked forward. Rising, she nipped the treat from his fingers.

"You must be starving, Okay, just one more time."

The animal tilted its head as if to say, "I don't speak your language." In a blink of an eye, she filched the delicacy from his hand.

"Yeah, you're welcome, but that's all for today. If you want more you're just gonna have to wait 'til morning."

For a few seconds the coyote stared, as if trying to communicate with Travis. Then the moment was over. She turned and hobbled away, disappearing into the dark.

The night air was transparent, cool, and as always in the northwoods, scented with pine. Stars began twinkling overhead. Thousands glittered like diamonds displayed on black velvet. For a time Travis kept a hot fire burning. He was hoping to chase sleep away, at least until moonrise.

But it had been a tiring day and he was bushed. He'd nodded off several times, waking when burning wood snapped or popped. At last, a slice of lunar light shared the night. The sliver of moon looked like a stage prop as it climbed above the distant smudge of shoreline. Travis felt a tinge more secure. A smidgen of the black blanket had been pushed back.

He was ready for sleep—and he did—all night long.

Jack Frost was the only overnight visitor. When Travis poked his head from the tent, the view took his breath away. The sun was rising—an orange beach ball where the moon had hung a few hours earlier. It promised to be another fantastic autumn day.

The clearing looked as if it had been sprinkled with powdered sugar. Every branch, leaf and blade of grass had a paper-thin coating of white frost. Lake fog— tinted gold by the sun's early rays—cloaked the water's placid surface.

For a time, Travis remained motionless, savoring Mother Nature's artwork. But when he began to shiver, he returned to reality. It was time to finish dressing.

Having had a full night's rest, he was impatient to be on his way. He blew on his chilled hands, stirred the coals and added tinder. Then he warmed by the fire, waiting for his morning meal to heat. He wasn't surprised when the coyote came slinking into the clearing.

"Come for a bite of breakfast, have you?"

Travis cut a fist-sized chunk off the remaining roast. Then he stepped toward the coyote, stopped and lobbed the offering. With a grin, Travis looked at his scrawny companion. "Enjoy. It's the last free meal you'll be getting from me."

Finishing his own portion, Travis broke camp. With the gear stowed in the canoe, he pushed off and hopped in. He turned to have a last look at the clearing. The coyote was standing near shore, watching him glide away.

"So long, friend. Have a good winter." Travis hollered. A grin cracked his face as his voice echoed back . . . "So long, so long, so long."

From far off, another sound caught his ear—the distant drone of an aircraft. Travis stopped in mid-stroke, hoping the airplane was winging his way. But it wasn't, and soon, like fog in morning sunshine, the vibration vanished.

"It's so quiet this morning, that airplane is miles and miles from here," Travis mumbled aloud, pulling hard on the paddle. "Probably some rich dude flying in for a day of fall fishing."

* * *

The small Cessna flew over the runway, then like a nimble bird, banked to the left. It banked twice more as it lined up with the long strip of blacktop.

From the front seat of their Suburban, the Larsens watched Bob Ritzer gently touch wheels to tarmac. Roger waited until the aircraft taxied to a stop and shut down before opening the car door.

Roger approached as Bob helped his wife step out of the plane. "Hello again, Bob. Greetings, Betty. Thanks so much for coming."

"No need to thank us, Roger," Betty Ritzer replied, giving him a hearty hug. "Just wish we were visiting under a happier state of affairs."

Once everyone was seated in the SUV and buckled up, Roger started the engine. He put it in gear and headed for Grand Marais. Friends and relatives were to gather in the church parking lot. From there a deputy would lead the caravan of cars, pickups and boat trailers. They were to head down the main highway and then up the Caribou Trail. Their destination was the boat landing on Brule Lake.

Everyone would be ferried to the clearing Roger and Doug had brushed-out the day before.

A half hour later the Suburban pulled up in front of the church. Vehicles had flooded the parking lot and were spilling onto side streets. And departure time was still nearly an hour away.

Many early arrivals were hoping to get an opportunity to exchange regrets with the Larsens. A few were just curious about a prayer service so far from the chapel. A smattering thought it unique to attend a wilderness service on such a gorgeous fall day.

The Larsens hadn't expected such a multitude. They sat in the Suburban, wondering how everyone could possibly be ferried across the lake.

Chapter Twenty-Three

C H A P T E R   T W E N T Y - T H R E E

Travis stepped into the water, pleased with his progress. The lightweight aluminum canoe had been so much easier to lift, slide and pull. Unlike the trip on foot, paddling the length of the swampy pond had taken only minutes. It was only midmorning but he was already at the last stream, and about to head to Brule.

A northerly breeze had risen with the morning sun. Blowing over the lake, it cast a nervous chill to the air. It was warmer in the channel, away from the wind's bite. Once there, Travis considered calling a timeout.

His shoulder hurt and his hands and arms throbbed. Adding to his discomfort, the crude paddle raised angry blisters on his palms. But he was eager to get home. He only rested a short while. Ignoring the aches, he headed downstream—pushing and pulling, tugging and lifting.

* * *

It was a most unusual service. More than a hundred people had been ferried across the choppy waters. They clustered together in the clearing, most with heads bowed.

After prayers and comments by church elders, it was Seth's turn to talk. He had been concerned that his vocal cords would fail him, and he would get too choked up to speak. But that hadn't happened.

Loud and clear, he gave a wonderful speech. Leaning on crutches, his voice only occasionally cracking, Seth thanked his missing pal. He spoke of how Travis found courage, how Travis had worried more about Seth's injury than his own. He told the group how unselfish Travis had been. And how Travis insisted on seeking help, not for himself but to make sure his friend would get medical aid.

When Seth finished there wasn't a dry eye in the crowd. Even the stoic sheriff's deputies found reason to use their handkerchiefs.

Sarah and Beth, helped by classmates, tapped the student-made cross into the rocky soil. Mourners unwrapped flower bouquets, then patiently waited to place each near the marker.

Finally, after everyone had a chance to pay their respects, the minister distributed song sheets. When the last words of "The Old Rugged Cross" drifted over the lake, a group prayer was said. The service was over. The assembly began shuffling toward the waiting fleet. It was time to depart.

Seth didn't want to go. He begged his mother to let him stay. "Mom, I need to say some things to Trav by myself."

"Oh?" she replied, feeling her son's grief. "What kind of things?"

"You know . . . for taking care of me and stuff. I can catch a ride with one of the deputies. Please?"

Lynn walked over to one of the uniformed men. She repeated her son's request.

"No problem," the deputy answered. He understood the boy's need for closure. He told Lynn not to worry. He'd be happy to bring him back to town.

Seth settled on a blowdown and waited for the boats to

depart. His eyes were misty, and tears streaked his face. He had been so sure there had been a mistake. That Travis was okay. That he was out there waiting. That he would be found alive and well. But this . . . the ceremony . . . it all seemed so final, so unreal.

Out on the lake, Search and Rescue began taking a last look. Each boat held a person in the bow, scanning the surface for anything out of the ordinary.

Seth rose slowly to his feet. With the aid of the crutches, he hobbled across the opening. He stopped in front of the cross. With head bowed, he began talking in hushed tones. "Trav . . . Trav . . . Trav, what did you do? I can't believe you'd try to cross Brule in a boat with a broken bottom. You're smarter than that. You weren't a rookie anymore."

Seth's words were interrupted by a faint clank. He paused, looked up and listened. What had caught his attention? But he heard only the wind whispering through broken boughs of the tattered pines.

He was about to say a final goodbye when the metallic clank echoed again—louder, more distinct. Seth had heard that sound many times before. It was the sound of metal bumping boulders. Somebody was coming down the creek, letting an aluminum canoe bang against the rocks.

Seth hobbled from the clearing, his crutches scarcely touching the ground. He limped toward the stream. His curiosity was a pot bubbling over. Who could possibly be coming through the rapids, abusing a metal canoe?

* * *

With hard work and resolve, Travis had reached the place where the stream raced downhill. Now he needed a different strategy. He needed a way to slow the canoe, some way of keeping it in one piece as it tumbled and banged through the rapids. He tied the pull rope to a limb, plunked his butt on the bank, and wracked his brain.

The inspiration came while watching the canoe strain against the line. It wanted to surge ahead on its own. The cord . . . the limb . . . maybe he could tie the line to a bundle of branches. They'd act like a drag, like an anchor. Plus, they'd keep the canoe pointing one direction—not allowing it to turn sideways.

Suddenly, as if someone had opened a church door, music filtered through the forest—a chorus singing his favorite Sunday song.

How could Mother Nature pull off that trick? The melody was like mist across a valley, soft, but untouchable. As quickly as it came, it was gone, and only the wind whispering its own verse stayed behind.

Sitting perfectly still, straining to hear, Travis wasn't certain it had been real. He must really be losing it, he mused—imagining the wind as a choir. Call in the men wearing the white coats, 'cause that was totally nuts.

Shaking his head, ready to move on, Travis started gathering broken branches. He stacked a dozen or more in a pile. Then he untied the canoe and pulled it up on land.

Next, he took the line and began knotting limbs along its length. When the rope ran out, he stood back and appraised his work. The cord reminded Travis of a prickly kite tail. The limbs had smaller branches sticking out like walrus whiskers.

If his plan worked, they would catch on rocks and windfalls. Each should help keep the canoe straight as it dashed through the whitewater.

Travis was about to put the canoe into the current. A new noise caught his attention—the whine of outboard motors. It sounded like dozens of engines—accelerating—then fading. He stood quiet, listening, perplexed.

Were they still looking for him? Was he just a little too late? From the sound of it, the boats were leaving. He must be too late. If it weren't for bad luck, he wouldn't have any luck at all!

He was disappointed but not discouraged. He had the Alumacraft, and even the wind was from the right direction. It would help push him across the open water. All he had to do now was get the canoe down the rapids in one piece. He'd be able to finish on his own.

The knotted limbs worked better than he'd imagined. They almost worked too well. Unlike the earlier trip, this time Travis stayed along the bank. He watched as the canoe bounced and bumped on its way downstream.

Twice he had to wade into the water to untangle the tail from windfalls. Despite cold feet, Travis was thrilled. The canoe didn't seem be suffering much damage. Only occasionally would it bang and clatter as hit bumped bottom.

It bobbed along like a dog on a leash, straining to break away but held tight by the rope. His transport would make the trip without life-threatening injuries.

Unmindful of his aches and pains, and in spite of being dead-tired, he was feeling great about the day. Things were finally working out. His mouth watered at the image of french fries and a big, juicy cheeseburger. Or maybe he'd ask for crispy fried chicken and mashed potatoes.

Travis couldn't decide which would taste best.

* * *

Seth hobbled to the edge of the inlet. The rapids finished their rush a short distance upstream. Where he stood, the creek flattened and the current slowed before emptying into the lake. He spotted a comfortable-looking spot alongside a fallen tree. He sat down and waited—crutches at his side.

The crunch of metal bumping rock came again—much closer now. Seth was certain it was a canoe. But who would be using the stream this time of year? Search and Rescue?

Peering over the log, Seth caught a glimpse of the Alumacraft. It had finished the whitewater race just a few yards upstream from where he was resting. Just then, its tail branches snagged a windfall, jerking the canoe to a stop. The boat bobbed in place as if it were a taxi waiting for a fare.

Seth was confused. Why didn't the canoe continue floating his way? All Seth could see through a snarl of limbs was the boat's bow. And it wasn't moving.

This was becoming more of a mystery every minute.

* * *

Travis was trying to untangle the cord but his feet were freezing. After several attempts, he gave up. He took out the tool and cut the rope. Clutching the leftover line, he scurried up the bank. After wrapping the line around a sapling, he sat down, dried his feet and put on his shoes.

Then he stood back and studied the canoe. Except for a couple of dents, it appeared seaworthy. Down the channel opening he caught the reflection of big water. What a sense of relief. Both he and the canoe had made the journey none the worse for wear. All that was left was to let the Alumacraft finish the trip on its own. He'd rush ahead and be at the lake to catch it.

He'd made it to Brule. It was time to take a break, maybe make a fire. He could have a last go at the moose meat. But first things first—get the canoe to the beach, and then worry about lunch. Who knows, someone might see the smoke and investigate. Maybe he would still catch a ride.

Travis untied the rope, held tight, and let his eyes roam the last stretch of channel. Few trees had tipped here. It looked fairly clear of debris. Since the current had slowed, he let the canoe drift ahead on its own. Propelled by the gentle flow, it bobbed forward at the speed of a slow walk. Suddenly it jerked to a stop. The single trailing branch shoot was caught on a submerged limb.

Travis was able to hook the rope on the fork of a long stick. A couple of sharp tugs freed the snag. The canoe started moving again. He decided to hold the rope the rest of the way. There'd be no need to do any more wading. Cold feet were a nuisance he could live without.

Seth saw the canoe move ahead, but couldn't see anyone controlling it. This was more than spooky. If it wasn't daylight he'd of thought it was the work of goblins. After all, it was only a few days to Halloween.

He hunkered alongside the blowdown and watched. He'd stay out of sight, let the canoe float by, and see who was following it.

As the canoe glided past Seth's lookout, it stopped again. Seth remained motionless—confused. The boat seemed familiar, an old Alumacraft. It was like the one used to take him to Winchell Lake.

He raised his head for a better angle. That's when he spotted the pack-frame. It had a green tent bag strapped above the canvas packsack. Recognition! Seth grabbed a crutch and struggled to stand.

Travis was about to step over the log when Seth popped up on the other side. Startled, he almost let go of the line.

Both were speechless. Instead, they stood grinning at each other. After a long moment Travis spoke. "Hey, you just gonna stand there or are you gonna help me?"

"Ahhh...rookie, can't you do anything by yourself?"

"Yup, but it's always nice to have help."

"So tell me, did you have a nice time without me?" Seth croaked, unable to mask his emotion.

Travis continued to grin, with a smile that nearly touched his ears. "Let's just say it's been quite an adventure—a really wild experience."

Chapter Twenty-Four

C H A P T E R   T W E N T Y · F O U R

The deputy was about to beach his boat. Two boys suddenly appeared in the clearing. He was surprised to see more than one. He thought only Seth had stayed back. But he was shocked when he learned the identity of the second teen. The man took a moment to check Travis over—to ensure he was okay, that he could make the trip to town without medical aid.

Putting a hand on the boy's shoulder, the deputy grinned and then declared, "Dang it all, kid! There were a whole lot of tears shed for you today. Now I expect there'll be a whole lot more. You must be one tough kid, making it out here by yourself. Especially with the weather we've had the last few weeks."

Travis turned to look at the man. "There's something I'm not sure about," he said seriously. "Why did you stop looking for me?"

"Haven't you figured that out?" the deputy asked, pointing to the big water. "Once we found your canoe and life jacket floating in the lake, we figured you fed the fish."

The man turned and nodded in the opposite direction. "Over there. That cross and all those flowers, they're for you."

"Not everyone, sir," Seth said quietly.

"What's that?" The officer asked.

"I said not everyone thought he was in the lake. I didn't believe it then, and I sure don't believe it now." Seth said, a mile-wide smile cracking his cheeks.

The deputy walked over to his rig to use the radio. He needed to broadcast the news to the boats still searching offshore. While he was doing that, the boys had pulled up the cross. A throaty whimper sounded from the far side of the clearing. Travis trotted to the canoe. He retrieved his pack and removed the remaining meat.

Carrying the roast in both hands, he rushed across the opening. He stopped in front of a pile of cut brush, plopped the meat on the ground and boomed out, "Here, little wolf. You'll need this more than me. Thanks for the company. Have a good winter."

Seth was completely confused. When they were together again he couldn't help razz his buddy, "Well, one thing's still the same."

"Yeah, what's that?"

"You're still talking to yourself. You must have really bumped your head the day you dropped the canoe."

Travis slugged Seth on the shoulder. "Yeah . . . well, like you told me a couple of weeks ago, sometimes things just happen."

* * *

The luncheon was almost over by the time the deputy pulled into the church parking lot. Strapped upside down on top the black Blazer was a dented, but still usable, aluminum canoe. The boys were in the backseat, busy swapping stories of their portage adventure.

"Well guys, how do you want to do this? Travis, we don't want to give your folks a heart attack," the deputy stated.

"How about I limp in first and get everyone's attention. I'll have them close their eyes and imagine Travis is still with us. Then Trav can slip in the door beside me," Seth suggested.

"Seth, I don't care how you announce it. Just make it quick." Travis grinned.

"Why's that?"

"Because I'm really hungry and they might be running out of food in there."

"You've got it pal. Let's go in and eat."

"Sounds great . . . but Seth?"

"Yeah?"

"Please tell me they're not serving fish."

Epilogue

E P I L O G U E

To say the congregation was stunned would be an understatement. Linda couldn't believe her eyes. She grabbed her tall teenager and despite his filthy jeans and fishy odor, refused to let him go.

For the second time that day, most of the crowd had misty eyes. Except now they were tears of joy. Roger was equally thrilled despite being upset that he had given up the search so soon. The memorial turned into a celebration of life; prayers of thanks filling the large room.

Except for a weight loss, Travis appeared healthy. Later, at the clinic, an x-ray showed a hairline crack of the collarbone. Given care and time, the shoulder would heal fine.

His hand was also examined. The photo showed no breaks or cracks. With a few hearty meals and a good night's rest, Travis could return to school.

Later, after the excitement waned, Sarah shared with her mom. She explained how Seth and she felt toward Doug Davis. Sarah beamed when she reported that both approved of Doug's marriage proposal.

It was a good day for everyone. Lynn announced that

there was to be a wedding in the future—sometime after the last snows of winter had waned. And the fact that there would be two handsome young men to give the bride away thrilled her as much as saying yes.

Many of the group had predicted correctly. This turned out be a most unusual memorial—an event they'd never seen the likes of before, and probably wouldn't again.

J
GAM

Gamer, Ron.

One last chance.

LHW

about the author

Minnesota native Ron Gamer has held a passion for woods and waters since early childhood days. Now retired after thirty-four years of teaching in the Robbinsdale School District, he continues to be active in the outdoors. When not out fishing, bow hunting, or piloting small aircraft around the state, Ron can be found at his computer—creating realistic adventure stories he hopes will be enjoyed by readers of all ages. To read more about the Chance series and Ron's school presentations, visit www.RonGamer.com.